# THE ELEMENTALS RUSHED FROM THE DEEP BLUE CRACK IN THE SKY ...

I saw three or four white creatures with long limbs and thin skull-like faces dominated by large mouths with sharp teeth. Their long, sharp fingers opened and closed, seeking something, anything to grip.

Shouts of alarm rang through the air. The Theran sailors scrambled to untie the net connecting their two ships, but their efforts came too late.

For just a moment I felt oddly safe in the slave hold, protected somehow from the creatures that rushed by me toward the upper decks, their long bodies like milky water. It seemed as if it were all happening in a dream and that retribution would be swiftly dealt to my enemies.

That illusion of safety ended a moment later. . . .

# EARTHDAWN: THE AGE OF LEGEND

In an ancient age of magic, heroes re-explore their world. Emerging from their self-imposed imprisonment in underground shelters, the people of the land of Barsaive battle remnants of the Scourge known as the Horrors, creatures from astral space that have ravaged the earth. Now humans, elves, dwarves, trolls, orks, the reptilian t'skrang, and the mysterious obsidimen work together to rebuild their home. Become one of the heroes of *Earthdawn* in this new fantasy roleplaying game from FASA.

# EARTH DAWN

# Mother
# Speaks

*by*

*Christopher Kubasik*

A ROC BOOK

ROC
Published by the Penguin Group
Penguin Books USA Inc., 375 Hudson Street,
New York, New York 10014, U.S.A.
Penguin Books Ltd. 27 Wrights Lane,
London W8 5TZ, England
Penguin Books Australia Ltd, Ringwood,
Victoria, Australia
Penguin Books Canada Ltd, 10 Alcorn Avenue,
Toronto, Ontario, Canada M4V 3B2
Penguin Books (N.Z.) Ltd, 182–190 Wairau Road,
Auckland 10, New Zealand

Penguin Books Ltd, Registered Offices:
Harmondsworth, Middlesex, England
First published by Roc, an imprint of Dutton Signet
a division of Penguin Books USA Inc.

First Printing, January, 1994
10  9  8  7  6  5  4  3  2

Series Editor: Donna Ippolito
Cover and Interior Illustrations: Robert Nelson

ROC   REGISTERED TRADEMARK—MARCA REGISTRADA

EARTHDAWN, FASA, and the distinctive EARTHDAWN and FASA logos are
trademarks of the FASA Corporation, 1100 W. Cermak, Suite B305, Chicago, IL
60608

Printed in Canada

For Mom

# PART ONE

## My Sons

# 1

My sons,

Strange that you should ask me now about your father. Just a week ago I received a letter from him, asking if he could come visit. If he has written to you with the same request, I understand your need for more information. Decades of silence is strange enough; a sudden breaking of silence even stranger.

Strange is the only word to describe all of this. All of my love for J'role. All of our history as a family. All of J'role. The day you two emerged into the world his eyes filled with joy. They floated above his smiling cheeks like clouds against a blue sky. Yet he also remained hesitant, as if some secret fear ate at him. As with most of his past, he never revealed these concerns to me. Perhaps he will do so now if I decide to let him come visit. It's hard to say. I'm so old now.

Do I love him? I don't even know anymore. There is a point where lives become so intertwined that names and words and labels lost their potency. Although we have not seen each other since the Battle of Throal during the Theran War, he has always remained a presence in my life.

But not in yours. I know that your memories of him must be shadowy and uncertain. Your letter said that someone told you of our first adventure together. I will tell you then of our last.

We spent several years after the discovery of Parlainth

wandering Barsaive, exploring ancient kaers and deserted citadels. We guarded dwarven caravans between the kingdom of Throal and the Serpent River. We escorted mining expeditions to Death's Sea, and battled elemental creatures that rose from the molten lava to attack our employers. We watched the world turn green again after the devastation of the Scourge, the lush jungle growth returning to the world in splendid force. We were very much in love. Traveling together this way we saved each other's lives time and again, becoming legends.

J'role kept his secrets, but I could sense them, and often their intensity frightened me. Occasionally the secrets revealed themselves, wordless, in your father's dark eyes as he stared off at memories I could not see. But he was charming, too, and brave, and as the years passed, the melancholy so deeply rooted in him when first we met began to lift.

You see, I thought I could save him from his darkness. I thought I *had* to save him.

Ah, hubris! It can lead one to fame and fortune. But in personal matters it is definitely a liability.

We decided in our mid-twenties to have a child. Our exploits had garnered us a small fortune that would have permitted us to cease our wandering if we had wished. And so we did. To this day I don't know if J'role spoke the truth about his desire to settle down, but we couldn't have been happier after the two of you were born. We considered ourselves doubly blessed by the Passions. The names we gave you, Samael and Torran, were those of friends we had made in the time of our adventuring. You were both so beautiful. Even after all these years, I can still see so clearly your small hands and fingers, constantly grasping and flexing, preparing to hold tools firmly. Even then, I suppose, your desire to grip a sword was strong.

Cries in the night. Stained clothes to clean. The constant feeding. (Two of you at the same time for me, remember!) All of these nuisances dwarfed by the intellectual demands of an infant turning into a human being, unleashed without warning into an amazing world that mystifies the child's curiosity. "Mommy, why is the sky blue?" "Mommy, why is Death's Sea all hot?" "Mommy, why *five* toes?" There is so much to explain, and adults, who the child views as all-knowing and all-powerful, are expected to have ready and at hand all the answers to all mysteries.

It all seemed too much. Yet how we adults re-learn our sense of wonder through the eyes of a child!

Excuse me. Your father.

Can you tell I'm circling the subject? It's strange. The older one gets, the less one cares about embarrassments and mistakes, yet the more embarrassments and mistakes accumulate. In the balance I suppose it all comes out even. I feel like a fool in this tale, for so much should have been clear. I had only to look. I feel as if I failed you two, for I should have known better. The remorse comes to me late at night, and I wonder again and again how I could have been so foolish.

I'm going to tell you things you might once have known but have surely forgotten, and for good reason. But before you agree to see your father, you should know about them.

# 2

It was only months after you were born that J'role told me he must go with Samael to help search for an ancient sword. The abruptness of the departure surprised me, but I didn't try to stop him. He was gone for half a year, then returned with gems looted from an ancient tomb. Samael had stopped by during the intervening months, telling me he had simply given up trying to find the sword after the third month.

When I asked J'role about this, he laughed, held up the booty, and said, "Well, it wasn't a total waste of time!"

He stayed with us two months, then was off again, this time gone for three months. Then he only stayed two weeks before going off again.

Each time he came back I really believed that surely he must have purged whatever it was had compelled him to leave. Certainly, upon each return, he would hold me as if he never wanted to let go. He also would stand for hours and hours at a time, just watching you two sleep at night. And how he would play with you all day, swinging you in the air, tickling you, running around with first one and then the other of you on his back so you bounced and bounced and bounced. You laughed and laughed. He loved to—needed to—make you laugh.

He kept the house clean, practiced juggling and acrobatics, and seemed so content.

But then would come another abrupt departure, and after awhile he would leave without even revealing his intentions. Months later he'd be back again, smiling sheepishly.

Finally I couldn't stand it anymore, and ordered him out of the house. He nodded sadly, telling me I was right. Hardly the reaction I sought. But he left.

For a while.

For years he would return as before, always telling me he wanted to stay. Apologizing profusely. Holding me in his strong arms, his eyes so full of open hunger for my love.

He never stayed. I started putting better and better and better locks on the doors, desperate for him to stop confusing me. But your father was one of the better thieves who ever lived, and it became a bad, grinding joke.

It would have been a boring joke, without variation, for the rest of our lives, had not a flying castle passed over our home one night and the Therans returned to Barsaive. You two were only seven. I don't know how much of the story you can recall. So I will tell as much as seems necessary for you to know your father.

# 3

Hours before the castle floated over our village, the three of us were at Horvak Smith's. His new forge needed to be prepared for firing, and I had taken you two along with me. It had just rained (when in Barsaive had it not just rained?) and the ground was soaked and muddy. Torran, you splashed through the mud outside Horvak's home, while daring Samael to imitate you. Within minutes you were both covered in mud—but that was the way of it. I had only so much attention I could give at any one time, and you knew I was busy using magical powers to ready Horvak's forge.

I believe that back then I was still wearing my scarlet wizard robe, the one festooned with silver and white birds taking sudden flight. At that time I needed it to protect me from the Horrors when casting spells. It was a temporary solution to the shambles the Horrors had made of astral space, and we've done better in the intervening years. But back then, a magician's robe was the lifeline to magic.

I was busy at work on Horvak's furnace, drawing on my knowledge and power to make it hold flame and heat longer than its fuel would normally allow. I had to keep watch for Horrors seeking me out on the astral plane, while also keeping an eye out for Horvak's fingers and for you boys. From the distance came the laughter of children, like metal chimes in a very light breeze. I thought nothing of it until I heard the children laughing and shouting as they ran by Horvak's. But even these thoughts amounted to little more than, "Hmmm, something is happening that children like."

It wasn't until you two came into Horvak's shop and Samael jumped up and down and shouted, "Mama, Mama, the clown is here!" that I actually took notice.

The clown.

My thoughts numbed and I dropped my connection with the astral plane, giving up the ritual for the moment. I stood up straight, and Horvak's mouth formed into a disappointed pout.

Your little bodies stood a few steps away from me. You each stretched an arm toward me, but the rest of you leaned away, as if you were already on your way to see the clown. And in a way you were. For the past three years the clown had shown up every few months, to the delight of the village children and to my displeasure.

But you didn't know about my displeasure, and you didn't know it was your father. You had not seen him as your *father* for at least four years. "No," I said. "I'm here now, and I must take care of the furnace."

Torran began stomping around the mud, purposely splashing it up to his chest.

"STOP IT!" I screamed. I'd just done the clothes that day. "Stop it!" But you didn't stop, Torran. You just continued to parade around in the mud, raising your knees high and slamming your feet down hard. Samael, you eyed your brother carefully, weighing the risk, and then decided to imitate him.

I tried to grab you both, to somehow settle you down. But you moved like weasels—an unflattering comparison, and I mean it that way. You squirmed with ridiculous energy. "I wanna see the clown!" Torran demanded. You ran in wild circles around me, and it seemed you would never stop. Villagers on their way to see the clown stared at our little circus, and I felt so ashamed. Why couldn't I keep control of my two boys?"

I tried to reason. I stopped chasing you, lowered my voice to a calm tone. "Please. We're not going. I must finish this."

Samael came to rest, knowing that my tone meant I felt bad. But Torran placed his hands on his hips, a gesture stolen from me, and stared back defiantly. "I wanna see the clown."

"Too bad."

A shriek ripped from Torran's throat. He raised his hands skyward and raced around as if possessed by a Passion. He screamed and screamed and screamed. A headache seized my temples. I could fight it and waste hours, or give in just to get some peace and quiet. If only I could have rested sometimes, had someone to share the burden of raising you two, I'm sure I could have been stronger. But I didn't. "Yes," I said finally, "we can go."

I explained to Horvak that I'd return soon, and taking one of your hands in each of mine, we headed off toward the clown.

We walked along the narrow path through old Jayara's rice fields, and made our way to the clearing at the edge of town. The big leaves overhead glistened bright green, sparkling with the special radiance of life that rain brings. The sky above cut clear blue, not a cloud marring the sky. At such moments I wondered—and still do—how our lives had become so complicated with sadness. I had steady work as the village magician, I had the two of you (troublesome, perhaps, but the lights of my life), and the world around me, so beautiful in its colors and shapes. The Universe held me like a mother holding a babe, cradling me in the crook of its arm, cooing to me with delightful, gentle sights and sounds.

Why can't we be content with simply being alive?

Your father had a crowd of children around him, at least two dozen. They sat on the damp grass, rolling back and forth with laughter, slapping the ground and looking around at each other to confirm that, yes, indeed, this clown was very funny.

He wore a costume of black and white patches sewn together in a criss-cross pattern. Around his right eye he'd drawn a dark-blue diamond and on his left cheek a small red heart. The tiniest bells jingled on his boots, tinkling almost inaudibly when he approached to pickpocket someone, but loud enough to give him a challenge. Challenges drove him like the lash of a whip.

He juggled three small balls of wood and one knife. As the knife flipped through the air he grimaced at it with panic, completely ignoring the three balls he also kept in circulation. The two of you wanted to get closer, but I held my ground. I did not want to give J'role the impression I wanted to get closer to him. You both leaned forward, bodies hanging limp as I held your hands.

Then J'role saw us. His eyes met mine across the distance. For just a moment something unspoken and undefined passed between us. Then, as if we did not know each other, J'role was back at work, shrieking in terror as the knife approached his right hand, then his left, over and over again.

I wanted so much to be stern-faced and to show how displeased I was with him. But he was too good. I couldn't help but smile.

He finished the juggling routine, set his props aside, and then, as if noticing the children circled around him for the first time, gave a huge smile. He clapped his hands together and sighed an exaggerated sigh. It was clear he loved nothing so much as entertaining children. Just as clear was his desire to make sure the children knew it.

They did.

Children loved J'role.

He was a clown. That helped, of course. He didn't stay at home and make up rules and tell them what they had to do if they wanted to survive and grow up to be able to take care of themselves. He just showed up every once in a while and made them laugh.

He extended his arm to shake hands with one of the children sitting several feet ahead of him. He took two steps forward, and then let his legs fly straight out from under him as if he'd slipped on the wet grass. His arms flailed, and his mouth opened wide in exaggerated terror. For a moment he seemed to float in the air, suspended not through magic, but comic practice. Then, SLAM! he crashed into the ground.

Screams of laughter cut through the peaceful afternoon. The children could not contain themselves. If they'd ever seen anything funnier before, this certainly made them think they hadn't.

J'role acted as if he wanted to get up, but again his legs slipped out from under him. Over and over again he struggled to stand, only to find the ground so wet he could only fall. His legs flew out to the left. To the right. They spread apart. They slid out backward.

Again, I tried to keep my jaw tight, showing only anger and displeasure on my face. But as the falls went on and on, I too began to laugh. The other adults were also laughing along with their children. And you two—you laughed until tears came from your eyes.

The show continued with more falls, more juggling; handsprings, rolls, and cartwheels. Finally it ended. The children and the adults applauded. You two let go of my hands and joined in giving praise to your father. He bowed low, several times, happy for the attention. He rose, and our eyes met again. But this time he held my gaze.

I panicked, frightened of having to deal with him, to speak to him, to have his warmth anywhere near me. He could trick me, you see. Turn my anger into sadness, my fury into laughter. And more than that, there was a part of him that terrified me. I never saw it clearly for what it was, always thinking instead it was something wrong with *me*. Only later would I know the truth.

I grabbed your hands and stormed away from the clearing, back to Horvak's to finish the furnace, and then home for supper and sleep.

Back home I locked the doors, sealed the shutters, turned off the lamps.

And waited.

He would come.

Of course.

# 4

You fell asleep quickly, not suspecting a clown would come calling. I remained awake, staring at the thin lines of moonlight formed by cracks in the shutters. The night was cool, the bed large. I held one of Mopa's brightly colored pillows against my chest, barely breathing, waiting for some noise to tell me J'role had arrived.

A strange paranoia buzzed in my thoughts, for, of course, there would be no noise.

I tried to remember how I had known he'd gotten in all the other times, but I couldn't. Would he get in at all this time? I'd put in new locks, augmented by magic. The magician who sold them to me had seemed very confident of his wares. But when I asked him if his magic could hold against the skills of the half-legendary thief rumored to dress like a clown, his smile dropped. He made no guarantees, he said.

A noise? Was J'role outside? I strained, trying to become perfectly still so as to hear any sound. The jungle insects formed a pulsing breath. I tried to ignore them, and found myself confronting the formidable buzz of silence. The more I concentrated, the louder the buzz grew, until I could no longer stand the strain.

I relaxed, only to discover I desperately needed to take in a breath of air.

I waited and waited.

Was he already inside the house?

Would he come? I had no way of knowing. He always did. But would he come *this* time?

I told myself I didn't want him to come. In fact, I begged the Passions—all of them, not caring which one heard me—to keep him away. If he didn't arrive, then it meant I was probably done with him forever.

Finally, the suspense and tension drove me out of bed.

Stepping as quietly as I could over the floorboards, I walked as far as the beads hanging in the doorway and listened. Nothing.

I parted the beads and looked through into the gathering room. Standing across the way, in the door frame of your bedroom, was your father, beads hanging down over his shoulders like frozen raindrops.

He'd already heard me, of course. He was like that. He heard everything, but no one heard him. But he didn't react.

I knitted my indignation into a tight and tense spine and marched across the floor—quietly, so as not to wake you up. I reached him and still he did not turn. I looked past him. Samael, your small hand gently rubbed your nose; Torran, you turned over, your lips softly moving, speaking the silent language of dreams.

"Why do you keep doing this?" I asked him quietly, tersely.

His body was so close. All I had to do was place my arm around his waist. He would place his arm around my shoulders. Do you understand? Even now, *in my flesh*— not in my thoughts, but in my flesh—I feel him so much. How our hands fit against each other, how his arm curled over my body when we lay in bed together, the touch of his lips against my neck. There are no images. Just the echoes of touch from decades past. That night, the echoes sounded even stronger, and I longed—I admit it—for the source of the echoes once more.

"I wanted to see them."

"Why do you sneak in?"

"That's what I do."

"Why don't you ask?"

"Would you let me in?"

"No."

"I love you."

I laughed. Not that what he said was funny, because I think he did love me. I know he did. But by laughing at him—without him first doing a pratfall—I put him on the defensive. I didn't want him to confuse me anymore. Leaving his side, I walked to the gathering table and sat on a stool.

He turned and followed, saying with great pain, "I do." The pain was fake. He added that to support his indignation.

"You want. You don't love." Cruel, but I wanted to hurt. I opened my hand and a golden flame burned from my palm. His dark eyes caught the light and they glowed like two stars. He looked handsome. "You're looking well. The smooth features of the young and insane."

"I try to have a pleasant outlook."

"Samael almost died of fever last season. Did you know that? Did any of your late-night visits reveal that to you?"

He remained silent. He didn't know that. Then, "He's all right now?"

My voice became louder. "Of course he's all right now, you idiot. If he were ill, I'd be up, worrying!" I caught myself, remembering you two, and dragged my voice down to a harsh whisper. "That's what parents do!"

"I can't be a father to them. You know that."

"I know nothing of the kind. In fact, I know nothing. Each day I live, I know less and less. Know, know, know. That's what you want, isn't it? You have to know everything will be fine before you take the first step. Coward." I closed my hand; the room fell dark. "You've got to stop coming back here."

"Part of me is here."

"Parts of you are everywhere! If you want to be here, be here. But don't leave a scrap of yourself behind every time you walk out that door. Take all of yourself out, or stay."

He swallowed. "You'd let me stay?"

I hesitated, trying to stop the words from coming out. "Yes, I'd let you stay. If only so you might figure out whether you really *wanted* to stay. My guess is you'd learn you *don't* want to ... But then we'd be done with this!"

"You don't know ...," he began, hinting once again at that dark past of his.

"No. NO! I don't know. I've never been privileged. I have no idea what you've been through. I doubt I ever will. Now get out and stay out."

He remained still.

"I mean it. Stay out. I will not tolerate this anymore. This is not your home. You left. You're out. I'll have you killed."

He froze, stunned.

My face became a mask. The truth sneaks up on us now and then, mugging us like a rough thief. "I really can't put up with this anymore, J'role. You've got to get out. Please. Never come back here. I think I meant what I said."

At that moment the moonlight through the cracks vanished and darkness filled our home. Loud voices, shouts, came from somewhere. We remained motionless, expecting something terrible to happen, but having no idea what it might be. Then we went quickly outside.

J'role saw the castle first. It floated several hundred feet in the air, heading north. Voices drifted down from it, and the sound of drums as well. Long oars protruded from the base of the castle, rowing back and forth. He pointed it out to me.

"What is it?"

"I don't know. I've never . . ." His voice trailed off
with boyish wonder.

The castle flew on.

"It's like an airship, like the crystal raider ships."

"But it's made of stone. It isn't shaped like a boat."

"The magical cost must be tremendous."

"Theran?"

As soon as he spoke the word, we looked at each other.
I think he was as surprised at the thought as I was. But
there seemed little doubting it. The Therans could do
such a thing, if anyone could.

Excitement passed up and down my spine; my hand began to shake, as if I'd cast one too many spells that day.

I don't think you can understand exactly what this
meant to us, to everyone in Barsaive. You, of course, en-
countered the Therans at an early age, and your impression was forged during the subsequent events of this
story. But for those of us from the first generation after
the shelters, raised on the tales of Thera, the thought that
they'd actually returned was overwhelming and exciting.
They were the world's saviors, but also rich with strange
customs, including slavery. They were the master magicians and adepts, but also the profiteers of despair.

"I've got to go find out," said J'role. His mouth formed
into an excited, boyish smile—a smile that years earlier
had given me so much pleasure, but at that moment filled
me with frustration and sadness.

"J'role," I said, "I'm curious too. But we can't go out
every time something interests us. The children . . ."

He stared down at me. The hot life had vanished from
his eyes, replaced by a cold analytic stare, as if I'd just
spoken a strange language he did not understand, but
found fascinating. It chilled me.

"But, we have to know."

"Others will find out."

"But I won't be there to *know*. I won't be there to *live*
it."

"What about the life *here*?"

The stare shifted and he looked past me into the house. His voice tightened. "I know this, already. I don't . . ." He looked away.

I touched his shoulder. Suddenly he'd become the sad, silent boy I'd met in the underground prison of the elf queen. "How can you know . . . ?"

He turned from me and out the door. "Releana, I have to go," he said firmly. Manly.

Then he smiled again. "A castle that flies!" He looked at me for a moment, then ran off into the night, vanishing into the arms of the night-black jungle. A few moments later I heard Jester whinny and then the distant sound of hoof beats rushing away.

# 5

I stood a moment at the door, wondering what horrible thing I'd done in my past to acquire such strong feelings for such a ridiculous man. I wanted so much to be able to pluck all thoughts of him from my soul, like splinters from a fingertip. But our passions are not foreign objects, jabbed into our flesh. They are as much a part of us as hearts and lungs, and just as alive and blood-soaked.

For a long while I stared into the night, the huts of the village lit by gray-silver starlight, the jungle deep and dark.

Finally my thoughts came to rest on the astounding sight of the castle floating through the air. Could the Therans have returned? A mix of thrill and fear bubbled up through my body. Then, agitated by not knowing what such an event might mean for you two boys, I turned from the door, from my thoughts, from the night, and returned to my bed. Alone or not, I was tired, and soon fell asleep.

The town buzzed, of course, when I told of what I had seen. Things had been quiet in the four months since the ork scorchers had raided the village. Theories abounded. The Therans had indeed returned; they would bring a new age of peace and prosperity. The Therans had been killed by the Horrors during the Scourge; the castle was a Theran vessel, but piloted by ghosts of the Therans. The Therans had become monsters, and were coming to finish the work of the Horrors. The Therans had been destroyed by the Horrors; this was just another strong magical empire come to claim land, as is bound to happen again and again.

Torvan the Scarred, Elasia Raven Hair, and a few others rode off in the direction I'd seen the castle flying, but came back a few days later, unable to pick up the castle's trail. I had wanted desperately to go with them. As village magician, it was, in fact, my place to do so, and arrangements could have been made for your care, as on other occasions. But I did not, and even then I knew it was only from an incoherent desire to spite your father. By not going, I thought I was somehow proving he should not have left that night.

Yet as the days passed, my curiosity grew and I knew exactly why he had gone. I thought again and again of how lovely it would have been to ride off with him in pursuit of the castle, the night rushing by, closing toward the unknown.

Weeks passed, the odd event drifting to the back of our thoughts. We had run out of gossip and theories. There was nothing more to be said without new information, and getting that would require a traveler passing through our village. Of course, the world was even less traveled in those days than it is now, and visits by outsiders were few and far between.

A month after your father went chasing after the castle, we did in fact have a visitor; a swordmaster adept whose name escapes me now. She had fresh scars on her neck and arms, wounds made by sword blades. She told of how a town had hired her to defend against raiders from the north.

"Scorchers?" I asked. We had gathered in Tellar's home. You, as well as some other village children, lay asleep on a thick carpet before Tellar's hearth, the red firelight casting shifting shadows upon your soft cheeks. Also lighting the room were several candles. About a dozen or more villagers had gathered to listen to the adept.

"No," she answered. "They came from a town called Mebok, or so the villagers who hired me said. Humans and some elves ..."

"Corrupted?" someone asked.

"The elves were not of the Queen's Court, if that's what you mean," the woman said with a rueful smile. "And no visible signs of corruption. But then Horrors do not always make signs upon the flesh." She shrugged.

"And they came for prisoners?" I asked.

"They killed, make no mistake about that. I haven't seen such fierce fighting for some time—not by folks not trained in combat. But their leader, he was a tough one. A swordmaster adept as well, from the way he fought. He rallied his people hard. The village I tried to protect ... Well, they didn't have much money, and it was me, three other warriors, all mundane, and the village smith. They ran roughshod over us. A hundred or more charged us."

Several of those gathered gasped.

"And they came for prisoners?" I repeated.

"Yes. They stole some goods. But for the most part they tried to disarm everyone and gather them up. They succeeded quite well."

"You escaped?" someone asked.

"I did. When I'd taken so many wounds that I could no longer raise my sword, I retreated." She looked down. Shamed.

I touched her hand. "Did the villagers know why the people of Mebok attacked?"

She shook her head. "A few farmers from the village had gone to visit a neighboring village and found it empty. All of its inhabitants had vanished or lay as corpses on the ground. They became afraid, and hired me when I stopped at their village."

A silence wound its way through the room. I asked,

"And you heard nothing of such raids while you traveled?"

"No. But then, I am new to the area."

"While you traveled, did you hear any word of a . . ."—I paused, realizing how odd the idea would sound to someone who had not been speaking of it for the last month—"a flying castle," I finished.

She looked at me with surprise, and then half-smiled, curious. "Yes. But I didn't think anything of it. How could anyone get a castle to fly?" She looked directly into my eyes, the smile gone now. "Does such a thing exist?"

"Oh, yes." My chest tightened with anxiety. "What have you heard?"

"Some people said that someone they knew knew someone who knew someone who'd seen a castle fly through the air the day before, or two days before. Some people knew someone who knew someone who was related to someone who had actually gone off to follow the castle. And none of these people ever returned."

# 6

That night I prepared to search for your father.

I left you in Tellar's care, the two of you still asleep on the floor. I planned to depart in the morning, saying goodbye to you then. Back home, I folded my traveling clothes, and gathered my magical components, placing them in small bags. It was late, I was tired, and every fifteen minutes or so I would stop, sigh heavily, and wonder why I was going to try to find your father. If he wanted to ride off into danger, that was his business. Why did I have to involve myself?

The reason was this: Although our reasons would be different, he would do the same for me. It was impossible to turn my back to him.

As I was placing the clothes and bags in Wisher's saddle bags, the first screams came.

Thoughts tumbled through my mind. I thought a wyvern, or possibly even a Horror, had entered the village. I started for your bedroom to make sure you two were all right, only to remember as I ran that you were at Tellar's.

I stopped, uncertain where to go next, listening. More screams and shouts filled the air, and I heard people calling for help. Then more cries, gruff and charged with the desire for battle. I grabbed my magician's robe and slipped it on. Barefoot, I rushed out the door and across the moist ground.

Across the village I saw dozens of torches, some bobbing in the darkness, carried by raiders on horseback.

Others rested on the ground, flung forward by the raiders
and illuminating the eastern half of the village. Swords
flashed harsh red. I heard screams. Someone in a white
gown was being carried off by two of the raiders. Those
who ran through the fields were chased down by raiders
on horseback.

Two raiders, a thick-bodied man and a woman, rushed
toward me along the small road through the village. They
laughed, but only until they recognized my magician's
robe. That's when they pulled up on their reins, trying to
bring their horses around.

Too late.

I grabbed two pebbles from my pocket and tossed them
at the man. As the pebbles crossed the distance between
us, I transformed them into maces of ice linked by a
chain of ice. The man's eyes widened as the frozen
weapon caught him around the neck. The maces swung
past each other, the chain biting deep into the flesh of his
neck.

The woman turned her horse back toward me when she
saw her companion endangered. She raised her sword,
obviously no longer concerned with taking me prisoner.
As she charged, the panic that always struck me in combat seized my mind. I thought of every possible spell I
knew, desperately searching for the best way to use my
magic, but meanwhile taking no action at all.

I gave up on thought when the woman was only a few
steps away. I dropped to my knees and touched the puddle of water her horse was splashing through. I concentrated, opening my thoughts to the astral plane, where
magic flows across our reality. As I had shaped the pebbles into maces and a chain, now I shaped the ground and
water before me. It bent to my will, the puddle becoming
deeper and deeper until the horse finally fell forward, surprised.

Whinnying and sinking up to its chest in the mud, the
horse threw the woman forward. The sword flew from her

hand, and she landed in the mud beside me. I pulled out a dagger from my robes, opting for a simpler method of conflict for the task at hand. As she scrambled to get up, I drove the dagger's tip down past the collar of her stiff leather armor and into her neck. Blood sprayed up, washing me warm. She cried out for mercy, and I pulled the dagger away, releasing more blood from her body.

You see, I had only you boys in mind at the moment. And anyone who threatened you or who prevented me from getting to you, would die.

The man had removed the ice maces from his neck, and rode back to the east side of village, toward the brunt of the attack. Again I shifted my thoughts to the etheric plane, and again I used my skill to change the nature of the world. I drew my hand back behind my shoulder, and as I did so a spear of ice formed, gripped in my palm. I flung it forward, and it cut through the air, leaving a trail of ice flakes in the air as it shot forward.

The spear drove deep into the man's back, then snapped, leaving a portion of the shaft buried in his body. He was alive, but disoriented. I ran up and dragged him off the horse, then mounted the beast myself, rushing off toward Tellar's home, desperate to protect the two of you. It took less then a minute to get there. The swordmaster who had brought us news of the raiders fought four of them outside Tellar's door. The raiders, a mix of humans and elves, cut at her savagely with their blades. She fended off their attacks, but could not make a successful strike.

Seeing me approach, she smiled in relief. I dropped the horse's reins, cupped my hands together and produced a flame, which I tossed to her sword. Her opponents pulled back, startled. In that half-beat she struck two solid blows with the enchanted sword, sending two of the raiders to the ground, bleeding heavily.

Then I heard you calling for me, Samael. I looked up toward a window on the second floor of Tellar's and saw you both looking down at me. Flames leaped behind you and smoke poured out the window.

In that moment I forgot all but my concern for you. A mistake. A fireball thrown by a raiding wizard splashed into my right side, blinding me with its fiery light and numbing me with incredible heat as it ripped into my skin.

I screamed—the sound of a thousand birds screeching filling my ears. By that time I had fallen from the horse. The left side of my body, from my face down to my waist, felt horribly cold even as a burning sensation cut through my flesh. My left arm shook violently.

I looked up at you in the window, saw your startled, horrified faces. Tears formed in my eyes. I didn't want you boys to see me like that. I felt shame mixed with fear.

My fingers dug into the soft ground and I tried to raise myself with my right arm. Pain cut through me as I moved my body. But still I tried to rise.

Then a pair of tanned leather boots stepped up in front of me, filling my vision. I suddenly felt like a child confronted by an angry adult. One of the boots pulled back to kick me in the face. I rolled to my right, but not fast enough. The boot swung forward.

My vision flashed to black, and for a moment I couldn't remember what was happening. Then I felt the ground slam into my face. I tried to get up again, focusing on a spell—a fireball, I think. I tried to bring my thoughts to the astral plane, but it was no use. I could not think properly.

The booted foot came for me again, and I tried to catch it with my right hand.

There was not a chance. It slammed into my face once more.

I rolled onto my back. A huge man stared down at me, his features angry and dark, though he smiled with dirty teeth. I turned my head and saw the swordmaster adept surrounded by enemies, her melee illuminated by fluid red torchlight. One of her opponents suddenly drove a sword point through her abdomen. She gasped, her face freezing in pain, then another sword slashed down into her shoulder.

Something, another movement, caught my attention to the left of me. Just as I was shifting my gaze, I saw the boot rising high over my head. After that, oblivion.

# 7

I awoke in pain. Darkness ate at my vision. The floor beneath me seemed to be made of stone, though I could not be sure. The burns on my body confused my sense of touch. Memories of movement—riding in a cart, and even walking, came to me, but I couldn't remember any images.

My voice cracking and barely audible, I spoke. "Hello?"

No reply came back. But as I listened carefully, I heard the sound of breathing, a few whispered words, soft crying, and a gurgling laugh no louder than water running slowly over a rock.

Gingerly I touched my right hand to the left side of my body. The burns had hardened—like thick scars. Someone had taken the trouble of healing me with magic. I tried for a moment to get up, but the pain bit too deeply into my flesh. A wave of dizziness passed over me. I put my head down against the stone floor and fell back asleep.

When the door opened, the room flooded with dim red torchlight. The noise of the door opening startled me awake. The flames, though not bright, hurt my eyes and my vision blurred. I saw figures in the doorway. Around me people of many races—dwarfs, elves, humans, orks, trolls, and others—stood up and made their way toward the door. Someone by the door shouted at us, but in a language I didn't recognize. I tried to get up, but could not.

A whip cracked beside me, and I cringed in surprise. Again came words I couldn't understand. Shadows moved about the room. Suddenly someone grabbed me and pulled me up. The rough jostling cracked some of my scarred flesh, and fresh pain coursed through me. At that moment, all I could think of was, "What did I do? What have I done?"

I was standing now, being pushed forward by someone, forcing me to walk weakly toward the door. To my right I saw an old man on the ground, crying. The man with the whip snapped it against the downed man again and again. Drops of blood rained against my face as the whip snapped back. The sight drove me into a fury, albeit a quiet one. I could barely walk, let alone rescue the old man. I thought for a moment that I had to do *something*— rush the slave master, shout at him to stop. But I could find no energy to do anything. The sight only inspired me to move faster out the door, wanting to avoid the same fate.

Down long corridors lined with smooth marble stones, up perfectly carved stairs with bright silver hand rails. We walked a long time—or so it seemed in my weak state— and I wondered where I was. It might have been the ruins of a shelter from the Scourge, but such places were seldom so well preserved.

We reached a large door leading outside. Bloated gray clouds churned overhead. Thick drops of rain fell. Our escorts herded us into the courtyard of a castle. The castle, of course! Memories came back to me. Were we flying? Maybe not. The clouds didn't seem any closer.

Rain ran down my ruined skin like horribly cold needles. I remember worrying over where the two of you might be—but only for a moment. The constant pain stole my attention, and tears rolled down my cheeks, mixing with the raindrops.

Dozens and dozens of thin, weak people of all races stood in groups all around the courtyard. I realized that my chamber had been only one of many holding prisoners. The features of the people were strange to me: some had skin darker than I had ever seen before, others had thinner noses, or higher cheek bones, or countless other small, unfamiliar traits. It seemed that my fellow prisoners must have come from many, many different places.

Standing around the prisoners were soldiers in scarlet armor, a mixture of elves, humans, orks, and trolls. In contrast to the prisoners, they carried themselves with strength and confidence. Their faces were expressionless, but their eyes betrayed energy and alertness.

You know that I am speaking of the Therans, for you have seen them from a young age. But I must tell you how I felt seeing them at that moment, seeing them for the first time.

Never have I beheld people so *beautiful*. Each seemed a perfect example of his race, each unique, but each an ideal. I had seen the graceful beauty of the elves, of course. Even the corrupted elves of Blood Wood are stunning in their own disturbing way. But the Therans washed me of preconceptions about how people can look. Their poise, lean builds—even though the orks and trolls were large, they were all muscle and bone. Purity. That was it. Purity. And in a world that was still trying to scrub the remains of the Scourge from the land, such people seemed as if they could only have been created out of my imagination. They looked like ideals that I might have dreamed for the day when the world was once again clean.

As my gaze passed among the soldiers, fascinated by their features, wonder alleviating my pain for a moment, I saw a familiar face.

Your father.

He stood in a group on the other side of the courtyard. Ragged rips carved their way through his clown costume, and red welts lined his flesh. He stared down, and never had I seen him so lacking in energy, not since the time before he regained his voice years and years earlier.

It was then that I realized how strangely powerful these people were, powerful enough to contain J'role the thief and to break the spirit of J'role the clown.

But these thoughts broke off sharply when the ground suddenly shifted first to the right and then to the left. Then it seemed to jerk up violently and my knees buckled. I collapsed and realized in a panic that we had left the ground.

# 8

I knelt on the white marble flagstones of the courtyard, the rain pouring down on me. Above, dark clouds
churned in a circle. The castle not only floated, but ro-
tated. As it turned, a huge white stone platform set on
thick, incredibly tall pillars came into view. Hidden behind me only a moment before, it now dominated the castle, dwarfing it. We floated up toward the platform. My
captors were masters of magic.

The platform stretched some eight hundred by twelve
hundred yards. Six buildings, each several stories high,
stood on it. The design of the buildings—the curved
lines, the repeating motifs of mirrored angles and circles, the sweeping balconies and awnings—actually made
my spirits rise. Perfect white marble, sanded soft like
flesh, folded on itself, hiding gentle recesses and seem-
ing to promise that the building would come to life at
any moment. I immediately recognized elements of the
architecture from Parlainth, the hidden city J'role and
I had discovered years earlier. No doubt now lin-
gered about whether or not these were Therans who
had captured me, for Parlainth had formerly been the
Theran capital of Barsaive. But how could the Therans build such lovely buildings and yet be so dreadful?

Several of the buildings looked like barracks, for
they sat low to the ground with less ornate designs.

Three of the buildings, five stories each, with large windows and railed balconies looking out over the platform's courtyard, probably held the quarters of the Theran officials. The last building rose taller than the rest, and atop its highest floor floated a ceiling—but neither walls nor pillars held the building's roof in place. A woman dressed in blue robes looked down on the rising castle. Then she turned and walked out of sight.

Docked around the mining platform floated airships, bobbing as if docked in the blue-green waters of a bay. Thick ropes kept the airships in place, and walkways made of rope and wooden slats spanned the distance from the platform to the airships. Each ship was about a hundred feet long, with a thick, long hull, made of stone. On each deck was a center castle and an aft castle, made of the same gray stone as the hull. Two masts, also made of stone, rose from the deck, each supporting wide yardarms. All the sails of the ships lay folded along the yardarms. Theran sailors were everywhere, the rain pouring down on them, guiding slaves loaded with metal barrels on and off the ships.

I looked toward J'role, who was staring at the platform with an odd expression. I was to find out later that he had, in fact, helped build it. It was at once a point of pride and despair that he had used his hands to create such a magnificent structure. I longed to call to him or draw his attention in some other way, but, certain of a beating if I did anything but wait passively with the other slaves, I did nothing.

The castle gate came level with the platform. Guards on the gate towers signaled to guards below, and the drawbridge was lowered. The red-armored soldiers began to herd us across the platform, keeping us in tight groups. For a brief moment I wondered why a rebellion had not already taken place. The slaves outnumbered the captors; the soldiers and guards seemed only half-aware of our presence. Yet when I secretly stole glances at the other slaves, their faces only echoed a desperate emptiness. They all seemed to me like children, lost and without their parents, numbed from too many weeks struggling to stay alive. Children do not know how to rebel. They have no idea that they *can* rebel. Somehow captivity had broken these adults back down to a time of childhood, before they were responsible for their own lives and so could risk their lives for what they wanted.

I looked down and realized that my wizard robes had been removed, replaced by the same kind of coarse black cloth worn by the other prisoners. Casting a spell would be dangerous, for Horrors on the astral plane might be drawn to me. Could I take the risk? Physically weak as I was, I decided it best not to.

The rain stopped, and I missed its hum in my ears. As we crossed the drawbridge, I glanced over the side and saw that the ground was hundreds of feet below. A broad plain surrounded the platform, the deep grass turning emerald green as the clouds broke and the bright noon sun came forth. In the distance I made out the city of Vivane, with its blue-green spires and glinting gold of its massive walls. So I was in Barsaive after all. I had worried that the Therans might have transported us to a strange land.

All the slaves filed onto the platform. Sunlight sparkled off the rain-damp white marble, and the delicately sculpted buildings reflected the light pure and white.

The soldiers moved us to edges of the courtyard formed by the half-dozen buildings sitting on the platform. The man who had entered the dark room to get my group of slaves, the one with the whip, made the rounds. I saw now he was a small man, thin, with very red hair and a sneering face. He cracked his whip at everyone as he passed. Sometimes he struck someone, other times the whip simply struck the air in between people. The rule, however, seemed to be that if you flinched he would definitely lash you with the whip. Everyone tried to remain as still as possible as the madman walked the edge of the open square formed by the slaves and soldiers.

The slaves raised their eyes toward the castle gate. A dozen soldiers in scarlet armor emerged in a three by four formation. Behind them, flanked by four soldiers in disturbingly black armor that seem to suck sunlight from the air, strode a tall, horribly pale man. Something in the way he walked instantly made me think of a fat, giant worm, but to this day I cannot tell you why. He was old, but showed no signs of decrepitude. A ring of short silver hair circled his balding head from temple to temple. He walked with an absolute confidence, as if the universe itself had whispered to him one night, "And, by the way, all that I have created—it is for you." So it was that I first perceived Overgovernor Povelis.

And behind him walked the two of you.

I sucked in my breath, confused, surprised, and overjoyed. You lived!

You looked extraordinary. The Overgovernor had dressed you both in pure white togas. On your faces, artists had drawn intricate patterns of spirals and curling lines, using silver flakes that glittered in the sunlight. The patterns on your faces was identical, serving to accentuate the similarities between you. Your hair had also been cut short and identically. The effect of all the cosmetics was so dramatic that even I, separated from you by more than eighty feet, could not tell you apart. You held between you a purple pillow upon which rested a white scepter.

I shouted your names and tried to push my way through the other prisoners to get to you. The red-bearded slave master immediately appeared before me and snapped his whip at me again and again. I struggled to get through the whip's blows, but they drove me back and I fell to the ground, cowering. "My children . . . ," I mumbled, but I could do no more. I could not move for the pain.

From the courtyard I heard my two boys crying for me. I looked up, through the legs of the slave master, and saw two Theran guards rush up and carry you toward the castle. I called out your names again, and again I was whipped. I began to black out, and fell flat to the ground.

I could no longer hear your cries when the guards roughly hauled me up to my feet. The slave master stood in front of me, shouting words I could not understand. The meaning, though was clear. "Behave!"

From the tall building at the head of the courtyard came Chancellor Tularch, the woman in robes who I'd seen earlier. She emerged from massive doors carved with a map. Lines radiated from an island in a sea, and I assumed the island was Thera. The woman, an elf with bronze skin and silver hair, walked down a stairway from the map door.

The guards escorting Povelis widened their formation, and the soldiers in black increased the distance between them, making a large square that could contain both Tularch and Povelis. The Chancellor and the Overgovernor faced each other. I saw a smile pass between them. Oddly, the smile did not contain vile secrets or a smug lust, as one might expect from such masters of miserable slaves. Instead, their exchange seemed to me one of true affection and pride; specifically, a teacher, Povelis, gazing upon his student, Tularch.

The pale Overgovernor held a thick white scepter of stone that seemed almost an extension of himself. He raised it high, spreading his arms wide, as if about to laugh with unbridled joy. Instead he shouted to the blue sky above, "And here, now, we have returned!" He spoke the dwarven tongue of Throal, though with a strange accent. A few guards posted around the platform, the castle walls, and the stone airships shouted out a translation that I did not understand. Some standing among the slaves repeated the Overgovernor's words in several different languages, apparently for our benefit. "Let the people of this province know that they are once again part of Thera, and receive the many blessings that rain down for all the people of the Theran Empire!" A cry went up from the soldiers and guards around the platform.

The slaves remained silent, but the Therans seemed not to mind.

Povelis lowered his arms, looked deeply into Tularch's face. "You have done very well, Chancellor Tularch." He spoke loudly, so that all might hear. "This mining platform, a symbol of our permanence in Barsaive, was completed three weeks ahead of schedule." Another cheer from the crowd. I noticed that the small, redheaded slave master smiled broadly and took a half-bow during the shouting. "May your success continue, as I appoint you commander of Sky Point." A final cheer, especially from the sailors on the stone ships.

Povelis handed Tularch the scepter, and she turned to face the cheering Therans and silent slaves. She opened her mouth to speak, but faltered, overcome by emotion. She paused, collected herself, then simply raised the scepter high, and shouted in Throalic, "For Thera!"

Behind her, the Overgovernor smiled, but hid the smile behind one of his old white hands. The soldiers and guards took up a chant that became louder and louder. Firmer and firmer. "Barsaive. Barsaive. Barsaive," they said again and again, emphasizing each syllable.

# 9

The ceremony completed, the Theran officials and ranking military officers made conversation and congratulated one another. I saw the Overgovernor call a guard over and speak to him. The slave master began cracking his whip once again, but the Theran leaders took no notice. Soldiers and the castle guards began herding the slaves as before. They forced some groups toward the castle and others toward the barracks on the platform. J'role's group headed back to the castle, mine to the barracks. We walked closer and closer, and at just fifteen feet from each other, only an instant before we would pass, J'role saw me. He had probably heard my voice earlier when I shouted your names, for he seemed relieved when our eyes met.

I began to open my mouth to speak, but he shook his head and patted the air at waist level. This was an old signal from our first days together, when he was mute and we'd had to forge a language of gestures to communicate. It meant: Wait.

Only a few steps separated our groups as we passed. J'role and I were on adjacent edges of our respective groups, and the crowd of slaves around us provided momentary cover from the guards. Just as we passed he slipped into my group, then grabbed a small female elf by the shoulders and said, "Please, switch with me." I turned, saw the elf's face become tense with fear. Then she nodded quickly and joined the other group as it trod on.

I tried to take his hand, but he waved me away, stared intently at the ground, ignoring me completely.

Just as we reached the barracks, the guard the Overgovernor had spoken to walked up to me. He was an ork, with piercing black eyes and bright white teeth that protruded over his lips. He grabbed me by the shoulder, firmly but not necessarily roughly. Turning me to face him, he studied me, then spoke in heavily accented Throalic. "You are the woman who shouted for the boys?"

I hesitated, not certain which answer would be better, but finally nodded.

"Come with me." He stepped aside so I might leave the group and walk ahead of him.

I turned my head to look at J'role for clues as to what to do. But from the corner of my eye I saw him shake his head slightly.

I stepped out of the group. The slave master looked disappointed, as if he'd just lost status by having one of his victims called away without his permission. This gave me pleasure even as this lowest moment of my life.

# 10

The guard led me to the castle, across the drawbridge, across the courtyard, and into the castle's great hall. Tables, finely carved from dark wood, lined the hall. At the head of the hall, set upon a dais of black marble, was a large throne. Tall, wide windows of colored glass lined the walls, casting extraordinary patterns on the floor. After a moment of staring at the colors I realized that they shifted. Looking up from the floor to the windows, I saw that the patches of color—reds, yellows, blues, greens, and purples—moved around each other, like clouds shifting against the sky at sunset. I had never seen anything so beautiful made by the hands of name-givers before, and nearly wept at the sight. I was becoming horribly confused—too much beauty and pain and fear all at once.

I turned to the ork to ask him why I was here. "Do not speak," he said firmly, but not curtly.

I remained silent.

The doors of the great hall opened, and the Overgovernor swept in, still carrying the stone scepter. His robes billowed around him as his brisk steps carried him past me and up the hall toward the throne. When he reached it, he twirled around and dropped into it, almost playfully.

"Bring her to me!" he shouted. Not waiting for the guard's prodding, I began to walk up the hall.

Against the dark wood and dark throne, the Overgovernor's pale flesh seemed ghastly; dead flesh just short of decaying. He smiled at me, his pale lips pulled back in what seemed a parody of pleasure. But when he spoke I realized he truly was happy. The grotesqueness of his appearance was just the way he happened to look. And more than that: the more I looked at him, the more I realized he was, in fact, attractive. But his attractiveness was of such an extreme degree that it seemed almost inhuman. His face was perfectly symmetrical, an anomaly in most faces; his features as cleanly drawn as if molded from smooth, shiny clay. His white flesh seemed bleached to whiteness, as if to prevent any blemish.

"You know Samael and Torran?"

This stranger speaking the names of my boys with a familiar tone made my knees weak. It was as if you two had lived a whole different life from the one we had known together.

The ork behind me said softly, "Speak now."

"Yes. They are my boys. My children." I clenched my hand, trying to stay focused and strong.

The Overgovernor tapped the scepter against his open palm. "Yes. I thought as much. I wanted to tell you something."

I nodded, suddenly thinking that he might be about to say something wonderful to me. Was he about to let me see you again?

"Put them out of your mind."

My mouth hung open, loose and useless.

"Now, now. They'll be safe." He smiled a strange smile. "I won't let anything happen to them."

"I'm sorry," I said. "But what do you . . . ? What do you mean put them out of my mind?"

"Just that. Put them out of your mind. It may sound harsh, but you will not be seeing them again. It's better for you . . ."

"Just put them *out of my mind*?"

"Your life will be hard enough as it is. I'm just trying to . . ."

"They're just boys," I pleaded. "Little boys. How can you make them prisoners?"

"I promise you, they will be well cared for."

"They're slaves!"

He sighed as if he'd heard it all too many times before. "Yes, that is what they are. You, their mother, committed a crime of some sort or other, and so they were enslaved. The children had to be looked after . . ."

"What do you mean, I committed a crime?"

"Well, you wouldn't have been enslaved if you had not committed a crime. That is Theran law."

"My entire village was attacked. My entire village consisted of criminals? All the people who had grown up together, raised families together, helped each other—we were all criminals? What crime did we commit?"

He looked flustered for just a moment, then said, "I don't have the records here. I don't know the village . . ."

"Yeras."

He glowered at me. "I'm not familiar with it, actually."

"Then how do you know—"

"We depend on local authorities to convict . . ."

"The slavers convicted us?"

"No. The slavers simply gathered you . . ."

"Who convicted us?"

"We depend on local authorities . . ."

"You took the word of people who attack and enslave other people for a living?"

"I'm not here to argue the point, woman. I just wanted to tell you your boys will be safe."

"What do you mean by that? You keep saying that."

He paused, uncertain if he wanted to share a secret with me. Then he smiled and stepped down the dais toward me. "They're twins, you see. Twins . . ."

". . . yes . . ."

"You've lost a great deal of the ancient lore, here in Barsaive, and part of that lost lore involves twins. Not a spell that can be cast. But something deeper. More mysterious."

The guard moved subtly, as if trying to warn his liege away from danger. "What does it matter, Yerv? She loves them. What will she do?"

"What are you . . . ?"

"Look. Twins are magical, and that magic is enhanced with proper rituals. I've bonded with your boys. They're *mine* now. As long as they remain perfect twins I am charmed. Not indestructible, mind you, but the ill fates of life and death that should befall me will be held at bay. I just . . . I just wanted to thank you. For bearing them. You yourself are a special woman for such an act."

My tone became deathly level. "I'm not a special woman. I'm a mother. And I want my boys back. You're treating them like animals . . ."

"No. Them I will treat as honored guests. The rest of you I will treat like animals." There was no clever malice in his voice when he said this. Just a statement of plain fact. He turned from me, clearly disappointed that I didn't share his enthusiasm, and sat back down on the throne.

"How can you enslave people?"

"It doesn't appeal to me, actually," he said, dropping his tone. "It's a terrible thing. But our economy depends on it. Our politics depend on it. Our continued existence depends on it."

"But they are name-givers. They are your equals in life. It's abominable."

"Yes. I've said as much. But I will do nothing to stop it. Do you know why? Because it works, and we will make the lands we conquer quite comfortable for us. Many people will suffer at our hands, but then, we won't be suffering at their hands." He looked away, then at me again. "Anyway, there it is. I'm sorry you can't accept the facts as they are. Your boys are no longer yours. I just thought . . . If you try to put them out of your head . . . Don't harbor hopes of trying to get them back. Your life will be easier."

# 11

A windowless barrack waited for me on the platform, as dark as the large cell I'd woken up in, and the ork ushered me inside. As he shut the door, J'role leaped up and cut across the room toward me. He moved so that the ork did not see him move, but by the time darkness had shrouded the room once more, he stood beside me.

"J'role?"

"Shhh," he said softly.

"What . . . ?"

"Shhh."

I raised my right hand to his and pulled him close. Instinctively he embraced me. His hug sent lancing pain through my burned flesh, and I gasped.

He pulled his body away, still holding my hand, and asked me if I was all right. His hand held mine lightly, as if it had little strength. When he spoke, it was in a whisper as dry and cracked as burnt wood from an evening fire.

"I know where the boys are," I said. "There on that flying castle. The Overgovernor has taken them as pets." I then told him everything the Overgovernor had told me about his charm. When finished, I asked, "Have you tried to escape?"

He was a silent a moment, then said, "It's hard here. No shadows except here. I've tried twice. Caught. Beaten. They do things to us. Beat us."

"Who was the elf you spoke to? The one you switched with."

He sat us down on the cool stone floor. "One of the few people here I could talk to."

"What?"

"Many languages. Talking is hard here. Therans, they pull people from all over the empire. We're not allowed to talk ... even if we know same language. And the ... Overgovernor pulls people aside. Tells people they'll be freed if they report to him."

"Report to him?"

" 'Are people talking?' 'Have you heard any plans for escape?' Anything of interest. Fear lives with us. We don't know who we can trust."

The way J'role spoke worried me. His uncertain words and cracked sentences coming out of utter darkness turned him into someone else. Never, in all his years of odd behavior, had he seemed so different. He had only been here a month, yet they had broken him completely.

I took his hand. "What happened? What happened to you?"

"Left our home and followed castle. Days. Rode up and saw slaves building this platform. Mining platform, for elemental air. I approached the castle. Soldiers came to me. Escorted me to castle to meet Povelis. To have dinner with him. Pompous ass. Other people—farmers, people from Vivane there, too. He asked me to be his clown. I refused. I asked about slaves. He said they only slave criminals who break Theran law. But they *buy* slaves from people who sell them. Left. Riding out, saw an old man being whipped to death. By Redbeard. To death. Bloody strips of flesh sliding off the muscles of his back. The old man was ... on his hands and knees. Screaming. Other slaves stood and stared. I said I'd take the old man if they didn't want him anymore. If they were going to kill him anyway, I'd take him. I pleaded. They said he was an example. I tried to rescue him. Rode

in and tried to grab him. Almost made it. Had him on
Jester. We rode. Soldiers chased us. Magic lances and
spears cut into my back. We fell. Old man died. Jester
died." He paused, half-laughed. "You know. I saw old
man clearly when we fell to the ground, our faces near.
He wasn't old at all. Boy, younger than me by five
years. I could see it in his eyes. They'd ruined him."

A silence fell between us. We sat and held hands.
Around us I heard the soft whispers of others talking
softly. A man crying. A soft moan.

"We have to escape," I said.

He said nothing, but I imagined he nodded.

"We have to find our boys."

He began crying softly. "Our boys. I was so worried
about you and the boys . . ."

"J'role. Listen. We have to escape."

He stifled his tears. "Yes. Yes. We have to find them."
Then a deep tone of resolution filled his voice. "We have
to save our boys." The quick change of emotion frightened me, for it seemed, like so many of his words and actions, inspired only by the moment, as shallow as a
brook. I wanted his sentiments as deep as the lava of
Death's Sea.

"Can you get through the lock?"

"No lock. It's something I've never seen before. No
knob. Nothing."

"Can we get the help of others?"

"No."

"What are they going to do with us?"

"We're going on the ships to mine for elemental air."

"We could take over the ship."

J'role snorted derisively.

I felt a strong impulse to ignore him, to leave him to
his despair and to proceed without his help. But I knew
if I could bring the old J'role back, he would help me im-
measurably. And the story of his capture, how he had
tried to save the boy from death . . . There is something,

my sons, true and good about your father, despite everything.

"J'role," I said. "We escaped from the elf queen together. We found Parlainth together. We can take over a Theran ship."

"Releana. They are different than anything else. They are Therans."

"And we are parents," I insisted. "We're going to find our boys."

# 12

The next day armored guards led us out of the darkness into the glaring sunlight.

The slave master—Redbeard, J'role called him—cracked his whip at us. At first I remained resolute not to let the man make me flinch as the others so readily did. I kept my spine straight and my face expressionless, forcing myself not to react. But then the whip's tip cracked against my back. I jumped forward, the pain ripping through my flesh. I thought for certain Redbeard would whip me again, but he didn't. He moved down the group, continuing to crack the whip. Most of the time, he struck no one.

When he had gone down the line, he returned, coming closer and closer. I stared ahead, not wanting to give him the pleasure of my attention. As he passed he snapped the whip against me. Again I jumped and cried out.

I did not want him to whip me again, and was terribly afraid he would. He was behind me, and I waited and waited for the snap of the whip. It never came. But now I was not so certain of my ability to avoid flinching.

They led us to a swaying gangplank of wooden slats stretched over rope, with rope railings on either side. The forty of us walked across to the gangplank and onto the stone ship.

I smile as I write these words, for I remember that despite the pain and worry I felt at that moment, a sensation of wonder overcome me as I stepped onto the stone deck.

How strange that our sense of wonder remains alive even during the darkest of times. I had never been on an airship before, and had only seen them in the sky once or twice in my whole life. As I stepped onto the ship, the same tickling of my soul occurred as when I cast my first spell and a golden flame sprouted from my palm.

The boat swayed slightly, and I looked to J'role. We had made sure several people stood between us, for he had explained that the Therans would immediately separate any two people who seemed to have made some sort of contact. As he stepped onto the boat he smiled slightly and lifted his head, pleased. His gaze met mine, and we allowed ourselves the exchange of a subtle smile. A strange moment, for we had not shared such enjoyment for years. That kind of smile, given in shared wonder—like the strange experience of stepping onto a flying ship made of stone—was what had drawn me to your father to begin with. It was that kind of smile that had made me want to spend the rest of my life with him.

As we quickly turned away from each other, lest any of the Therans spot our brief connection, I wondered what had happened to J'role's smile. I had not seen it for years. Then I realized the smile had never left. I simply had not been around him during his adventures. I never discovered *with him* the surprises the Universe held.

They led us along the deck to a door built into the central forecastle. Then down a set of stairs to a lower deck illuminated by glowing spheres of moss. After two more flights of stairs we reached the lowest deck on the ship. Only a few moss lanterns, dim and aged, illuminated the corridors. The walls were rough and streaked with smoke from torchlight.

The corridor ended in a doorway, and through the door a long room with ten benches on the starboard and port sides of the ship. Each bench sat next to an opening in the hull, through which extended oars. The imitation of sea-going vessels would move us through the air.

Redbeard and the other guards arranged us on the benches, shackled our wrists to the oars. J'role sat across the aisle from me, three benches up. He did not glance back at me once. Redbeard stood before us, the open doorway framing him. He cracked his whip twice. A bare-chested man at the back of the room, another slave as far as I could tell, began beating a drum slowly.

# 13

Redbeard cracked his whip and walked up and down along the aisle between the benches and shouted something at us in words few of us could understand. But the meaning was clear. We all gripped our oars and began to row, using the beat of the drum to set our rhythm. Redbeard backed up to the doorway and turned to us. He looked up and spread his arms wide, his eyelids fluttering wildly. When he looked back toward us his pupils had rolled up.

My muscles tightened, and though I continued to row, I had lost control of my body. It was as if my mind sat trapped in my flesh, my body now an alien thing. Detached, I watched my arms as they continued to row.

For a while I thought that somehow, through the use of a magic I knew nothing about, Redbeard could make us row without tiring. But after an hour, despite my sense of dislocation from my body, my muscles began to fatigue. I remembered some questors of various Passions talking about such a power. Vestrial, they'd said, had gone insane during the Scourge, driven mad by the Horrors, and his powers had become those of slavery. Redbeard, I realized, was a questor of Vestrial, and could make us perform the same mindless task again and again until we simply died.

Out the oar's hole in the hull I saw the ground drop lower and lower until the jungles below seemed a huge green sea, the ripple of the leaves in the wind like water gently rolling on a calm day.

The pain in my arms grew, and, nightmarishly, I could not even slow my pace in response. Above us I heard the shouts and cries of the sailors at work. I could understand nothing of their native Theran. We, of course, were not allowed to speak while we rowed. With my body no longer under my control and my ears filled with words that had no meaning to me, I truly felt as if I'd entered another world—someone else's life—by accident. It seemed that all I had to do was swim up from a deep dream, wake up in my own bed at home, perhaps on the very night J'role had come to visit. The castle we had seen flying overhead would have been part of the dream, and the Therans would not have come to Barsaive.

These useless wishes ended suddenly when a tremendous explosion erupted off the port side of the ship. I craned my neck to see out the hole, even as my arms ceaselessly rowed. Outside I saw another of the stone ships floating a hundred yards off port. During the journey a huge net had been strung out between the two ships. The net was made of thick rope, but bits of silver glinted in the rope. I knew enough about mining for magical elements to know the Therans had laced the rope with orichalcum.

More shouts bellowed from the sailors. I saw Therans on the other ship shouting toward our ship, and heard the loud responses from above me. The winds were fierce, and the sailors clung tightly to mast lines and railings. A sailor appeared on the other ship with two red flags. After a few moments another sailor appeared on the stairway behind Redbeard. He said something to Redbeard, who in turn shouted instructions to the drummer at our backs.

The drumming ceased, and suddenly we could stop rowing. Terrible pain cut through my arms, as if someone were dragging the tip of a knife over my flesh and into my muscles. I and many others cried out in agony. Tears formed in my eyes. Gasping for breath, I doubled over, collapsing onto my chained hands.

I turned my head and saw the other ship bobbing in the air. The netting strung between the two ships loosened and tightened. The sailors on the other ship had dropped the ship's sails. As I watched, two sailors from the other ship heaved a black sphere over the edge of the ship. A Theran wizard in an emerald robe stood by the edge of the ship casting ritual gestures as the sphere dropped. They seemed elemental, but I did not recognize them.

The sphere fell through the air, then suddenly exploded in a fiery red blossom. The red glare of the explosion washed the edges of my small portal with light, and the image burned into my eyes. Jagged edges erupted in the air at the point of the blast, curling like flower petals opening to the sun. The momentary hole revealed a patch of absolute, pure violet light. I knew what they had done, but gaped at actually seeing it. The Therans had ripped a hole as big as a cart into the plane of elemental air.

The hole quickly closed back up on itself, but I saw a shimmer of elemental air rise up from the tear. It resembled the wavering air over a fire, but with a silver sparkle to it. Rushing up, it slammed into the netting strung between the two ships. Immediately the vessels began to rock wildly, knocking me first right, then left. The netting rose up quickly, causing the ships to list sharply and rush toward each other.

Several of the lines snapped from our ship, falling down and dangling between the two ships. A sailor trying to catch one of the ropes as it trailed overboard abruptly dropped into my view, clinging to the end of the rope, his face darkened with tension and fear.

As the two ships rushed toward each other, I thought for certain he would be crushed. But then our momentum slowed and the two ships stopped moving toward each other at about forty feet apart. The sailor on the loose rope came to rest at eye level with me. He saw me looking at him and smiled. He'd not only lived, but he'd helped keep one corner of the net down, preventing the elemental air from escaping the orichalcum-laced net. He'd won.

Above, on the decks of the two ships, barked orders tumbled from excited mouths. Lines were thrown back and forth between the two ships, locking them in place at this distance from each other. I saw sailors swishing orichalcum jars through the air under the net, drawing the elemental air out and trapping it.

Gathering the elemental air from the net took several hours, for the Therans wanted to mine every last bit they could. As they worked, the net slowly dropped, eventually reaching deck level, then fell below that.

By this time the sun had sunk behind distant mountains. Over the jungle rooftop a violet twilight had spread darkness across Barsaive. Clouds in the distance appeared like bloody castles.

Redbeard snapped his whip. I gripped the oar again without thinking, as if I'd been born for the task. The drum beat began, and I lifted the oar, fearing the snap of the whip against my flesh. The oar moved slightly, heavier than before. I thought exhaustion had finally taken its toll. I would collapse and be pitched overboard for my uselessness. Then I glanced to the right and saw that my partner, a thick-muscled man with brown skin, had still not lifted his head. A moment ago I'd thought he'd been resting from exhaustion, but his chest still lay on the oar and his head hung down.

I turned to call out to Redbeard, but he was already marching down the aisle, glaring at me as if I'd caused the man's death. He grabbed the man's head, jerked it back. The man's mouth hung open, slack and lifeless, the eyes half-open.

Redbeard called up the stairs and a sailor arrived shortly. He came down the aisle and held the dead man as Redbeard took his key ring and unshackled the corpse from the oar. He smiled at me and said something with a sneering tone, then laughed. The sailor dropped the corpse into the aisle, and Redbeard cracked his whip. The drum began again.

I couldn't believe that they expected me to row alone. But there seemed little doubt, for Redbeard glared at me and cracked his whip against my chest when I showed hesitation. That was painful, but what hurt more was the helplessness. I wanted so much to wring his neck. The thought of casting a fireball on him rushed into my senses. But what would that get me? I might snap the chains with another spell. And then what? Trapped on a ship with dozens of opponents. And without my robe, I would surely draw a Horror to my thoughts with one too many spells. No. I decided to wait. I had to think, come up with a plan, not act simply on the angry desire for revenge.

# 14

By the time we returned to Sky Point I was ready to die. The greatest pain was in my shoulders, which felt like they were bleeding.

As we approached the platform I looked out my oar hole. In the starlit darkness I saw that beneath the platform stood troops and a military camp. Even if I got *down* from the platform, how would I escape an army? J'role's weariness made more sense to me now. I remembered my promise to myself that morning not to let the Therans get the better of me, and all I could think was: *Had it only been this morning?*

They led us to the lightless barracks. Above, the stars filled the sky, glistening like grains of sand at noon. I saw Redbeard pass his hand before the featureless door. It opened, and we entered. J'role and I made sure to be near each other by the time the door closed, and took up a space on the floor together. I was too tired for words, and he seemed to be as well. We curled up, holding each other carefully against the pain of the day, and fell asleep together for the first time in years.

It went on. And on. And on.

The fear of the whip grew. The labor that brought each one of us to near-death never ended. The mind-numbing realization that escape might be impossible took firm hold. A fight, yes, but no escape.

"We have to try," I said to J'role one night. Others

around us slept, or spoke softly. "I'll kill Redbeard. You'll get through the shackles . . ."

"And then what?" he asked.

I was crying, and only realized it now. "We have to do *something*."

"There's nothing—"

"You told me we'd try!" I shouted. He put his hand toward my face. I pulled back in pain and anger. "Were you just saying that?" I asked, now speaking in a harsh whisper. "Just to placate me?"

"I really . . ." He was crying now, too. "I want to do something." He paused. I thought he might get up and stumble away. He didn't. "But I don't know what to do. We need something new. Something to throw the circumstances our way."

"We could be dead by then."

"Then what is your plan?" he snapped.

I remained silent. J'role had always made the plans. His daring had allowed him a certain good luck. I had been content to follow him on the adventures. "Are we going to die here?" I finally asked.

"Don't know. Don't know," he answered, his voice flat and level. He hadn't given up yet, but he didn't know what would happen. He stifled his tears and said, "People can't live like this."

Yet, as he said the words, I thought I heard something odd in his tone. A pleasure. In that moment I suddenly thought of smiles I'd seen J'role make over the last few weeks. It suddenly occurred to me that part of him liked the life we were living. As if it proved something he'd known all along. Yes. That was it. This life of misery was somehow confirmation of a dark secret he thought others were too weak to see clearly, but that he knew only too well.

# 15

We remained silent a long time, until, finally, we held each other against our fear of death. We kissed.

J'role's fingertips slid down my neck, along my breast. My body was so weary, but so longed for the gentle touch. The palm of his hand pressed lightly against my nipple.

"J'role. No. Not . . . not . . . here." In the darkness, in our private, whispered conversations, it was possible to think we were alone. But we weren't. Forty other people shared the room.

"Releana," he sighed, making his desire for me so clear.

"No. I . . ."

"Just some pain?"

"I . . ."

"Yes." He raised my hand to his neck, pressed my fingers against his flesh. "Just some scratches."

I'd never liked the hurting. Never had thought of love-making involving pain—not until my first time with J'role.

"Please," he sighed.

I pressed my fingernails into his shoulder and raked them away from his neck.

"Again. More."

"I . . ."

"Yes."

I did it again, this time with one hand on each shoulder. He sighed with pain and pleasure.

"More."

Something about his enjoyment dragged me into it, as it always did. I dug down deeper, could feel the thin furrows of raked flesh producing blood against my fingertips. I was sighing with him, a matched rhythm forming in our breathing.

"Teeth."

Without thinking I leaned down toward his right shoulder and caught up some of his bleeding skin in my mouth, squeezing it between my teeth. He groaned loudly. The taste of blood pressed warm against my tongue.

And I did like it. I did. Now it seems all so ... But then ... I could not even tell you why. I can't even believe I'm telling you this, but it's ... I think it's important you know ... for what's to come. And I think you should know I was a part of it in my way.

He touched himself, rubbing harder and harder, and as I continued to hurt him his breathing increased faster and faster until he finally climaxed. He sank softly against me, and mumbled something like this: "Scars are what make us who we are."

I held him while he fell asleep, the enjoyment quickly draining from me. I stayed awake, feeling wrong and lonely.

# 16

I sit at my desk, as I have for several days, writing this strangely long missive to you. It is morning. The air is warm, the day gray. When I search my thoughts for the next word, I look up and out the window into the lush green treetops of the jungle. My hut sits among the branches of a giant tree, as do the other homes of my village. Countless raindrops splash against dark green jungle growth. From leaf to leaf they fall, one short fall after another, until their final plummet to the ground.

Children, far below, run and laugh, splashing their small feet through mud-rich puddles and chasing each other with half-understood threats of monsters.

I think of you two. Your childhood had moments in it I had not planned. I think of the young children below, and consider them so lucky, for they have not had to face the terrors you lived through. Then I remind myself you were seven when the Therans came. Some of the children swooshing water in puddles with their feet or carefully crafting castles of mud are only three or four or five years old.

There is time yet for tragedy in their childhood.

# 17

Weeks passed.

I felt my spirit splitting into several pieces. It was harder and harder to find the energy to think of plans of escape.

Worse, it seemed that J'role did not want to escape. He seemed content to be trapped with me. I would discuss plans and options, and he would listen, and then change the subject. Having me in his life, without the possibility of me sending him away, actually made him content.

# 18

We sailed into the sky, again and again, the thrill of floating in a stone ship now long gone. I no longer looked out the oar's small hole. Neither did I pay any attention to the task of rowing. Redbeard cast his powers granted by Vestrial, my muscles left my control, and I had little to do but make my mind wander as far as possible from the pain.

One day as I stared forward, a red-haired woman glanced back at me. She nodded slightly, then quickly turned forward once more.

Was she one of the Overgovernor's spies? Was she a potential ally? Had she overheard J'role and I talking in the darkness? Did she know how much I wanted to escape? To get to my boys?

Our ship was following one of the five established routes over now-familiar landmarks, and had risen to our standard mining altitude. It seemed that certain portions of the sky were more rich in elemental air than others, just as a mine in a mountain might have some veins richer in silver.

Sailors strung the nets out between the ships, and dropped charges of elemental fire to rip holes into the plane of elemental air. I watched these operations, for it was during these breaks that the Therans usually fed us a mix of gruel and water. I needed something to keep my mind off the mess I ate.

On the day the red-haired woman looked at me, storm

clouds, dark and forboding, rolled quickly toward us from the south. Rushing winds and rain-soaked clouds usually sent us back to Sky Point. But this day the captains of the vessels decided to stay, for they had yet to gather any elemental air.

The day turned from bright and blue to gray and dismal. Sails fluttered wildly and the snapping of their cloth sounded like Redbeard's whip. As the sailors quickly lowered their sails, long streaks of rain began to rush by my oar's hole. The drum started up—a steady, slow rhythm, designed to hold us in place and parallel with the other ship as the winds pushed us through the sky. The Therans refused to return to the platform empty-handed.

Another charge went off. I glanced out the window. The tear appeared, finally, the red blossom of flame cutting into the dark purple of the elemental plane. As I stared I gasped, for within the hole cut into another world I saw something move.

# 19

My bowl of gruel slipped from my hands and splashed to the floor as I craned my neck to get a better look at the things rushing up from the deep-blue crack in the sky. I saw three or four white creatures with long limbs and thin, skull-like faces dominated by large mouths lined with sharp teeth. Their long, sharp fingers moved in and out of a grip, terribly desirous for something to rend.

Already, shouts of alarm rang through the air. Sailors scrambled to untie the net connecting the ships, but their efforts came too late. The elemental air rushed up from the hole in the sky and snagged the net. It shot up like a blanket over a rambunctious and sleepless child. The two ships lurched and rushed toward each other. As our ship jerked to port, some of my fellow slaves cried out in fear. Redbeard, always ready with just the right response, cracked his whip to silence us. Then he, wide-eyed with concern, called up the stairs. No answer came back.

As the two ships nearly crashed into each other, sailors on the other ship dropped their end of the netting. The elemental air drove the loose netting up and then rushed out from under it, a strange, amorphous glitter of silver shunting aside raindrops as it raced toward the gray clouds above. A treasure lost to the skies.

For just a moment I felt oddly safe in the slave hold, protected from the rain like a child staring out the window of her hut. I also felt somehow safe from the creatures that rushed by me toward the upper decks, their long bodies like milky water. It seemed as if it were all happening in a dream, and that retribution would be swiftly dealt to my enemies.

The sense of safety ended a moment later.

The first scream came from directly overhead. Dark drops of blood fell with the rain, startling me. I pulled back just as the corpse of a Theran sailor fell from the deck above, cartwheeling through the air, his chest an open cavity, the ribs shattered and pulled opened wide. The rag doll body slammed into the hull of the opposite ship, bounced off, and began its nightmare plummet to the ground below.

On the other ship I saw several sailors gathered against one of the things. They had surrounded it, their blades flashing strange light as they swung at it. The thing raked the air with its claws, and they could neither strike it nor avoid the tips of its sharp claws. Lines of blood appeared on their faces. The sailors cried out in pain, but the pain only seemed to strengthen their resolve to destroy the thing.

A palpable panic filled the hold as slaves on the port stared out at the carnage through the small oar holes, their backs tense with terror, while the other slaves uselessly craned their necks for a view outside. Some of the slaves cried out questions in a variety of strange tongues. A few answers came back. One slave, the red-haired woman, shouted in Throalic, "Elemental monsters. They're attacking the ship!"

Redbeard walked the aisle, snapping his whip, but his heart wasn't in it, the gesture more like a reassuring habit. The snapping of the whip quieted us, but the anxiety did not abate.

I realized that if the sailors lost the battle, we might well be the next victims of the terrible elemental creatures. Chained to our oars and weaponless, we would be easy prey. More than that, it seemed that the chance J'role said we must wait for had arrived. If the creatures won the battle, then the Therans would be dead and we would only have to face the monsters. No simple task, but possible. If the monsters lost, the Therans would be wounded and their numbers reduced. An even better opportunity.

"J'role!" I shouted without looking at him, so as to not call Redbeard's attention to him. "Now's our chance!"

The tip of Redbeard's whip slapped into my face, blocking my view of J'role's reaction. For a moment I could think of nothing as blackness stuffed its way into all my senses, blocking any sight, sound, or touch. When I came awake again, it seemed that hours had passed, but I knew it had only been seconds. I felt a thin, ticklish stream of blood dripping down my cheek and soaking into my black slave robe. Redbeard shouted at me, his face close and red, his mouth wide in frantic panic. More screams came from the upper decks. The other slaves began screaming as well, holding up their chains to Redbeard, pleading for their freedom.

I glanced past Redbeard, and saw J'role huddled over and quiet. I breathed a sigh of relief. He was working on his lock, using his thief magic to free himself.

My sigh of relief was the first mistake I made that day.

Redbeard saw my reaction, whirled around, searched for what had given me moment of respite. He spotted J'role and rushed toward him. "J'role!" I cried. Your father ignored me and continued to work.

When close enough, Redbeard snapped the whip at your father's back. The clown outfit was long gone, replaced now by a black slave robe already pockmarked with ragged holes from the whip. J'role's body jerked in response to the blow, but he kept working, his attention—as much of it as he could retain—focused on picking the lock.

Again and again Redbeard snapped his whip at J'role. Blood rained down on the slaves behind your father.

"Stop him!" I screamed, standing. "Stop him! J'role's our only chance." I do not know whether it was from fear or lack of understanding, but no one stirred to lend a hand.

In his frantic desire to stop J'role, Redbeard gripped his whip with both hands and slid it around J'role's neck. He jerked the whip back and began to strangle your father. Panic seized me, and then rage at all those around J'role who refused to help. Options for spells raced through my mind; I had to risk drawing a Horror to me. If a risk must be taken, now was the time. Air blast was unavailable, for I could not fling my chained hands wide enough to cast the spell. Earth darts would have been wonderful—but of course I had no dirt. In fact, I had no spell components of any kind near me.

J'role called out for help, his breathing like the gurgle of a drowning man.

Then I thought of icy surface. Could I lean down far enough? I could only try.

Straining my spine as much as possible, I brought my face as close to floor as I could. The oar squeezed deep into the flesh of my stomach and thighs. I focused on tapping into the astral plane with my thoughts, drawing the magical energy needed to collect the moisture in the room's air. My mind slipped into the strange place between our world and all the worlds around ours.

Were Horrors near? Would they sense me in my weakened, magically exposed state?

The ship tossed back and forth in the rough winds of the rain storm. Screams filled the air during the tiny gaps between the storm's howling. I heard someone shouting from up the stairs, making Redbeard look up and call back. Then he returned his attention to J'role.

I exhaled, my breath turning as misty and white as it might on the upper reaches of a mountain. The mist flowed down from my mouth, and a thick layer of ice formed on the floor. It spread out five feet across, then rushed forward, a blue-silver carpet of ice unfurling, slipping around the legs of the benches the other slaves sat on, racing toward Redbeard, who was still struggling to strangle J'role.

# 20

The ice rushed up under Redbeard's feet. In that moment
he tugged hard on his whip, making J'role gasp sharply.
The momentum of the tug rocked Redbeard back, and he
uttered a cry of surprise as his feet slid out from under
him. Falling backward, he dragged J'role with him, bend-
ing your father over backward to the floor, the whip still
wrapped around his neck.

J'role used that moment to wriggle free of the whip.
With the deft motion of a well-practiced thief, he slipped
the keys from Redbeard's belt. He then swung his upper
body back up and began searching for the right key. But
Redbeard was already scrabbling to stand. A slave stuck
out his foot and tripped the slave master. Redbeard
scrambled for balance on the ice, then fell back down.
The slave smiled, something I'd never seen him do before
in the two months he'd been with us.

A cheer went through room.

J'role found the key, undid his shackles, and stood. Another cheer and a rattling of chains filled the room. A
charge of thick energy passed through us all. Suddenly
we could remember the taste of freedom. We needed our
chains undone *now*. J'role dodged a kick from Redbeard
and tossed the keys to some people on benches behind
him. Immediately they began fumbling with the keys to
free themselves.

Meanwhile, Redbeard had scrambled up, avoiding the
clawing hands of nearby slaves and the quick kicks of

their legs. He stepped off the ice, whirled his whip back, and snapped it at J'role in three quick, successive blows. J'role moved quickly right, left, then right again, each time just a hair's breadth from the snap of the whip.

The keys made their way back along the benches. Prisoners found their freedom, passed the keys back, then rushed forward to help J'role. A few of the slaves slipped on the ice patch, but most flung themselves into Redbeard, knocking the slave master to the ground and burying him under their bodies.

The keys reached me, and I undid my shackles. I jumped up—realized that was a mistake in my weakened condition—and staggered a moment. I covered my eyes with my hands and drew in a long, slow breath.

Footsteps came from the stairs. J'role turned, and a Theran sailor, his hair heavy and wet with rain, his silver and white clothes streaked with stains of blood, stared in horror and disbelief at the rebellion before him. In that pause J'role rushed up the stairs. The sailor swung his sword. J'role ducked beneath it and drove his right shoulder into the man's abdomen. The sword slammed into the stone wall, and the two men tumbled down the stairs and out onto the floor.

Redbeard screamed harsh words—obscenities, no doubt, and orders for us to free him. I moved quickly to the front of the hold, intending to ignore Redbeard in my desire to help J'role. I hadn't even gotten that far, however, before a group of slaves grabbed the guard's head, a dozen hands all at once. No word or signal had been given. A perverse communication of pain had passed from mind to mind. As a single, writhing entity of arms, they twisted Redbeard's head, first to the left then to the right. A sharp crack, much like the sound of his whip, resulted from the first twist. The second produced a simple grinding.

I rushed past the horrible scene and came up to J'role and the sailor rolling back and forth on the ground, each seeking the final, decisive advantage over the other. The other slaves were still enraptured by the fate of the Theran they hated most, and paid not the slightest attention to my husband's skirmish with an unknown sailor.

The sailor's sword lay on the ground. I picked it up and shouted at him, ordering him to surrender. My plan had been to use Redbeard as my hostage. That possibility removed, I decided to replace the slave master with the sailor.

Although the sailor did not understand my words, he turned quickly to find me standing behind him, sword raised high. He paused. In his eyes I saw him weighing a decision. Then he tensed and rushed at me. I am no swordmaster, but I swung the blade down well enough, catching him in the shoulder. A splash of blood cut an arc through the air and spattered the gray stone wall. The sailor cried out in pain as J'role used his legs to knock him down to the floor. Then other slaves swarmed over the sailor like waves crashing onto a rocky shore.

I rushed toward the stairs, desperate to escape the man's screams. The sword still in my hand, I led J'role and a few other slaves up from our prison.

# 21

We worked our way along the corridors of the next deck up. No one stood in our way, nor seemed to be in any of the cabins. The ship shifted left, then right, and I had to place my hands against the cool gray walls to remain upright. I wondered for a moment if the stone airship was horribly damaged somehow. Were we plummeting to the ground?

A rush of fierce wind and harsh rain met us as we approached the door to the main deck. It slammed open and shut over and over. A crack of lightning illuminated the downpour: a thousand drops of silver rain whirled in the air. The deck seemed empty.

J'role came up beside me, placed one hand on my shoulder, the other hand on the hilt of the sword I carried. "My love," he said, "unless you've practiced the use of this weapon since last we traveled, I'll take this, and you use magic." I felt annoyed, for I had the suspicion that whoever held the sword would lead, and it seemed that J'role was asking to lead out of habit. But it was true he would put the sword to better use. I gave him the weapon, then turned to the crowd of slaves behind us, signaling them with a raised hand to wait. Their eyes burned with intensity and a hunger for violence, but they kept their passions in check. J'role held the door open and the two of us stepped out onto the deck.

The rain drenched us immediately. The wind pushed us to starboard, and we had to crouch to keep our balance.

Lightning cracked through the sky and thundered terribly in our ears.

The lightning illuminated eight Theran corpses fifteen feet ahead, their blood mixing with rainwater to stain the stone of the deck a light red. All had suffered improbable wounds to their limbs and chest. One woman's face had been crushed, leaving nothing but a smear of bone and torn flesh. Others had portions of their bodies scooped out. J'role signaled for a half-dozen of the slaves to follow us onto the deck. He pointed out the swords lying near the corpses, and the slaves hungrily picked among the dead.

I looked off starboard and saw the other airship floating far away. The entire sky churned gray, and we rocked uselessly back and forth. It occurred to me that even if all our enemies were dead—the elemental creatures and the Theran sailors might have killed each other—we still might die on board a magical vessel we did not know how to use.

But everyone was not dead. J'role tapped my shoulder, cocked his head to one side. I followed him around the ship's central castle. As we moved, working with great difficulty to keep from slipping on the rocking, rain-soaked deck, I heard sounds. Cries of battle, cries of pain. And a horrible shrieking.

With the other slaves following, we rounded the center castle, and saw a battle waged between a dozen Theran sailors and two of the elemental creatures. The things stood more than a dozen feet tall, with long, thin bodies. Their limbs were elongated as well, giving their sharp claws a long reach while their bodies remained safe. Their arms had suffered nicks and cuts and even a few long gashes. Deep blue liquid dripped from the wounds, but the strange blood fell *up*, floating high into the sky. The huge, curved mouths of the things seemed to be smiling.

I noticed that they did not stand on the deck, but floated near it. Darting around the sailors, first they would attack from the rear, then from the top. The sailors twisted themselves around in confusion. One fell, his abdomen gouged by the creature's claws.

And then one of the creatures spied us.

# 22

It smiled. I am certain it smiled.

It rushed toward us, arms spread wide. J'role held up the sword, though I feared the weapon would be little help against the monstrosity.

Without thought I held my right hand up, letting rain-water collect on my fingers. I rubbed the water between my index finger and my thumb and created a pair of storm manacles. I cast them forward just as the creature reached me. The manacles wrapped themselves around the wrists of the creature. Confused, it stumbled into me, sending me slamming into the stone railing of the ship.

I flailed my arms desperately for a grip on the rail, the thought of an endless fall filling my mind. I grabbed the thick wall of stone with one hand. My body swung wildly with momentum, and my grip slid across the railing, which was slick with water. My fingers let go and I experienced the strange sensation of not being supported by *anything*.

J'role caught my wrist just as I let go of the vessel. The elemental creature came up behind him and slammed its manacled hands down into J'role's back as he struggled to get me on board.

The blow dropped J'role to the railing, and I slipped out of his grasp, falling a second time. J'role caught me, this time by the shoulders of my ragged black slave robe.

At the same instant my spell drew a lightning bolt down onto the creature, for as long as he remained manacled he could not strike an ally of mine without being hit by lightning. The monster shouted in pain and cried up to the sky, its body arching in pain.

I grabbed J'role's wrists as my robe began to rip. He shifted his grasp and took hold of me by the arms. Again he began pulling me on board.

The creature struck once more, and again lightning crashed into it. It let out a high-pitched scream and stumbled back. J'role was prepared this time. He winced from the pain, but his grip on me never loosened. I looked down and saw a dizzying void that faded into rain-swept gray. Looking up I saw the face of a man who, for a moment, looked like no one I had never seen before. J'role was simply frantic in his desire to save me. His eyes were wide, his mouth muscles pulled back in a grimace. It seemed likely he would begin to cry the moment I either fell to my death or finally reached safety.

With the monster momentarily stunned, J'role hauled me back over the railing. The catharsis I expected him to experience did not come, however. Instead he whirled toward the other slaves gathered in a semicircle several yards back from the elemental monster. They held their swords up, but all quaked with fear.

"What are you doing?" he screamed at them. "We've got to *fight* it! Not hold it off! Kill the thing!"

The creature roared and struck at J'role's turned back, sending your father sprawling across the deck. I pulled back, preparing to shackle the creature's ankles, when the second creature floated over the ship's central castle, arms wide, claws and teeth gleaming with bright blood.

A scream went up from the slaves. "Back! Back!" I cried, waving my hands at them, directing them toward the doorway of the central castle. They scrambled without hesitation.

"J'role and Releana!" I shouted, protecting the two of us from the spell I would be casting. I had sent the other slaves away because I didn't know any of their names, and didn't want to harm them. I raised my hands even as the second creature raced toward me. J'role jumped forward, swinging his sword at the monster. The blade shimmered silver as he swung and caught the monster in the belly. The edge struck home, and the monster cried out as it drifted up to the riggings.

My arms swept wide and I gathered magical energy and changed the world. The raindrops around us suddenly transformed into drops of sizzling heat. They pelted the creatures, and the things cried out as countless plumes of steam rose from their flesh.

The first creature, already shackled, flew into a rage and charged J'role and me. J'role blocked me with the sword, and I cast shackles on the thing's ankles. It twisted a bit, surprised once more, screaming with rage, steam rising from all over its body. Dozens of red welts lined its blue-white flesh. As J'role swung his sword I heard another scream from above. The second creature raced down toward us. I rubbed the rain water between my fingers once more, and cast the storm manacles on the wrists of the second thing.

The first creature attacked J'role, the second attacked me. We both jumped out of the way of their claws, but they tore flesh from us just the same. The pain from their claws was like hot metal against my skin.

Twin bolts of lightning slammed into the creatures. They screamed with rage and retreated from the ship. Thirty yards off port they floated in the air, bobbing and staring at us. We had moved out of the area where I had cast the death rain, and I wondered how much further I could push my luck with another spell. Losing so much blood from my wound had begun to make me dizzy.

The creatures charged at us, their horrible screams roaring over the wail of the storm winds. I called forth a death rain once more. The creatures entered the range of the spell and immediately the rain burned at their flesh.

They screamed in pain, but I had little time to feel relieved. I felt something slide through my thoughts, like fingers passing under my skull and massaging my brain.
A Horror.

# 23

Whatever was happening around me no longer mattered. I had cast too many times, taken far too many chances without the safety of a magician's robe. I clutched at my head, thinking blindly I could somehow force the thing out. It slithered through my mind, breathing heavily, like a fat man with lechery on his mind, picking its way through my memories and fears.

And there the Horror found the two of you.

I really can't tell you what it did to me. Words would not do. It turned thought and memories into muscle spasms and physical pain. Everything I'd ever thought I'd done wrong by either of you came crashing up into my skull, like boiling water escaping a covered pot. Foremost in the nightmarish thinking was the possibility that I was somehow responsible for whatever was happening to you now. That somehow I didn't do enough to keep J'role at home. That I should not have left you two in Tellar's care. Then it bounced back to your births, and it seemed horrible that I had even given you life. How could I have done so if only to let such terrible things befall you now?

I thought my eyes were bleeding. Hating myself so much at that moment, I clasped my hands over my face and began dragging my nails down my cheeks, scraping into my flesh. I could think only of you two dying somewhere, wondering where I was, wondering why I had betrayed you. I should have died for you!

The thing in my head drove me to my knees and I be-

gan beating the stone deck with my hands, and then with
my forehead. Anything to drive the pain away. I would
keep doing it until I was dead.

Suddenly someone was holding me, embracing me.
Rocking me back and forth. "Shhh, shhh," someone said.

The creature hissed, dragged me away from the comfort. Seared my thoughts with more pain. J'role's de-
partures. Memories of our bloody lovemaking. My
loneliness.

"Here," a distant voice said. "Here. Releana. Come
back here. The world, the real world, is not wrapped up
in your thoughts. The love of others waits for you here."
I floated toward the voice, recognizing it as J'role's. The
Horror clawed at my thoughts, but J'role's pull was stronger.

The sky above was gray. Raindrops fell against my
face, cleansing me. The wind howled. "Shhh. It's all
right." I looked up. My back rested against J'role's chest.
He held my hands, and I let him comfort me. "It's all
right," he said. "They're gone. Your rain and lightning—
you frightened them away."

I spoke quickly; a child trying to get a word in edge-
wise. "Yes, but in my head. Too many spells . . ."

"Shhh," he said again. "I know. I know. Is it gone?"

I nodded. "I think so."

In his voice I heard clearly that he did know. But he
had never told me of any encounter with a Horror. As he
was not a magician, his encounter with one would not
have been one of the brief strikes the creatures often
make against spellcasters. It would have been a longer
torture. But J'role had never mentioned it. Why?

# 24

Why has he never told me? Why did he keep so much to himself?

# 25

The storm carried us another hour toward southern Barsaive. The golden sunshine of daylight drifted ahead of us, and we eagerly anticipated getting out from under the thunderheads. An hour later, when we had finally cleared the storm, the absence of pelting rain and roaring wind created a delightful aural void. Too weary to attempt to figure out what to do next, we lay on the deck, wallowing in the lack of danger, tending to wounds, listening to the delightful silence, letting the sun dry and warm our wet skin. Some of our group even slept.

After this we were up and about. Free from Theran supervision for the first time, we made awkward, and nearly useless, stabs at communicating among ourselves. Out of the original forty, twenty of us were still alive. We discovered later that one of the monsters had entered the lower decks and slain most of those waiting for instructions. Of the twenty, six were from Barsaive, and roughly five other languages were spoken by the rest of the group. We broke up into our local groups for a while, exchanged names, and found out who had sailing skills.

Of the representatives of Barsaive, there was J'role, the small red-haired woman, who came to be called Aunt Wia by you boys, an ork, a dwarf, a human male, and me.

None of the twenty survivors had experience with airships, and only some of the bronze-skinned slaves who spoke a harsh language of nasal vowels had any sailing experience at all. They became our captains, and put the rest of us to work. We raised the sails, learned how to set them for maximum speed, and soon controlled the ship well enough.

It didn't take long, however, to realize that none of us knew how to get the ship *down*. And the moment the realization hit, a silent, subtle panic gripped our motley crew. The thought of sailing endlessly through the skies until the ship's supply of elemental air ran out and we finally plummeted to whatever terrain lay below, far from any of our homes, sent us pacing, searching the skies and the land below, as if some sort of knowledge waited for us, scribbled in the earth or air. The Theran sailors had obviously used some sort of adept talents to control their ship. We could never learn these, for we had no teacher. To the south was the red glow of Death's Sea. What if prevalent winds carried us there? Could a stone ship withstand the heat of the molten sea?

Ultimately the decision was never ours to make. We spent the day floating in the sky, deciding finally, after much pointing and hand-waving, to put as much distance as possible between Sky Point and us. This meant traveling southwest, for that seemed to be the direction in which the winds gave us the greatest speed.

We traveled without incident, and night fell. After we split into two watches, those of us from Barsaive took our turn sleeping during the first watch. Weary beyond belief, I went below deck with the others to find a bunk.

We had cleared out the bodies hours ago, though blood still stained the walls. I pushed open a door of a cabin, found that it held a bunk bed, and stepped inside. J'role was at my back, and said, "Let's find something bigger."

I paused, uncertain what to say, because I did not want to sleep with him. I could not say exactly why. But with freedom mine again, I don't know . . . The rules of being trapped allowed me to enter his arms. Without those rules in place, there was no need to pretend everything was all right; to stifle myself at the expense of risking being alone.

"What's wrong?" he asked.

"I just don't think we should . . . Right now . . ."

"Did you see how everyone was working so well up top?"

"Don't do that."

"What?"

"That changing . . . I'm too tired to fight."

"Who wants to fight? Let's find a bed."

Wia arrived then. "Any room in here?"

"Yes," J'role said. "All yours."

"Good," she said, and squeezed past J'role and me into the room. "Oh, good," she said to me. "You want the top or the bottom?"

A wave of relief washed through me. "Top."

"But," began J'role.

"Let's all just rest," said Wia. "We've got to go on watch soon."

She pushed him out gently and shut the door behind him. But I didn't see him go out. My back was turned and stayed that way.

We stretched out in our respective bunks, the ship rocking gently, the cabin's darkness comforting.

"Don't you hate that, the way they think they can just sleep with you any time, just cause you've done it before."

"Yes," I said quickly, happy to have a sympathetic ear. And then suddenly I was uncomfortable, embarrassed by the love-making—if that was the term—back in the Theran cell. I didn't *know* this woman.

"You two knew each other from before. Before being prisoners."

"Yes."

"Sorry. I'm prying."

"No."

"Yes, I am. I'm doing it, so I should know." A silence fell, and then she said, "I got to tell you. He's attractive. But there's something about his eyes. Kind of spooky."

"Yes."

"You like that, don't you?"

I laughed. "Somewhat."

"Here's my question to you: if you saw those eyes on someone else, not this man you've known for so long, but a stranger, would you still find him attractive?"

Another long pause. I thought of J'role's eyes. They hung in the darkness before me, large and luminous, separated from J'role, from all the memories of joys and adventure and laughter. They frightened me.

"No. I don't think so."

"I know what you're feeling. My first love. He and I . . . I thought we were destined. But ever so slowly I figured out things were wrong. That they weren't going to work. But it's hard . . ."

"Yes. Hard. Giving up something you think is right and . . ."

"So you think something's wrong with you, because you keep thinking it should be fine."

"But it's not."

"That's hard."

"I want it to be right."

"It's good to want to to be right. We all want that." She paused. "But is it?"

"I don't know," I answered. But I saw J'role's eyes, and all I could think was, No, things are not all right.

We remained silent, each sunk in our own thoughts, the pause lengthening and lengthening until I dropped imperceptibly into the well of sleep.

# 26

Some time later—it seemed only minutes—a woman with long hair tied into elaborate loops shook me awake. I didn't recognize her at first, then realized she must have changed her hair while up on deck. A cultural custom of a different land.

I staggered out of the room with Wia, and we made our way to the deck. Surrounding us on all sides were stars, dipping down even below the ship's hull so that from the center of the ship it looked as if we had entered a world consisting only of star. The effect was at once chilling and exciting.

With words I was beginning to recognize—and many, many gestures—our resident sailors gave us quick reminders of how to keep the lines taut and the wind in the sails. Speed was imperative, for the Therans would, of course, send ships to recover our vessel. We all knew a flying stone airship was not something anyone would give up easily.

We settled in for our watch. J'role and I stood on the ship's rear castle. My rest and talk with Wia had relaxed me, and I did not feel uneasy in his presence. J'role stared up at the sky, drawn by the stars, as he had been since first we met.

"Still looking for your destiny?" I asked.

"It might be there," he answered without looking at me.

His theories had always bothered me. I always picked

on him for them. "What makes you think there's any truth about you or the future in the stars?"

With his back to me, still looking over the edge of the ship, he spread his arms wide, like a wizard showing off his newest, most amazing creation. "I can't imagine all of this is just for show!"

"What if it is?"

He turned, smiled, did a cartwheel or two across the deck, and ended up beside me. "Then I'm wrong. I've been wrong before." He took one of my hands from the wheel, brought it to his lips, kissed it lightly. Still holding my hand, he looked into my eyes. "But not about many things."

I pulled my hand away. "But about enough."

He twirled away, oddly back to his blithe self despite our circumstances and the fate of you two. I tried to ignore him. But he leaned against the railing and I wondered if in his carefree attitude he would lean back too far and fall to his death. The thought frightened me at first, but then filled me with a smug pleasure. It would serve him right.

We remained silent for a long time. The stars were indeed beautiful.

"Why can't you just be happy with me?" he finally asked.

"I'm not in a happy mood."

"We'll find the boys."

"And what if we don't? What if they're already dead?" I spat the words out without thinking. The moment I did, I felt despair rise in me. Giving the fears voice seemed likely to make them truth.

I was not prepared for the horror of your father's reply. "If they are, they are. There's nothing to be done about that."

My hands dropped from the wheel, and I stood staring at him, my flesh feeling frozen. "How can you say that?"

"Because it's true, Releana. If they're dead, then they are . . ."

"Please stop. You're chilling me with your casual words of death."

His voice became very serious. "They are not casual."

"They sound casual."

He shrugged. "I speak the way I speak."

"I don't think you love them, you know." He opened his mouth, but I raised my hand to stop him. "I know you think you do. You really *think* you do. But that's not the same thing."

"What is love but something I think I feel about another person."

I didn't know if I'd ever say the things I wanted to say to him again, so I went on. "There's something . . . love—not the love of passion created by urges of the flesh—but the love between members of a family. The love a parent has for a child. That isn't found only in the love one *feels* for someone. It is buried in actions. It is the difference between someone who shows his loyalty to his village by waving a flag, and someone who builds a fortress of stone to protect the villagers if bandits come."

"I love them. I come to visit!"

I laughed, and the other members of our watch turned their gazes from the lovely stars to the rear castle. I stared them down and they looked away.

"Do you know what you do?" I asked finally. I did not wait for a reply. "You look at them."

"Yes . . ."

"That's all you do. You stare at them as they lie there unconscious, helpless . . ."

"I'm not threatening them . . ."

"Nor they *you*."

Now he laughed. A derisive sound. "What is that supposed to mean."

I had never thought the words before, but they came tumbling out of me now. "You don't have to be with them. Interact with them. Find out what they're really like. You don't have to be disappointed in them . . ."

"I'm not disappointed in them," he said defensively.

"How do you know?" I asked sharply. "They haven't had the chance to disappoint you."

"They're little boys!"

I wanted to shriek, but instead I spoke very calmly, carefully enunciating each word. "They are Samael and Torran. Two very different little boys. They are not what you think they are."

"And what is that?"

"Just what you said. Two little boys. Two little thoughts in your head of what they're like. You know, you don't love them. You're just sentimental. You have an idea of what little boys are supposed to be like. That's what you love. The idea. The idea of two children safe and asleep in their beds, neither speaking nor walking nor playing nor thinking, questioning, or demanding. What are you afraid of? That if you come and see them when they're awake they'll turn on you? Try to kill you?"

His face turned ashen white. His jaw and fingers shook.

"J'role?"

He turned from me, terrified. To this day I do not know what truth I had struck, but obviously I had struck home. He looked away, and then raised his head and said, "Sweet Chorallis."

I looked beyond him, to where he looked. Behind us, heavy storm clouds had gathered. They rolled across the sky from east to west, then crashed into each other and continued on toward us. It was as if powerful forces from the air and water planes had conspired to invade our world and destroy our ship.

"Get the sails down!" I shouted. "And get those sailors up here!"

# 27

What little we could do with our inexperienced crew, we did. It was not near enough.

The storm swallowed us up, shredding our sails as we lowered them. The center mast cracked at the base, tumbling to the deck, and crushing two of our crew beneath its weight. Whether or not they were killed by the impact we never found out. The wind swept the sail and the mast back up into the air and took the slaves with them. All of us nearly went overboard, for the improbable tangle of rope and riggings whipped and clawed at us like a strange sea creature. I only barely escaped being snared and carried over the edge. The riggings, the crushed slaves, and two members of our crew flew off over the ship and vanished into the darkness.

The ship listed sharply to port. Most of us on deck slid quickly to the edge of the ship, slamming into the thick wall that served as the deck's rail. The wind roared in our ears. The rain pelted our cheeks, stinging with painful clarity. I screamed for someone to do something. A useless command, I know, but it showed what state of mind I was in. I could not hear my own voice.

Someone grabbed me by the shoulders. Wia. She pulled my head close to her. "Below!" she shouted.

It seemed a marvelous idea.

Along with the others I made my way on hands and knees across the deck, each of us afraid that if we remained standing, the winds would grab us and toss us over the side. The stone floors became slick with rain, and the ship rocked to one side, sending us all over the deck. Sometimes we rushed toward the door we wanted to reach, other times we lost yards of hard-earned progress. I saw two of our number blown into the railings, and then over the side of the ship as the ship shifted unexpectedly. I numbed my heart to such sights—if I imagined the terrifying, endless plunge through the dark rain as a possibility I would become paralyzed with fear and would certainly meet my own death.

I pressed on, and finally reached the door in the center castle. Each of us threw ourselves into the castle, and quickly made our way across the small chamber to the stairs leading below deck. The ship rocked back and forth, the motion sending most of us tumbling down the stairs.

We huddled together, wet and terrified. "What are we going to do?" I asked.

"What can we do?" Wia said. "The sails . . . We don't know . . ." Her words faltered, reflecting her failing hope.

No one had a plan.

"We might just have to ride out the storm," said J'role.

Lightning cracked near the ship. A shaft of blue-white light shot down the stairs and illuminated our terrified faces. Suddenly pale and already gaunt, we looked like a group of corpses.

"We're going to die," said a dwarf.

The others from different lands also began to speak quickly in their tongues, but ultimately there was nothing to be done. The ship tossed and rocked in the wind.

Suddenly the ship lurched and a horrible scraping noise cut through the corridors of the ship. The vessel spun sharply to port, knocking us all against the wall. Then the ship floated on, still rocking wildly. We all looked at each other, startled and surprised, frozen for a moment in inaction.

J'role leapt up and began to run up the stairs. "Wait here!" he called over his shoulder. I paid no heed to his words, and shot up after him, followed by another woman, one who had experience with ships.

# 28

The wind attacked us when we reached the deck, gripping us by the shoulders and trying to throw us over the edge. We dropped to the deck. The ship traveled nearly sideways through the air as the winds buffeted us.

The woman, dark-skinned, with coarse, curly hair, shouted something I could not understand. But her pointing finger explained all. I turned and looked and saw, just barely through the haze of rain, the gray shapes of mountains all around us. They towered high above us, and spread out in either direction, finally disappearing into darkness. I slid myself over toward the edge of the ship and saw lower peaks around us. Suddenly a jagged wall of rock appeared, as if formed by the rain itself, and the ship slammed into it. Stone ground against stone, and the blow knocked me back to J'role and the dark woman. Lighting cracked through the air. The mountains glowed momentarily with myriad colors. "Twilight Peaks!" J'role shouted. "We must have reached Twilight Peaks!"

I nodded. Water drenched my clothes, covered my face. A chill set in, and not just from the water. I had never met any of the crystal raiders who made their home in the huge mountain range, and had little desire to.

"We've got to get the ship away from here!" I shouted back. "Get everybody to the oars! I'll take the wheel!"

J'role shook his head. "Two people on the wheel! I'll come with you!"

He turned to the woman and made a motion of rowing,

then pointed to her. I pointed toward J'role and myself, then to the aft castle, then made the gesture of holding the ship's wheel. She stared at us with surprise, but finally nodded and started down the stairs.

J'role and I made our way along the deck, gripping ropes set into brass hooks along the walls of the castle. A bit more work brought us to the aft castle. We climbed the stairs and I grabbed the wheel. I lost track of J'role for a moment, and panic coursed through me as I thought he might have been swept overboard. But he reappeared, now with ropes in his hand. Working quickly, he lashed our hands to the wheel. There we stood, my right arm crossed under his left; our hands close, but tied to different spokes.

"I love you!" he shouted.

My heart fell. He had no sense of proportion. "Shut up!"

I saw oars extended out from the sides of the ship. Fortunately we had pulled them back inside hours earlier at the suggestion of our seaworthy companions. Otherwise they would have been crushed against the mountains when we crashed. There were only a dozen or so on the oars, however, and I did not know what chance we had with such a weak crew. But the oars that could be manned were, and I saw them sweep slowly through the air.

J'role and I began to turn the wheel. Even our combined efforts, no matter how well meaning, seemed incapable of preventing a shipwreck. We pushed all our strength into turning the ship to starboard and away from the mountains, but it seemed to no avail.

"More!" J'role screamed, less, I think, to me than to himself. We finally forced the wheel to move an inch. It was only an inch, but the success brought forth a laugh from the both of us. We pushed harder and harder, and finally moved the wheel enough that a visible change could be seen in our direction. The grim gray shadows slid slightly to port. We had traveled close enough that I could make out cliff faces and cracks in the stone.

Then a horrible wind rushed up to the ship and lifted us up suddenly. For a moment J'role and I left the deck, our feet floating inches above the stone floor. When we came back down, the wheel spun suddenly, driving J'role to the deck, with me on top of him. I heard a sharp crack, and J'role screamed in agony as the bone of his forearm shattered and pierced his flesh.

I struggled to get up. My efforts dragged at J'role's arm, for we were still lashed to the wheel. He screamed out even louder. I hesitated, not wanting to rip his arm apart, but knowing that if I couldn't pull the wheel back we were doomed.

J'role cried out in horrible agony, but I had no choice. After more of his terrible screams, we were standing once more. The wheel turned easily now, and I smiled with great relief, for it seemed for one delightful instant that the winds had died down enough for us to get better control of the ship.

Then I realized the wheel moved too easily. The mechanisms connecting it to the rudder had snapped during our last encounter with the winds, and we no longer had any way of controlling the ship at all.

A crack of lightning illuminated the air. I looked up. A mountain face loomed before us like an angry parent rushing to slap a child.

# PART TWO

# My Passions
# Take Form

# 1

We smashed into the mountain with the aid of one final, massive wind. The ship rose into the air, lifted as if on a giant wave of water, and crashed against a cliff face. The impact threw me forward, slamming me against the wheel. J'role cried out in pain once more.

I lost all sense of balance as the ship dropped, scraping along the cliff as it fell. My wrists, tied to the spokes of the wheel, nearly broke as the ship crashed into the ground.

Sudden stillness attacked my senses. Happy that I was still alive, yet terrified that we had landed on the top of a strange mountain, far from home, far from my children, I found myself weeping, my tears mixing with the rain. I didn't really know where I was, and had no idea how I might get back to those I loved.

I looked down at J'role and saw that he had passed out from the pain. The sharp, shattered bone looked pale and glowing even in the darkness of the storm. I worked quickly to untie my bonds, then leaned down to help J'role.

Within moments some of the other slaves joined me. They were full of questions, but when they saw J'role's injuries, they quickly helped me bring him downstairs.

We cleaned the wound and set the bone. We had no questors of Garlen present, so we could not heal him. I searched through the ship, slamming open cabinets and drawers and checking small boxes, desperate to find a po-

tion or salve or any kind of magical means of curing him.
I found nothing.

I did not know what else to do, so we carried J'role to
bed and spread a blanket over him. A fever had set in,
and it seemed more than likely that he would die before
the night was over. He had lost so much blood, and we
had no way to properly treat his injuries for the other
sicknesses such wounds encouraged.

When I went to look for the others, I found the rest of
the slaves had gathered in the ship's galley. We had eaten
earlier that day, but in small clusters, all over the ship.
Now everyone had gathered in a group, with our oranges
and corn and peppers carefully placed in silver bowls,
bits of dried meat on plates, and wine held in metal jugs.
As I entered, the little conversation taking place broke off
into silence.

I nodded to them, uncomfortable, and took a seat.

Everyone took food and ate quietly, the silent meal
cloaking us in comfort. We were, oddly, a family, bonded
through trials of misfortune over the past few weeks, and
especially by the successes and failure of the last few
hours.

We decided there was nothing to be done until daylight. We posted watches. I went to sleep.

I awoke with a start. No motion. No wind. No sound of
rain. Everything seemed wrong.

I propped myself up on my elbows, then looked over
the edge of my bunk. Wia still slept. When I placed my
feet on the floor, I found it cool. Golden, morning light
cut through the room's portal and formed a perfect circle
on the wall.

Thoughts of J'role rushed into my head. His wounds! I
gave out a gasp at the memories of the night before, and
rushed out.

One of the group, bronze-skinned and still strong,
stood by J'role's bunk, holding water to J'role's lips. He

kept his eyes shut. I knelt down beside him and placed my hand on his forehead.

His eyes fluttered open, and he turned slightly to look at me. He smile weakly.

"Alive," he said. A matter of declaration.

"Shipwrecked."

His voice cracked. "But alive." He took pride in any victory, even if others might see it as defeat. He once said to me, "There's enough that grinds us down each day. We've got to acknowledge anything that seems like good news."

The man got up and left the room. I took his seat.

"I'm dying?"

"No."

"Releana. I'm the liar."

The statement stunned me, so I said, "We've got to find you help."

"On a mountain?"

"If we're on Twilight Peaks . . ."

"Excellent. We might be able to get some help from troll barbarians."

"They're not barbarians," I said quickly, though I had never met any of the crystal raiders.

J'role closed his eyes. "Yes. Whatever." His face contorted with pain. Then he relaxed slightly. "Releana," he said hesitantly, and opened his eyes. I felt he was on the verge of saying something significant.

"Releana!" someone shouted from above deck. The cry carried panic.

"I'll be back." I gave him a peck on the forehead and rushed out of the room.

# 2

As I ran through the corridor, others were awakened from
sleep by the cry of my name. Each one looked startled
and sleepy. Each let me pass and then followed. I realized
I had become the group's leader. When exactly had that
happened? My crew followed up the steps and out onto
the deck.

Dozens of trolls dressed in armor made from gleaming
crystal approached the ship off the port side.

The ship had landed with the deck nearly perfectly
level with the ground. A huge fissure ran through the
foredeck, up along the forecastle, and over the sides of
the hull. It seemed that if the airship had suffered a hull
breach, it would sink just as a sea vessel would. The
ground around the ship was barren, and covered with
small rocks and a few boulders. The mountain we sat on
continued far above us, and I became dizzy looking toward the peak. Around us stood many other mountains
forming the Twilight Peaks. Beyond the gray mountains
grew the jungles of Barsaive, now nothing more than a
blur of green.

The trolls stood still and silent, gathered in tight clusters. Each stood about eight feet high, with horns growing
from their foreheads, and large teeth protruding from
under their lips. Their bodies bulged with muscles, and
there seemed a kind of exaggeration of masculine quali-
ties about them, in the females as well as the males. From

their stance and build, it seemed they could do little but bash things.

For the most part they wore thick furs for armor, and a few had robes or cloaks fashioned from tapestries they'd acquired on their raids of the lowlands. However, many also had the astounding crystal armor that had made the trolls so famous.

Their crystal armor did not cover their entire bodies, as I'd been led to believe from the stories I'd heard. Instead, most of the thick, colored crystals grew from the fur or cloth armor. Sections of crystal armor covered the shoulders of some trolls. Others had shields made of crystal. A few had breastplates strapped on with thick strips of leather. And there were weapons made of crystal as well. Spears, swords, maces. The colored crystals were smooth and shaped with many facets. The sunlight struck the magical weaponry and arms and shimmered deep reds, twilight blues, jungle greens, and other colors.

The trolls stopped their advance a few hundred feet away, taking up positions behind boulders and tucked into huge cracks in the cliff.

I tried to think.

I failed.

Around me my crew shifted. I noticed that they had gathered the swords taken from the Theran sailors.

Good. That was good.

We were outnumbered, under-armed, under-muscled, still weak from our slavery. That was bad.

I wanted very much to turn around and foist responsibility for the next few minutes on someone else. But I had seen leaders panic at the moment of crisis before, and it usually meant defeat. I was the leader. Being the leader meant being alone. I had to make a decision. I had to do something. That's all there was to it.

"Greetings!" I cried out. My voice sounded weak.

A huge troll, monstrously large, a dozen feet tall, at least, stepped forward. He carried a crystal sword as tall as me, which glimmered ice blue. Heavy fur boots covered with crystal shards covered his feet. Crystal bracers made of hundreds of facets covered his forearms. He wore a giant fur cape.

Four trolls flanked him, each armed equally well.

I had little doubt that those five alone could kill us all. The other thirty or so would have a good time watching.

"Greetings!" I shouted again. I wondered if the trolls spoke Throalic.

The massive troll stopped and stood as solidly as any rock. The words from his mouth were Throalic, but broken and uncertain. "You. From stone ship?"

"No!" I replied, hoping against hope that it was the answer that would bring a quick end to the threat of violence.

The five trolls turned and looked at each other. After a short discussion, the leader asked, "Where stone ship warriors?"

"Dead."

"Dead?"

"Dead."

"How?"

"We . . . we killed them. And some elemental air creatures attacked the ship." The troll looked at me, curious. "Elemental air creatures?" I repeated. Still they looked confused. One of the trolls, an old fellow with a few strands of white hair growing from his bald head, stepped forward to whisper into the leader's ear. I realized with a start that the troll wore the robes of a magician. The patterns on it showed jungle vines winding around one another.

The old troll and the leader exchanged words, and then the leader turned to me and with surprise asked, "Trecka?" He pointed to the sky and repeated the word.

As that was the best I thought I could do on the matter, I nodded my head and said "Trecka."

The troll's eyes opened. "Where trecka?"

"Dead."

"Who killed Trecka?"

My companions, gathered around me in a semicircle, pointed to me.

This bit of news had a great impact on all the trolls. They stepped forward as if to get a better look. "You?"

Their disbelief bothered me, and I placed my hands on my hips. "Me!" Then I jabbed my thumb at my chest. "I killed trecka!" It was only then that I remembered that I hadn't actually killed the monsters, just driven them off. I decided it wasn't a subtlety worth trying to communicate at the moment.

They stared a while longer, deciding whether to believe me or not. Finally the leader said, "Get off our mountain." With that he turned and started to leave.

"Wait!" I called. I had no idea how to climb off a mountain. I didn't know if anyone else in the group did either. And J'role was in no condition to travel in any case. We needed help.

He turned, his massive, fleshy face crinkling into deep cracks. He stared.

"We ..." I gestured to the others. "We need help."

This seemed to interest him.

"What you need?"

"We have someone who is injured. And the ship—it is ruined. We need help getting down."

"Ha!" he said pointing. "You no kill trecka!"

"I chased them away," I said, giving in, my voice barely loud enough for them to hear.

"That is still good. And better because true." The troll smiled, pointed to himself. "Vrograth."

I did the same, speaking my name.

"Come," he said. "You all give—" he stopped and thought—"two months' labor. We get you off mountain." He turned and started to leave again.

"What?"

He turned back, now clearly annoyed. "Come and get help. Stay and get off mountain. NOW!"

"One of our group is wounded . . ."

"Dying?"

"Maybe. Yes."

"Leave him. He dies. Way of things." He headed off to join the other trolls, clearly leaving the decision to me.

"STOP!" I screamed, suddenly extremely frustrated with the choice before me. I climbed over the edge of the ship and dropped several yards down to the ground. Vrograth stood, half-turned away from me. As I marched up to him, he turned completely toward me. "He's hurt. He can be helped! Do you have a questor of Garlen?"

"Not for him. He is outsider. No help to us."

One of the flanking trolls said, "Bad for us to take the weak. Weaken troll clan."

I reached Vrograth. He towered over me more than twice over. I recall I pointed my finger up at him, as if I had some authority. "I'm not asking you to make him a part of your troll clan . . ."

"No!" Vrograth thundered. "I tell you. You will be part of troll clan. Two months. Those who can help. Dying one cannot. He dies."

"NO!"

The massive troll stared down as if I were a child who had just spoken his first lie. "I make rules," he explained carefully.

"I understand. We will come. Part of troll clan for two months. But we'll bring the dying man. You heal. We'll all be part of troll clan."

One of the other trolls, a gray-skinned warrior with dark red hair, said, "It is bad to bring in the weak."

"But you could do it if you wanted to."

"I don't want to," said Vrograth.

I grabbed him by the fur on his cape as if I might yank him down to my height. "You will!"

The trolls around him laughed, and the old troll spoke

to him in the troll tongue. Vrograth's features crinkled into deep creases as he stared down at me. "You will contest me? For a dying man?"

"Yes."

He looked me over carefully, then said with a bit of pity. "We will fight until first blood. What is the combat?"

I must have looked startled, for he said, "You challenge me, we fight. I set victory, you set battle." He looked into my eyes, searching for comprehension. His eyes, I remember clearly, were large and green. As pure green as jungle leaves.

"I don't want to fight you," I said with an idiotic confusion. I spoke the words first from an ethical revulsion. I had learned to fight because the world was a dangerous place, not because I had any particular fondness for it. Then I realized I really didn't want to fight him because he could probably kill me with one awkwardly placed swing of his fist.

The old troll said to me in much better Throalic than his leader, "It is a custom. A custom of combat. Challenge the sarlord"—he indicated Vrograth—"and you must fight." He thought for a moment, then added, "Or anyone with more . . . power." He shook his head. "Authority," he said carefully, smiling at finding the right word. "Excuse me. It's been a while. I am Krattack. We are the Stoneclaw tribe. Our custom allows us to take in the homeless, but not the weak. If you want your dying companion to come with you, then you will have to defeat Vrograth in a contest to first blood."

The whole process seemed horribly archaic and nonproductive. I asked with a sigh, "But why?"

The trolls looked at one another, each searching the face of another for an answer. None was forthcoming.

"Because we do!" Vrograth exclaimed with frustration.

"Yes, but . . . ," I began.

The old troll leapt in to try to help me again. "Releana,

you are brave. You are capable. You killed Theran *poorchat* and drove off trecka. Very good. But this is not something you refuse. Vrograth has given . . . hospitality." Again the strange, boyish smile from the ten-foot-tall troll taking pleasure at his own vocabulary. "But the dying man cannot come. If you want to win argument, you must fight. You must. You can stay, or can come without dying man. No problem. But to come with the dying man is to . . ." He struggled to find the right words, gave up, and finally said, "It is to fight Vrograth." His eyes were old and kind, and he seemed less restless than the rest of the trolls, who continuously shifted and looked around.

It seemed I had a choice. The main reason I wanted to go with the trolls was to get help for J'role. If I refused their hospitality, he would die. If I accepted it without the fight, we would have to leave him behind, and he would die. However, if I fought and failed, I might lose Vrograth's hospitality. My motley crew, having put their faith in me, would join me in being stranded on top of a barren mountain with limited food, supplies, and no means of getting us home. This last point troubled me greatly, for who was I to make a decision for all these other people? Maybe I should put it to a vote? Here I surprised myself. If I put it to a vote, they might decide not to worry about J'role, and just leave with the trolls. That would leave me alone with J'role, a worse position than I already had.

So I decided not to put it to a vote. More than that, I reasoned that they had chosen to put their faith in me, so if I ruined us all, it was their choice to follow an idiot, and they could work their way through the consequences of my actions and decisions just as I would have to.

That was the valuable lesson I learned that day on the mountain. When you put your fate in someone else's hands, you have no idea where you will end up. Better to trust in yourself, insecurities and all, than think someone else—who might have completely different goals from you—can run your life better than you can.

"All right," I said, blundering forward. "I'll fight you."

Oddly, Vrograth didn't look the least bit startled. "Good."

# 3

Moments after I accepted the challenge the trolls surrounded Vrograth and I, forming a large arena. Some members of my crew worked their way through the circle of trolls for a better view, others watched from the deck of our ship.

"You accept my challenge," Vrograth bellowed, "a fight to first blood! Now tell me. What is the method of our combat?" Around us trolls stood ready to give us whatever weapons they had on them. Spears. Swords. Knives. Maces. Flunchents, which I'd only heard of before, their twin bone blades shiny in the clear, cold morning air. Nearly any weapon I could think of would be provided within seconds. And would be used to kill me just as quickly.

I thought for a moment of suggesting magic. I might be able to draw enough spells to drop Vrograth to the ground and make him bleed. But the sight of all the powerful magical items around me led me away from this plan. What if the trolls' armor protected them from spells? What if they had magic I could not counter? What if their magic was even more dangerous than their muscles? Something J'role had taught me years earlier came to mind:

"Unless there is no other choice, never, ever fight someone unless you know you can win. Why enter a battle you might lose?" The key was finding a battle I knew

I could win. I looked Vrograth over. Tall, muscular. Born to move. He shifted uncomfortably under my stare.

"CHOOSE SOMETHING!" he shouted.

Vrograth's declaratory style seemed designed especially for the moment, so I decided to mimic it. Drawing on the deepest tone I could muster, I proclaimed boldly, "We will fight with patience!" and promptly sat down on the ground.

A stunned silence followed. Vrograth then asked with sincere confusion, "What?"

"Patience," I said, still bellowing as deeply and loudly as I could. "There is no greater test of strength!"

"Yes," stammered Vrograth. "Maybe. But . . ." He paused, cocked his head to one side, then suddenly exclaimed, "How can one bleed from patience?"

"I take it you have no children," I replied flatly.

"Stupid!" he cried, completely losing his deep tones of formal presentation. "This is stupid!"

"You refuse my challenge?"

"Yes! No!" He stepped toward me, his large, green-gray arms spread wide. "How can we fight each other with patience?"

"We sit here. Whoever loses his patience first loses the contest."

"Bah! There is no blood. Without blood there is no first blood. Without first blood there is no loser. Your contest is bad."

He had me there. But the thought of actually fighting him to first blood seemed ridiculous. Not only was I certain I would lose—and thus guaranteed that J'role would not get the help he so desperately needed—but there was no assurance that Vrograth would stop at first blood. I wondered if he could control his strength enough to keep from driving his weapon through my body while seeking a drop of blood.

"Very well," I said. "We will fight with patience and knives." A murmur went through the trolls circling me.

"We will fight with patience, as I have already suggested. If one of us loses our patience, the other may take a swing with the dagger."

"So we fight with daggers!" exclaimed Vrograth, a huge, toothy smile on his face.

"Not exactly. The loser of patience may not block the blow, nor dodge, nor defend against it in any way." A gasp from the trolls. Wia and Krattack, the old troll, each raised an eyebrow.

"You are taken by creatures in your head!" he exclaimed. His Throalic deteriorated in his frustration. "This is not fighting, what you say. This is stupid!"

"Well, Vrograth," said Krattack, with a touch of slyness in his voice, "it is a contest, and it is to first blood."

"But not with weapons!"

"There are weapons, now," Krattack answered for me. "She has added knives."

"But no warrior's . . . skill."

"Oh, yes. The better the skill, the better the cut. First blood can be drawn then."

"How can I miss if she stands?"

"You probably won't. But that is her penalty for losing patience."

Vrograth stood in deep concentration. He narrowed his eyes and stared at me. "How do we compete for patience?"

# 4

We sat on the ground facing each other—Vrograth's massive frame still higher than my small body. He could have leaned forward and crushed me under his weight. Instead, he was forced to simply look into my eyes and try not to blink.

I'm sure you two remember the game.

I'd certainly watched the two of you play it enough times, though I'd never played it myself. I didn't know if I would be good at it, which meant I was not truly following J'role's maxim: "Never, ever fight someone unless you know you can win." I didn't *know* I could win.

But there was something in Vrograth's demeanor that reminded me of you—of boys in general. Your belief that sitting still and staring at someone was a challenge made me believe Vrograth would be challenged as well. For my part, I felt quite comfortable sitting still and looking at people. I hoped this natural inclination would survive the pressure of the moment.

From the moment Vrograth sat down, he seemed to transform himself into a rock. His immobile, nearly lifeless stance leant credence to the idea that trolls had been born from rock and were cousins to the obsidimen. Out of sight, but still a part of my perception, stood the crowd of trolls and former slaves, tightly grouped around us.

I sat with my eyes locked on his, straining my muscles in an attempt to relax. After a few moments I realized too much effort would doom me. I finally relaxed.

Vrograth's green eyes stared at me, lifelessly, as if they were somehow independent of his body; strange artifacts carved from elemental earth. But I saw one quiver of muscle in the flesh around his eyes, and then another.

The impulse to blink came upon me. I strained, opened my eyes wide, let it pass.

The longer the contest went on, the more I wanted to blink, and I became desperate. Perhaps I could blink just a little? So quickly no one would notice. I forced the thought from my head, knowing I could not take that chance, and knowing full well I was tricking myself if I thought I could blink without being noticed.

The strain built. It seemed like an eternity as I stared into his green pupils. They stared back at me—they were very beautiful, actually.

Longer.

I thought I might be willing to give in and risk the stab from Vrograth's dagger.

Then, abruptly, Vrograth blinked.

A cry went up from my companions. Vrograth raised his hands and shook them at the air, screaming uncontrollably. "Stupid!" he shouted at me.

Krattack interrupted him. "Yet you agreed to the contest . . ."

"YES!" he bellowed with such force everyone took a step back. He narrowed his eyes, and looked at me with a gaze full of death. "Still stupid."

We stood, and Krattack handed me a knife. The troll blade rested heavily in my hand. The late morning sun caught the yellow crystal and the blade sparkled like a brook rushing over rocks.

Vrograth placed his hands at his side and waited. He wore his armor, the fur boots encrusted with crystals, the blue-tinted bracers on his lower arm, but his mid-section was bare. I decided to swing the blade into his lower right side just above his waist.

I pulled the blade back. Krattack stared at me with a

strange intensity, as if deciding something about me. His gaze unnerved me for just a moment, then I slammed the blade forward, driving it up toward the troll's side with a straight thrust.

Vrograth did not flinch. Perhaps because I thought he would pull back or somehow block the blow. In the last instant before striking, I panicked and that slowed the blade just a little. I had still used enough force to split the flesh of any man. But trolls are tough. And more, I learned then that their crystal armor protects more than just the portions of their body covered by the armor. The magical crystals form a magical armor over their entire bodies, covered or not.

As I reached the last inch of my thrust toward him, a resistance worked against the blade. It pushed against the dagger and worked its way up my arm, like a powerful wind focused on only one portion of my body. Try as might, I could not overcome the resistance. Still, the crystal tip pierced his flesh, splitting a narrow, shallow wedge in his skin. He winced just a little, more from fear than pain, I suspect. The blade drove half an inch into his skin.

Nothing happened. No cry of pain. No blood. Nothing.

Vrograth stared down at me. Smiled. "We stare at each other again?"

We did.

Again the moments endlessly passed. Again the strain in my eyes sank into my thoughts and my mind tried to come up with schemes to blink without anyone noticing. Such a little thing—a blink of an eye—but in my case it meant a wound, possibly mortal, and a lack of help for J'role.

We stared. His green eyes bore into me. Green as green marble. Green as ruined flesh. I lost track of time. The world seemed to spin around me as I lost the awareness of my surroundings. My eyes began to feel itchy.

And then the remarkable happened. Vrograth blinked again.

More laughter, more cheers. Vrograth let loose a terrible wail at the sky. His cry echoed across the mountains. He pounded his massive fists against the ground.

We stood. Vrograth drew in a long breath of air, braced himself. He knew I would use as much force as I could possibly muster this time.

I drew the blade back, drew in a sharp breath of air. I screamed as I exhaled, throwing everything into the attack. I did not think this time; no distractions haunted me. I noticed the efforts of Vrograth's magical armor only as I reached his skin. It tried to push me away as before, but I was prepared for it this time. With all my remaining strength I slid the blade through the strange force, and then drove it into Vrograth's thick skin. In went the blade, deep this time, and the translucent handle quivered in my hand as it sank into his flesh.

When I could drive the blade in no more, I jerked it back out, twisting it as I did so. I, along with everyone else gathered for the contest, leaned down and peered at the wound. For a moment—nothing. Then from the lower tip of the vertical slit came a single drop of blood. Like a ruby turned to liquid, it rolled down Vrograth's gray-green flesh, slowly spreading out into a stain.

The delicacy of the blood's journey stunned everyone present into an appreciative silence. Then, the crowd went wild, applauding and screaming in appreciation and joy, as if they'd just witnessed a performance inspired by Astendar. A chill went through me—strange and exciting and warm.

I had done it! For an astounding moment I forgot about J'role's needs, my desire too for the trolls' aid in getting us off the mountain, and my desperate quest to rescue you boys from the Therans. Though I had many more tasks before me, in that moment I achieved success.

"We've got to acknowledge anything that seems like good news," J'role had often said. Exactly. Good news was getting what I wanted. Good news was not dying. Good news was accomplishing what I had set out to do. Not everything; not yet. But the first victory along a road that would require many.

We traveled to the Stoneclaw village. Vrograth himself carried J'role in his powerful arms. J'role winced from pain as the troll's steps jostled his broken bone. But most likely he enjoyed the pain. As you now know, he's like that.

The village was set on a series of cliffs. One was as large as a field, the rest smaller. Set on these cliffs were dozens of large tents made from the tanned hides of animals and the thin trees that grew on the mountains. The more powerful members of the tribe lived in caves. Tanned hides covered the mouths of the caves, which were the most secure shelters against danger. When raiders attacked or elemental storms brewed, everyone gathered in the caves. It was the duty of the strongest to protect the weaker.

About a thousand trolls, including children, made up the village. In the lowlands this would have been a town. But on Twilight Peaks the trolls subsisted purely by raiding. No farming, no trade. Their culture and economics was exceedingly simple. The wealth of the clan did not readily reveal itself.

The day we arrived, the sun shone brightly. Steam rose from kettles in which the trolls were cooking their noon meal. The children scampered up and down the cliff faces, their bodies the size of small men. The warriors who had remained in camp practiced with weapons and wrestled each other to the ground. I could not tell if these fights were for blood, for sport, or some violent sense of play.

Life with the Stoneclaw clan was one of the most draining experiences of my life. There is an impression that because trolls are so large they are slow. This is not the case. More, they are tireless. The trolls expected those of us from the shipwreck to match them, and they always looked at us suspiciously if we slowed, as if we were slacking off on purpose.

Tasks included cooking food, repairing the sails of their airships—called drakkars—forging weapons, hunting the sparse game on the mountain, cutting down and carrying trees back to the village, and so on. As the days passed, we slowly, very slowly, regained our strength while serving our time with the trolls. The compensation for our toil was that questors of Garlen healed us. Our recovery was much quicker for this.

Wia and I became quick friends. Every morning we worked on the ledges of Twilight Peaks, the sun catching her red hair and turning it bright as firelight. The Stoneclaws had settled on the eastern side of the mountain range, and each day the sun's arrival stunned me. We lived several thousand feet above the jungle floor, and nothing obscured the view of the sun as it pierced the horizon, a tip of orange flame that slowly revealed itself as a massive orb. Wia and I watched with open mouths as the clouds over the sun turned bright red, orange, and gold. When the sun rose high enough, the sky flashed harsh yellow for just a moment. The light washed the entire land, rushing over the mountain where we stood and covering our flesh with warmth and a wonderful glow that seemed to emanate from within us.

"It's so perfect," Wia said.

"I know."

"Once, when I was little, I tried to hold the sun in my hands. When I couldn't get it to stay, I cried and cried."

"Yes. One of my boys tried to walk along the reflection

of the moon in a deep puddle and became quite frustrated."

"I didn't know you had children."

The sun had risen, and the sky spread out a solid blue. I turned and found her fumbling with an odd-looking rock. "Yes. Two. Boys. They're seven. Twins."

She smiled at first, but looked into my face, and the smile melted to sadness. I knew that her face mirrored mine. It occurred to me that J'role had not done that at all since the boys were taken. Whenever I became upset about them, he looked away, or changed the subject, or simply told me I was too worried about the boys.

"Sorry. I didn't mean . . ."

I took the rock from her, turned it over in my hands. It was black, with rough edges. "The Therans have them. The Overgovernor. He's decided that they're good luck."

"Those are your boys?"

"Yes."

"They're monsters, the Therans."

"I *hate* them."

"Useless . . ."

"Wasters of . . ."

"Of life."

"Yes."

"He's serious about that charm, you know." She took the stone back from me. "I spoke to a man from Thera. A slave. He knew a bit of Throalic and we spoke. They really think twins, with the proper magic, can protect their masters."

"Maybe they can."

"Maybe. Magic is tricky."

I smiled, took the stone back. "Yes it is. So if I want to run a blade through that man's neck, I've got to get my boys back first."

"Looks that way."

"Well, I was going to get them back anyway. Killing him's just an afterthought."

She leaned in, a conspirator. "Do you want to kill him?"

"Kind of. Not really. But a part of me just wants to know he won't bother Torran and Samael and me again. I'd kill him to make things safe for my family."

"But not to win against him."

"What does that mean? Win?"

A troll near us shouted, "Hey! What are you doing!"

I dropped the stone. We got back to work.

# 6

The clan's healer, a stocky troll with green-blue eyes, took care of J'role, and within the week he was up and about. Now healed, he seemed to possess not only the abandon of a five-year-old child, but the energy as well, and somehow kept up with the trolls. It was a trick of his, and though I never asked him how he pulled it off, I think now it had something to do with hiding pain. Though he drew pain to him like a baby suckling his mother's breast, he didn't tell people about it. He wanted people to be impressed by his boundless endurance, and pushed himself to appear amazing in the eyes of others.

J'role quickly took charge of the clan's children. Not a difficult task, for while the trolls were not indifferent to their children, it was generally assumed their offspring would *manage*. Raising them was a communal affair, with any adult taking care of a child's needs as it arrived. Because the raiders were often gone from the village for weeks at a time, searching for plunder as they sailed through the Barsaivian sky in their drakkars, it proved a practical system. I could not empathize with it; I knew if the two of you had been present, I would only have wanted to look after you.

Troll children grow quickly, and by the time they are four or five, are husky and heavy. Their games are rough, and J'role threw himself into their play with his usual delight. He drew up games that involved tackling and running around, with a few elements of strategy new to the children. One of the favorite games he invented was an elaborate version of tag that took place all over the mountain around the camp. He divided the children into two sides, with each side having three large rocks that must be moved to specific locations. The object was for each side to get their rocks to their "nests," while preventing the other team from doing the same. Custom decreed that a tag was not enough. An opponent had to be wrestled to the ground. So as the children slammed into each other, often nearly plunging to their deaths off the mountainside, the adult trolls continued their work without interruption, happy that they had found someone who actually liked being with children.

At night, when the sun had set and the glow of Death's Sea turned the southern sky hazy red, J'role would gather to him those who wanted to hear stories. His father, he had told me, had been a storyteller. I assume that he borrowed many of his father's tricks when he performed— for he did not just tell stories, he acted them out. He became a troll. A mountain. An army. His face was terribly elastic, which always surprised people, for he usually wore it like a stiff mask. But when he told a tale, or when he was alone with me, the tension left and he became so full of—LIFE! There is no other way to put it.

He fought duels with himself, swiftly shifting his right side to the audience, then his left, so that, in the shimmering red light of the camp fire, his sword strokes and witty repartee (spoken with two distinct voices) created the illusion of two men fighting an exhausting battle right before us.

Monsters leaped out of concealed chambers; dragons flew down from the skies and consumed villages; magical swords shone bright in the moment of greatest despair. Conspiracies grew between whispering scoundrels shrouded in the shadows of the night. His characters concocted plots, planted poisons. Chance revealed treacheries. J'role became a swirl of people, each driven by maniacal emotions and a physical violence that would have staggered the more demure sensibilities in the court of King Varulus.

The crystal raiders are by temperament a violent and emotional people, so of course they leaned in hungrily as J'role spun his countless tales. It seemed that J'role had finally found an audience that could handle the truest aspects of his talents. Their huge faces—dark red and terrible in the firelight—watched with eyes wide. When they laughed or gasped, their enormous, yellowed teeth moved like mountains shaken by an earthquake.

I had never seen him do these stories, had never heard them before. His clown performances—those you yourselves had seen when he came to visit our village—contained nothing of the sweep of these tales, none of the anger and hope. These did not contain the black and white villains and heroes of his children's tales, with justice and triumph sharply defined. A woman noble and strong during one segment of the narrative would be revealed to be consumed by jealousy, her passion driving her to plot her lover's murder. A black-hearted warrior would be shown making clumsy attempts at affection toward a boy he realized was his own son. The internal world of the characters twisted and turned with moral ambiguity; everyone could define their actions as good or bad, but they themselves seemed constantly confused as to the true nature of their own hearts.

J'role did all this by himself, fashioning the tales from his imagination on the spot, propelled by creatures in his mind that would doubtless have torn my thoughts apart. He was the wind let loose over a volcano, carrying fiery ashes through the night sky, igniting the jungle with brilliant blasts. Fire and wind.

I caught him in a mid-air twirl, and he landed on one leg—a strong leg, well-shaped, I realized. His arms flew wide, the entire universe his audience. He smiled at us, the firelight casting dark shadows under his face—

perfectly dramatic; he knew exactly where to stand. "The heir to the throne," he said, "hung over the edge of the precipice, clinging to the thin root as the swordsman approached ... Ah! But it is late!"

A groan escaped the lips of those around me. "NO!" the trolls all wailed.

"It will keep. It will keep. Tomorrow night."

"No, no!" some shouted, but others smiled. J'role had done it enough times now. The enjoyment of delay was not lost on the trolls, and they stood and went off to sleep.

Wia stared with bright eyes at J'role, who in turn stood loose and happy, arms extended, firelight shifting against his skin and the furs the trolls had given him. With the strange sense people sometimes have when being watched, Wia turned to me, startled. She looked guilty for just a moment, then said, "He is wonderful, in his own way."

I nodded, oddly uncomfortable. Jealous. When I turned back, J'role caught my eye and smiled at me. He was very alert, very alive, very sexy. Yes, he could be attractive, but I knew all there was to know about him, so the attractiveness had worn thin over the years. Skin pulled horribly taut over the bones of his painful ways.

He worked his way through the crowd of dispersing trolls and came up to me, grinning as he had a decade ago, when joy had flowed between us like the swirling water of a river. Things had been in balance then, the harmony of the elements.

He took my hand. "Hello," he said, his eyes afire. I knew immediately he wanted to make love. I, however, had no desire to indulge; or rather, other matters outweighed the desire. Three weeks has passed since our arrival on the mountain—according to our agreement with Vrograth, we must spend another five more here. During that time J'role had mentioned you boys but once. I was furious at him, desperate to understand how someone filled with such passion could be so flippant about his own children.

I was furious at myself as well. Why hadn't I tried to escape yet? I had to find the two of you. Yet, to make my way down Twilight Peaks, alone, and then travel across Barsaive to Sky Point . . . assuming the Overgovernor's castle was still there . . . We had needed time to rest and recover from our battle with the Therans and the treckas. But we were better now, and it was time to move on, agreement or not.

All these ideas passed through my mind, though at the time they came not as words but as overwhelming emotions. I pulled my hand away from him and began to walk away, saying, "Come." He followed, and when we had found an isolated spot amid a few boulders, I addressed him with firm tones and a stiff body. "We have to go now. We can go now. We have to find Samael and Torran."

He put his hands on my shoulders, and I shrugged them off. How often do men try to replace intimacy with domination? "I might make it down the mountain, Releana," he said. "But I have the abilities of a thief adept. Without equipment I don't think you would manage."

"Enough. It will be difficult. Will you come with me to rescue our sons?"

"In just over a month . . ."

"Our boys may be dead! They might be dying right now. If you won't help, I'll speak with the others. I know some will come with me."

I began to walk past him, but he grabbed my arm and pulled me back. The muscles of his face became twisted and tight; a mask I'd seen hundreds of times before. The man who only minutes before had been a swirl of motion and impromptu tales was suddenly frozen and unable to speak. He struggled to form his thoughts into words, but as had happened so often before, the ideas clogged in his head, blocking one another from finding release.

"I want to help them," he finally said, softly. Whatever it was he needed to say, this sentiment was not it. It was a sentence carefully picked to keep me concerned for *him*. Not for our children, but him. He said what he thought I wanted to hear.

What I wanted to hear—what I have *always* wanted to hear from him—are all the ideas that so clogged his thinking and jammed his words. I wanted him to take his time and let them out slowly, one by one, so that I might listen to each one carefully, tend to them, like children, and finally understand what it was that had haunted my J'role for so long.

# 7

Perhaps this is why he has written to me. Is he finally
ready?

# 8

We stood in silence for a long time, he consumed by whatever monsters ate at his thoughts, I by frustration.

"I don't have time anymore, J'role. Either be a father to these boys, or do not. But stop thinking you can be a father off in a corner, without the problem of actually being responsible for your children."

His head snapped up then, and he looked straight in the eyes. I saw him become determined—a determination as affected as everything else about him, it seemed to me. He held my gaze for an appropriately dramatic amount of time, then said with a level voice, "All right. We'll get them."

Then, to make it clear he had assumed fully the responsibility at hand, he walked by me, defiant.

I think I sighed. I certainly sighed at the memory just now. Your father was an idiot. He knew only how to *show* concern, not be concerned. It never seemed to me a subtle distinction, but the number of people I've met who confuse the two is overwhelming.

He stormed his way to Vrograth's cave. Even in my anger I was relieved by this turn of events. Whether his heart was in it or not, one thing was simply true. When J'role set his mind to something, he usually got it done.

# 9

Dark furs and blood-stained shields and swords hung from the walls of the cave. Several large fires were burning, their red glow flickering across the ornamentation—sharp and bright on the arms, dull and dark on the furs. The shifting illumination and the odd combination of textures on the wall tugged at my attention, making me somewhat dizzy. The firelight pulsed with a rhythmic flickering, and its red coloration reminded me of the pulse of blood from a wound. The objects on the walls seemed arranged in a pattern, though I could not quite grasp it. The overall impression was that the mountain was somehow alive.

Vrograth sat on a large mound of furs, with several of his notable warriors surrounding him. J'role and I stood before Vrograth, having roused the chieftain and his followers from their sleep. The trolls had asked if it could wait until morning. I would have been willing to do so, but J'role would hear none of it. His chest puffed out, he made it clear the matter had to be addressed *now*.

Krattack supported J'role, arguing quickly that Vrograth should see us before any emergency situation got worse. Though the logic was sound, it seemed to me that Krattack simply argued the opposite of whatever Vrograth wanted. If Vrograth had wanted to listen to J'role and me immediately, Krattack would probably have advised getting a good night's sleep before hearing problems and making decisions. As was common in such situations, Krattack won the moment, and Vrograth convened a clan council.

The cave was hot. The breathing of the dozen trolls gathered echoed through the cave, adding to the impression of its being something alive. Vrograth stared at us, bored and looking somewhat stupid in his sleepiness. He treated us much as he treated the children of the clan— with indifference and occasional fits of annoyance. Only J'role's stories made him think of us as anything but servants, and that impression left him the moment J'role finished his tale.

He yawned—a massive yawn that turned his mouth into a cavern filled with large, sharp, yellow stones. His yawn ended, and he abruptly pulled back his shoulders, placed his huge hands on his massive knees, leaned forward, and said, "What you want?" Suddenly his bearing was powerful and worthy of a leader. His attitude and proportions turned me instantly into a child standing before my father, hoping he would find what I had to say pleasing.

I was taken aback. J'role, as usual, was not. He raised his hand, dramatically, the wrist slightly turned, his fingers pointed up the ceiling. He opened his mouth to speak . . .

"No, storyteller," Vrograth interrupted. "No story." He leaned even closer to us, and drew air audibly into his lungs. When next he spoke, his voice was soft and menacing. "What you want?"

It was at that moment I realized we were less than children to him; we were pets. And though pets must be given a certain amount of attention, that attention is limited. I realized that if we were to gain anything from our audience, it must be done quickly. Directness seemed an innate part of crystal raider culture, and I thought it the best tactic.

"Chieftain," I said, bowing, "the Therans—the people who fly the stone ships—stole our children several months ago. They have enslaved them. We want permission to leave and get them back. We must get them back."

When I looked up, I saw Vrograth staring down at the ground. His eyes seemed fixed on a distant point. I realized then that he was not stupid; but thinking did extract an enormous amount from energy from him.

Oddly, Krattack seemed impatient. He licked his lips. His eyes contained the realization of being on the other side of youth; the knowledge that whatever dreams he had would come true now or never. He took a step toward Vrograth, and this time there was no smile of the competitor or taunter on his face. Suddenly serious, he also seemed about to speak before Vrograth had made a decision.

Or, at least he wanted to. Without turning his head, Vrograth swung up his hand toward the old troll, a lazy swing that would have shattered some ribs if it had connected with me. Krattack pulled back at the last instant, then tried to step forward into the fist's wake. But Vrograth said, "No."

For a moment I held my breath, not certain whether he was speaking to Krattack, or telling me my request had been denied.

"No," he said again, more firmly this time, and suddenly I realized he was speaking to both of us.

"But Vrograth—" the old troll said with a gesture toward J'role and me.

Vrograth turned sharply on him. "I say NO!"

That last syllable echoed endlessly down the cave and then rushed back up, filling my ears with despair.

"Chieftain," I began again.

Vrograth stood then, leaping off the mound of furs, and stood before me, towering over me. He poked a finger into my shoulder and I staggered back. J'role leaped forward, in a reckless attempt to punch the troll, but Vrograth merely swatted him away. J'role slammed onto the ground, and two warriors pinned him down with heavy feet.

While J'role squirmed and tried to get away, Vrograth spoke loudly at me, his face inches from mine, his hot breath streaming down against my flesh. "I have spoken. You made deal."

Krattack made one more attempt for my case. "True Chieftain . . ."

Vrograth turned on the old troll, his face full of rage and suspicion. He cocked his head to one side, examining Krattack carefully. "Others warned me about you. You turn on me now?"

Krattack's body went still and stiff, and finally he shook his head. Just slightly.

"Good. I sleep NOW!"

With that he turned away from us. The trolls released J'role, and the warriors made a line to block us from their leader as he stretched himself out on a mound of furs. Krattack stood outside the line with J'role and me, separated from Vrograth. I saw him look with longing past the warriors. Then he turned to us and said, "I think you had better leave."

There was, of course, no choice—other than risking our bodies in a desperate argument with an adamant troll. We passed through the flaps of fur at the mouth of the cave and out into the cold night air. It chilled my flesh, but that was nothing next to the icy fear filling my heart for the two of you.

# 10

"We'll just have to go . . . ," I said under my breath.

J'role answered, "We can't. You know that . . ."

"I don't know that! Don't tell me what I know!"

"How are we going to get down a *mountain*?"

"I'd rather die trying than do nothing."

He grabbed one of my shoulders. I shook his hand off. He grabbed both my shoulders. I whirled around. "Don't do that?"

"Do what?"

"Try to force me."

"Force you? Force you to do what?"

"To . . . Just force. It's never what you're trying to make me do. It's the forcing. It's the forcing all by itself."

"We were talking about going down the mountain . . ."

"Now we're talking about this."

"What this? What's this *this*? What are you talking about? Forcing? What about the mountain?"

"Forget the mountain . . ."

"Isn't that what we were talking about?"

"It's not what's important right now."

"All right. All right. Tell me now. What's important right now." He crossed his arms and stared at me silently. There was nothing to be said. He wouldn't listen. I began to walk away. "Releana," he said, surprised, but I kept on walking. I wanted nothing to do with him.

I heard nothing after that, not even his footsteps pursuing me, and that made me even more furious. Was he truly so cowardly? Any idiot can face a monster—circumstances often demand it, whether for survival, a desire for glory or wealth, or a desperate, hidden desire for the final rest of death. But how many men fail to face their wife and children? Too many.

I made my way to a poorly made tent where my companions and I slept. I slapped aside the flap of fur, but calmed myself when I saw that my fellow former-slaves lay gathered around a dying fire, stretched out and fast asleep on their furs.

I turned back, one last time, to see if J'role followed. If we were going to have a scene, I would rather do it outside the cave.

He was nowhere in sight.

The stars shone bright, appearing at the edge of the cliff and rising up and over me. They reminded me of the fingers of babies—tiny and unique and magical in their mystery. No one else was about, and for a moment the deep quiet stilled my fury. It is odd how our passions, no matter how intense, can become snuffed and transformed in the face of the awe-inspiring magnitude of the Universe. We are but small specks in the face of history, which stretches backward and forward endlessly from the moment of our contemplation. I felt both chilled and warmed by these thoughts. It is not pleasant to acknowledge insignificance. But it is freeing. One can act as one wants, live as one chooses. Our passions and actions are glorious if only because they should not matter against the cold indifference of the Universe. But they do. *We* make them matter. We have that power.

I realized I was not alone. A large, still figure that I had at first mistaken for a tall stone now moved. A troll.

The shadow moved its hands to cast a spell, and before I could react, a shimmer of silver light formed itself around the caster, revealing Krattack. Strangely, I could see his face clearly, despite the distance and darkness. His eyes particularly. He stared at me, and it seemed as if we were very close to each other. "Will you speak with me?" he asked. His voice was soft, barely audible, yet I heard every word quite clearly.

# 11

I was not afraid. After the encounter in Vrograth's lair, I knew there was more to this troll than I had originally suspected. I knew now Krattack was an illusionist of some kind, and I would indeed speak with him.

He waited for me to approach, and then without another word, led me down a gently sloped path. When we were out of sight of the rest of the camp, I created a large flame in my hand so we might walk more easily through the night.

Finally we reached a collection of rocks resting against a sharp rise in the mountain. Krattack placed his hand against the side of one rock, then slowly lowered himself onto another large one. How old was he? In the last hour, age seemed to accumulate on him like raindrops from a stormy sky. Illusionists, I knew, were crafty, and did not always depend on magic to carry out their deceptions. Did he usually carry himself with more youth than he actually possessed? In the violent society of the crystal raiders, where strength mattered so much, such a ruse might serve him well.

"Apologies for such a late meeting," he said.

I spread my arms. "Please. Thank you for what you did in Vrograth's cave. I appreciate it."

"Nothing, at all," he said, kindly, like a faint memory of my grandfather. Then serious. "Something, actually. I wouldn't be honest if I didn't tell you I had my own reasons for trying to help you." I remained silent. I didn't know what to say. "You listen. That's good. I can't say I'm used to that around here. A noisy bunch. Deliberation is a rare commodity here."

The quality of his Throalic was very good, and I commented on it.

"I'm from the lowlands, originally. I was captured at the age of twenty. The Stoneclaws raided my village, killed some of my people, including my parents. You know of the custom of *newots*?"

I shook my head.

"Odd bit of business. Newots are prisoners taken by crystal raiders." He turned his bald head up, his old face searching the sky. "Not prisoners, really. They take you in as their own. Not just trolls. Anybody. But usually trolls. Trolls can survive the harsh life. Most other races might not make it out here. Exhaustion soon takes them." He paused, stared at me. "You look concerned. It happens. People die."

Once more his words confused me into silence.

"A harsh point of view, I know. But living with these people—the death of my parents—coldness can be acquired. At least your husband—yes?—he is your husband—?" I nodded reluctantly. "At least your husband is helping to reduce the work load for the rest of you. I don't know where he finds the strength. Humans don't usually possess the endurance, but he's going to keep some of you alive. That much I'm sure of."

"I'm ... What are you talking about?"

He looked at me carefully. "Those rests your people take while the trolls of the clan continue to work—you don't think that's normal, do you?"

I shrugged, embarrassed.

He laughed. "They're not. You're doing it because it seems normal to you. Not normal to a member of a crystal raider clan. No. But it's all right because J'role makes so much noise with the children all day long and then telling stories half the night that he creates the illusion you're all so busy. By representing the rest of you with his antics, he gives you the chance to do whatever you want. A simple manipulation of attention, but it works."

The words stunned me. I hadn't thought of it that way, but it certainly seemed possible. "I'm sure he isn't doing it on purpose," I said suddenly.

Once more he examined my face, as if looking for the solution to an intriguing puzzle. "Whatever do you mean by that?"

"I . . . I mean, he just plays with children. He just tells stories. He doesn't mean to be helping us."

"Us?"

"Well, not that he's not part of us . . . It's just that . . ." My words trailed off into confusion.

"What makes you think anyone does anything that he 'just' doesn't do?"

Now I stared at him. "We all do that. We all choose the things we do. I didn't have to come here with you. I could have ignored you. But I didn't. I followed you. I didn't *just* follow you. I chose to do it."

He smiled and nodded. Then he barked a laugh and stood up and looked out over the edge of the mountain— out at the stars ahead and down into the dark jungle below. "I don't think so," he said, still laughing, his back to me. "Though it's touching you think so."

I stormed up to him, frustrated by his derisive good humor. "Well, I think so. I mean, it's true."

"Then why did you come?"

I moved around to stand in front of him. "Because I was curious."

"Yes," he said, looking down at me, smiling, "you are curious. Your curiosity is so clear on your face, it's comic. Your eyes eat at the fabric of the Universe. Now, I'm not saying that if circumstances had been different you wouldn't have come. Say, if your boys were in danger in the cave where you were standing when I caught your attention. But given the circumstances, your curiosity took control. You had little choice."

"I had much choice."

"Only if you denied who you were. We *can* do that. We can stop being ourselves, and sometimes that's important. But at the root of it, we are who we are; tightly wrapped bundles of passions securely held in our flesh. And whether we know it our not, our passions drive us forward."

"Like the Passions? Like Garlen and Chorrolis? But we choose to call on them or follow them."

"We call on them or follow them because of who we are. A woman who isn't greedy isn't going to draw Chorrolis' attention."

"What if she needs money for her family? What if she doesn't have money, but *needs* it, and goes out to get money?"

"Then her love of her family requires that she become greedy."

"But she isn't greedy, she's generous."

"Ah. Now you're trying to couch everything in nice terms. I don't care about the reasons. What is she at that moment?"

"But she . . ."

"She's desperate for money. She might even be willing to lie for it, given the circumstances. Even kill. Chorrolis, his passion for greed strong in her now, will influence her action. Perhaps even inspire her to terrible deeds."

"Yes, but not everyone in need is willing to kill."

"Exactly. And why not? What prevents her from killing?"

"She chooses not to."

"And where does this choice come from?"

"She's decided. She's deliberated . . ."

"And where does this decision *come* from?"

"From her . . ."

"Thank you."

"But she decided it."

"How?"

"She just does." At this point my argument seemed weak, even to me.

"You said you're a curious person. I'd think on this matter if I were you. And I remind you that there are cases where the spirits manifest themselves without invitation. If a person is strong in a certain spirit, the spirit calls and invites him or her to be a questor."

"Who are you?" I asked, exasperated.

"I am Krattack, illusionist, accidental member of the Stoneclaw crystal raider clan, and advisor to Vrograth."

"Advisor? You seem to taunt him more than anything else."

"I do that. Yes, I do. I even enjoy it sometimes. I honestly don't know why he lets me get away with it. But I've got an odd look in my eyes. Some people confuse it with wisdom, and he thinks I'm good to have around. Oh, I'm not being vain. I'm just perceptive. People think I know what is happening in the darker corners of fate. Really, I'm just as confused as the next person. I just don't tell many people. So I'd appreciate if you could keep it a secret between us."

I couldn't tell whether he was joking or not, but when he spoke again, Krattack was very serious. "I want you to find your children. I truly do. I lost my parents when I was a child. The two situations are different, of course—my dead parents, your children enslaved. But the pain is comparable. So, out of compassion, I wish this for you. But I have my own reasons for wanting to set Vrograth against the Therans. I think your interests and mine intersect, and so I am asking you to wait before you go running down the mountain to try to rescue them yourself. I guarantee you will not survive. It will all be in vain."

His knowledge of my immediate plans certainly lent

weight to the idea that he knew the "darker corners of fate." I asked, "Why should I wait?"

"First, and, I repeat, you won't make it down the mountain alive. You don't have a magician's robe, so casting to protect yourself would be quite dangerous. No one here is going to give you a robe so you can reattune it, and I don't think you'd stand a chance of stealing one from anyone in the clan. Nor do we have spare resources for you to make your own. The trip itself down the mountain is ridiculously dangerous. There are monsters. Vrograth will come after you when he discovers you have broken your contract. Other raiding clans live on the mountain who are not as kind as Vrograth—trust me. And the mountain itself . . . Well, let me put it this way. There's a reason we travel in air ships. The second reason you should wait is because I think not only will you soon have the opportunity to free your children, but I think Vrograth will help you."

"Why? He seems to have no interest in the Therans."

"Except as potential targets for raids, yes. But I've been poking and prodding him for years now, and I think I finally understand how to get him to see beyond the limited confines of the clan."

Smugly, I said, "Why would he do anything he doesn't want to do?"

Krattack smiled. "You see. There's the difference. He doesn't have to fight the Therans to help you. If he doesn't want to, he won't. But if the right events take place, he will fight the Therans, exactly because of who he is. He'll have no choice."

"And what might those events be."

"Young woman, didn't you take any stock of the ship you arrived in? Compare its size against those of our drakkars. It outclasses our cargo and crew capacities immensely. And it's made of *stone*. The ship is sturdier than anything we've ever thought of building. My study of magical theory is haphazard, given the circumstances of my life, and I have *no* idea how they get a ship of stone into the air. The law of similarity mocks the idea."

I nodded. "As an elementalist, I should have some clue, but I'm flummoxed as well."

"Flummoxed?"

"Confused."

"Ah. My Throalic is, you see, good enough, though limited. Well. There it is. Vrograth didn't show his amazement when you met him—no crystal raider would—but the ship you arrived in stunned him. Word had reached us of the Therans from people we've attacked, but he had never seen one of their ships before. Vrograth has yet to encounter the Therans. His pride will demand he try to attack one of these vessels. And he will fail. And if he lives, his fury will consume him and he will have to strike at the heart of the Therans."

"Why . . . why don't you warn him?"

"And say what, you foolish woman? 'Mighty Vrograth, despite your pride and fury, you're no match for such opponents.' Anything I might do to argue the situation would only goad him further on into battle. No. He'll do what he'll do, and I'll try to steer him the right way. But if you would remain, I would be grateful. You will make things easier."

"I don't want to be a puppet in your plans."

"Puppet!" he barked. "I'm only offering to help you get exactly what you want."

"With your own desires pulling the strings."

"Working in agreement. What is wrong with that?"

I could see nothing wrong with it at all. "And what is it you want?"

"Me? I want the Therans out of Barsaive."

# 12

As Krattack and I walked back to the village, I turned the word "Barsaive" around in my thoughts. I knew, from J'role and others, that Barsaive was the name given to a huge swath of land at the edge of the Theran empire from the time before the Scourge. The region extended from the old Wyrm Wood—now Blood Wood—down to Death's Sea, and from Iopos to Travar. Though my travels had taken me across much of this land at one time or another, I rarely thought of it as "Barsaive." I only considered the local geography and the local names of the places I visited. That all these areas formed a whole had never truly entered my head. For many people, however, the boundary drawn by the Therans generations ago had taken deep root in their imagination, and they identified their interests with all of the province, not just the area where they happened to live.

We reached the village and said good night. Krattack lumbered away from me, his massive shoulders thrown forward. I turned toward my own tent. I would not try to travel down the mountain because Krattack's words had made sense. And now that he had given me something to share with him, I trusted him.

# 13

I awoke the next morning to find Stoneclaw village buzz-
ing with preparation. The presentation J'role and I had
given to Vrograth the night before had worked after all,
though not in the way we'd intended. Vrograth would not
free us of our obligations, but his pride had been
wounded, for I, a human woman, was willing to attack
the Therans, while he, up until now, would not.

The preparation kept us busy most of the day, and I had
no contact with J'role, though I could hear his laughter
and cries of victory and defeat as he entertained the children up and down the cliffs.

Several dozen trolls and I climbed up a steep slope to
a series of long, narrow caves that wormed their way in
from the slope. One of the trolls told me that the caves
had been dug out decades ago, specifically to store the
drakkars. By keeping the ships in caves carved out from
the middle of the steep slope, the drakkars were relatively
safe from thieves. Several trolls nevertheless always remained on watch in the caves. Fifteen caves lined the
slope, and I was assigned to work in one of the lower
ones along with a group of four trolls.

Though I knew the ship was an airship, the sight of it
levitating slightly off the cave floor still caught me off
guard and made me smile. The morning light streamed
into the long tunnel and illuminated the drakkar—an airship about a hundred feet long and fifteen or so feet wide.

The bright yellow light glinted off the shiny dark wood, which the trolls had carved with intricate patterns.

I suddenly realized that I had seen very little in the way of artistic endeavor among the trolls—a few large rings made of blue or green crystal, some carefully crafted cooking ware, also of colorful crystal. But everything else the trolls owned—tapestries hung on cave walls (all decaying quickly from lack of care), goblets, silver and gold rings (which the trolls wore as earrings after reshaping them a bit), statues of wood and stone—were prizes taken from the victims of their raids of the lowlands.

The ship revealed where their concerns rested. Unlike the Theran vessels, which were smooth and featureless, the wood of the drakkar was so covered with carvings it seemed to writhe. Swirls and knobs and pictures of the sun and clouds and mountains all flowed in and out of each other, so it was impossible to discern where one representation or pattern ended and another began. One might look at a piece of the pattern and think it showed the sun rising over Twilight Peaks, but they shift perspective only slightly and the Peaks were lost as they transformed into clouds hanging over a rising sun.

The thick mast rested between the two rows of benches on either side of the ship, waiting to be set into a well-braced slot at the ship's center. Approximately thirty benches lined the vessel, fifteen to a side. Oars rested on the benches, and two trolls sitting on each bench would use one row. It seemed odd to me that the trolls would require more oars to crew a much lighter vessel than our Theran ship, which was much larger and made of stone. But of course the Therans' magic let them build much more efficient ships. The Theran ships also drained the life essence out of their rowers for more power—a magical feat the trolls did not utilize.

Several of the troll sailors—that is, adepts with talents that allowed them to manipulate the vessels—climbed on board. One of them yelled at me to get to the back of the cave and untie lines that connected the drakkar to great metal hooks driven into the wall. The gruff voice of the troll, loud and harsh, did not frighten me. I heard in his voice impatience—an impatience to be airbound—and his impatience swept me up in its momentum. At no time during my tenure at the troll camp had I ever felt any particular connection to the work at hand. If I worked hard it was only so my people and I would have food and shelter while stranded on the top of a mountain. But this new task created a sensation that I have never experienced since.

We live in an age of magical thought. Certain records suggest that this magical thought has not always been with us, and scholars theorize that it may all someday vanish again. But it is ours now, and I do not think we always appreciate these wonders we possess. Sometimes it seems that if the world were encrusted with jewels instead of earth, we would search frantically for dirt. So, the idea of flying ships was not in itself spectacular—hadn't I already traveled on one? It was confusing to feel such excitement gripping my muscles as I undid the cord that would free the ship from the metal hooks. My shoulders tightened. The thick, coarse rope in my hand felt amazingly rich in textures as my flesh became more alive.

I pondered this as I coiled the rope, and realized that wonders in themselves do not produce wonderment. There was no wonder on the Theran ship—the vessels were smooth and stone gray and dull. The sailors had moved around on them as if they had stepped out from their huts onto some dry, empty field that held no interest. For the crystal raiders, however, the passions evoked by preparation for the launch of their fleet transformed the air itself. Their love of their vessels—of the splendor of flying through the air—filled the chamber and took hold of me, too.

We define wonder. We create it. Without us, the world would exist, but robbed of all beauty and splendor. To say that the stars would be just as beautiful without our eyes to see them is to miss the essential point of the exercise:

There would be no one to see the stars. They would be only what they are, objects without the investment of our meaning. That is why the Universe created we name-givers. To name splendor and create the true magic.

I placed one coiled rope, and then another, and then a third over the edge of the drakkar. The trolls on board the ship had unfurled the ship's sail, which had been neatly tucked under a section of benches. While they were busy, I touched the wood of the vessel when I was sure none of the trolls was looking. The smooth, polished wood rolled away under my fingertips, and it seemed that the hard wood would be comfortable to sleep on.

One of the trolls spotted me and shouted, "You done?"

I jerked my hand away, suddenly a child caught in the act of stealing some rice candy out of the bowl before dinner. I nodded quickly.

The trolls seemed not to notice my fondling of the hull, and two of them jumped out of the ship and grabbed it by the edge. "Help push it out," one of them said. She looked me in the eyes, then smiled at me, her massive gray-green face filling in the cheeks, the large teeth in her mouth sticking out as her lips stretched taut. She had seen my fascination with the ship and approved.

We all began to push.

I put my weight against the stern, expecting the ship to move forward easily. It was made of wood. It floated in the air. A troll stood on either side of the ship, also push-ing. But the ship moved only a few inches. In my surprise, I lost my grip and fell forward into the stern, slamming my shoulder against the hard wood (not nearly as comfortable as I had fantasized moments before), and cried out.

Four sets of large troll eyes turned slowly back toward me to see what the ruckus was about. I offered no explanation—not even a shrug—and they seemed content to let the matter drop. The two trolls on the outside of the ship gripped the edge of the vessel once more and I placed my hands flat against the hull, ready this time for the slow progress.

So we forced the ship forward, and as we moved closer to the opening of the cave the sun's light caught me full in the eyes, dazzling me with its brilliance. In that blinded moment I lost all track of my previous life—my children, my husband, the quests I'd undertaken. It seemed that all that I'd ever done was work among the trolls of Twilight Peaks, and that I was quite content in my life. The sunlight glinted off the dark wood, and the vessel's strange, carved textures sparkled like silver jewelry on a lady's fine-boned wrist. I had never seen anything so beautiful, and I smiled from sheer joy.

I wanted desperately to climb into the boat, slip under one of the benches and hide myself if necessary so that I might go sailing with it off into the sky. Away from J'role and his confused pain. Away from my concerns about the other slaves who I'd helped free. Away from the concerns about rescuing you two. I feel ashamed writing the words, but that is how I felt just then, and if I am to be honest about J'role, I must also be honest about myself. My only explanation is this—I did not want to leave everyone forever, just for a little while. I only wanted a rest from having to care so much about everyone else.

# 14

Have you two ever had such feelings? Have you ever loved someone so much, yet yearned to escape, if only for a brief while? I once believed love would not be capable of such a contradiction. While growing up I used to think of finding someone to spend the rest of my life with, and that I would do so happily with complete contentment. And though I would wish such a dream for every child, I do not think it can come to pass. It's true that in a way I did find J'role and spent the rest of my life with him, in my thoughts at least, for no one ever possessed my imagination as he did. I have been with many men since the end of the Theran War, for I tried to forget your father in the strong arms and gentle kisses of others. But none served well enough. They were all, by definition, not J'role.

Was your father worth such odd devotion? Certainly, when I think back on what I have written thus far, no. Yet how can we measure worth when it has to do with an intimate relation between two people? For whatever reason, I have always longed to be with him.

But now I realize something. All this time I have resented your father for his senseless wandering. Yet, did I not appreciate his absence as well? Was there not something perverse in my own behavior? Not just the fact that I always waited for him, but in the relief I found when he was gone. Your father was difficult to take—his passion and pain drove strange energy into my thoughts—like the embrace of a corrupted elf of Blood Wood.

Perhaps I enjoyed the spaces between our meetings as much as he did. Or at least needed them in a way I did not appreciate until just now.

Is it possible that the marriage we had was exactly the marriage we wanted? Or rather—for I doubt either of us wanted such a marriage—the only one either of us *could* have? I think now of Krattack's statements about passions and our lack of control over our actions. I have been bitter toward your father for so long, for I always believed him responsible for taking away our happiness. Yet, in my heart I stayed with him. Whatever happened belongs to me as well. How can I place sole blame on him for what happened in a relationship where my own behavior was so complicit?

# 15

The drakkar floated into the air, drifting out from the mouth of the cave, rocking gently against the splash of water not present. The two trolls who had been pushing the ship along with me jumped in just as it left the cave. They paid me no further attention, and I was left standing alone at the edge of the steep slope, watching the trolls lift the mast and slot it to its home. Other ships now floated around the mountain face. It seemed a wonderful way to live—floating along the insubstantial streams of the sky, with nothing to sustain you but the desire to get someplace new. My heart ached for the glory of it.

As some of the trolls worked on the sails, other sailors took hold of the tiller and brought the ships down to the village below. I still do not fully understand how the air sailor adept controlled the altitude of the vessels. But then, I never will unless I become an adept at the discipline of air sailing. To understand a discipline, you must live that discipline, moment to moment. The trolls, heavy and bulky though they might be, understood the odd magic of controlling ships of the air.

One at a time each ship moved in a wide spiral, like a bird languidly coming to roost on the large ledge below. Dozens and dozens of troll warriors waited. Some wore thick layers of fur and hide that would serve as armor. Others had stitched together scraps of leather armor taken from victims of their raids. And a few had breastplates and bracers made of metal. Most spectacular of all, though, were the furs and leathers and metals with crystals incorporated into them. Over the last few weeks I'd seen the clan work on enchanting crystals of all sizes and colors with spells I did not understand.

The crystals were red and blue and green and violet and orange. Some the size of pebbles, others as large as several fists. Many of the stones stood in clusters, while others stood alone. More still were sprinkled across the armor like glistening seeds in a field. Many of the crystals were long and seemed to have grown from the armor over years and years.

In their belts the trolls held swords and maces, also made of crystals, reinforced by magic and enchanted to stroke terrible blows against their opponents. These were more spectacular than the crystals scattered across the armor; thick and jagged, they retained their crystalline features, but could kill if used properly. Each was large and obviously heavier than a metal weapon of the same type. Only a people as strong as trolls could successfully use the weapons.

As the trolls moved about and finished the preparations for their ships, the crystals refracted the sun's light and turned the area below me ablaze with colors; like a broken rainbow in motion, but glittering with more colors than I'd ever seen at once in a single sky.

I sat down at the edge of the cave, for I feared that I would actually try to sneak on board if I got close enough. Against the rough splendor of the clan existence, my life seemed tawdry and dull. I'd had adventures, but not for some time. My latest quest had been trying to raise the two of you safely to adulthood.

Krattack appeared beside me. "I'm not here," he said. "So don't try to figure out how I sneaked up on you." He pointed down toward the village, and I saw him sitting beside a large fire set some distance from the ships. He looked up at me. I waved, amused by the deception, and he returned my wave.

"Do you want me to come down to speak with you?" I asked the illusion.

"No need. Anyway, I need the practice," the illusion said. The image was a bit younger than Krattack, and moved with more energy. It was either a mistaken ideal Krattack had about himself, or a well-thought-out ideal. "I noticed you looking with longing down at the preparations."

"It's beautiful."

"Yes. Astounding people."

"You speak as if you really don't belong here."

"Part of me does. But part of me doesn't. You never forget where you're from. You rarely forgive the murderers of someone you love."

"I don't think I could do that—forgive someone for killing my parents. Have you forgive them?"

"To tell you the truth, I really don't know."

The illusion and I sat in silence for a while. I looked out over the trolls. Looked once more at the real Krattack, who was sipping broth from a stone bowl.

"You want to go with them," the illusion said.

I nodded, embarrassed.

"You will. Soon. But not now. This expedition is headed for death. Not all. But enough that it would be prudent for you to wait."

His calmly spoken words so startled me that I turned quickly to look the illusion in the face.

It was gone.

I looked down at the real Krattack.

Then *he* vanished.

My chest tightened. I scanned the clan village for the real Krattack, suddenly afraid that the troll did not exist at all. I looked at the busy scene below for some minutes. When I finally found him again, he was walking casually through the village to speak to Vrograth. He did not look up at me, and I had the impression he was not even aware

I was there. I realized there was no way to know if this impression was correct, for he obviously could mask many of his features—physical and emotional.

I realized, too, that he wanted me to know this.

# 16

The fleet departed in glory. The trolls, wearing their glittering, glowing armor, took hold of the ship's oars and swept them back in wide arcs as the fifteen ships rose up into the sky. The sails all rested on the yardarms, for they would only be unfurled when conditions demanded using the wind for extra speed. The trolls, I learned, preferred using the oars, for the long, narrow craft could capsize when heavy winds slammed into the sails.

They left in late afternoon and headed west, their ships drifting lazily toward the sun, turning quickly into silhouettes of wonder. The commands of "Stroke! Stroke! Stroke!" in their troll tongue soon turned thin and soft. When the ships were no more than dark dashes in the sky, I made my way back down to the village. With most of the clan away on the raid, there would be more work for the rest of us until they returned days or weeks later.

I did not watch J'role's stories that night, but hid myself down the path where I had spoken to Krattack the night before. Though I told myself with loud thoughts that I wanted nothing to do with anyone, I secretly harbored the wish that Krattack would come along and have another discussion with me. Hearing the "oohs" and "aahs" of J'role's audience coming over the night air, I spoke bitter thoughts to myself about how stupid all of J'role's stories were and how he wasted everybody's time.

Below me the jungles of Barsaive lay as dark as diseased waters. they had grown thick and fast in the mere thirty years since the Scourge had ended. Before that, the world had become almost barren, devastated by the Horrors swarming over our world. When I was still a child and my people had just left the shelter that had hidden us from the Horrors of the Scourge, it was all we could do to create fields for our crops to grow in. But with help from the Passion of Jaspree we managed to grow food, finding in ourselves that strength and impulse to cultivate and protect the world around us. The earth itself seemed to demand life, and soon jungles sprang up everywhere. I had come to love the abundance of life that flowed over the world. But as I stood high above the jungles that night, they seemed nightmarish. Things were just too complicated, and the thick jungles of that complication were dark, impenetrable, and dangerous.

"Releana?" J'role said. The stories had ended, but wrapped in my cold thoughts, I hadn't noticed. J'role now stood above me, looking down from a path almost directly above my head "I've been looking for you." Ridiculously, he stepped off the ledge and slid down the nearly sheer drop that separated us, drawing on his thief magic to keep his balance. He slammed into the path where I stood, and I reflexively reached out to stop him from falling off the path. Such a dramatic slide would have carried almost anyone else over the ledge and into the arms of death. But J'role's abilities as a thief adept rescued him from the fate.

He smiled at me, amused at my outstretched hands meant to save him, as if saying, "So, you care about me after all, and I caught you at it." I jerked my hands away. I hated myself for once again underestimating his sense of balance, and for once again revealing my concern.

"You've been ignoring me," he said.

"Yes. I've been enjoying it." I turned and started further down the ledge.

A panic came into his voice now, rare for him, as he

called, "Wait! What . . .?" He ran up behind me, following closely. "I don't understand. I upset you last night. I did something wrong. I'm sure I did. I do things wrong with you all the time. But this time I really don't know what."

He touched my shoulder, hoping to get me to stop. I shook his hand off. Kept walking. How I enjoyed him coming after *me*, rather than me constantly longing for him.

"Releana, I really want to know. Please."

Still walking I said, "I'm upset because I could tell you were happy that Vrograth decided we wouldn't be freed to go after the children."

Behind me his footsteps faltered, then rushed to catch up. "I was . . ." Then, with actual confusion, he asked, "I was happy?"

"You skipped."

"I skipped?"

"In your step. A skip in your step as we left the cave."

We came to a small clearing—a cul de sac bound by massive boulders and a sheer drop. The dim light of the moon cast a blue pallor over our flesh. I turned to face him, as if he might try to strike me from the back.

"I don't think I skipped."

"You skipped, but I'm sure you weren't aware of it. You're strange that way. You're so used to controlling your face, presenting only what you want the world to see. But the truth of you leaks out in strange ways. I know you too well not to notice. A skip in your step. A subtle wave of the hand at waist height. The beginning of a spin on the ball of your foot, stopped at the last moment. You have too much energy, J'role. The stuff oozes out of you like smoke from fire. Try as you might, you can't control it all . . ."

"I think you're seeing too much . . ."

I held my hand up, silencing him immediately. "Don't you ever do that. Don't you ever try to tell me I'm missing the truth. I've known too many men in the village who did that all the time—dismiss the perceptions of their wives. If you knew who you were, I might discuss the matter with you. But you don't. You don't know who you are, do you?"

"I ...," he began, and faltered. He turned away from me, swinging his arms right and left. "I don't think I know in the way you mean. In a way that's really worth anything." He smiled at me, the tears in his eyes catching the night's slim light. "You expect more from me than everyone else. I love you for that. But I can't keep up, you see. I'm going to keep disappointing you. There's something wrong ..." His voice trailed off.

My first impulse was to leave, for he had slipped into that pitiable pose again, designed to draw my fury to his despair. It occurred to me, though, that I *did* expect more from him than from other people. All they wanted from him was to be moved by a story—to lean forward in excitement, to lean back with laughter, to shed a tear during a sad moment. I wanted him to be a human being who could be a father and husband. Maybe he simply couldn't do it.

"Why don't you want to rush after Torran and Samael the way I do?"

"They're safe. You said so yourself. The Overgovernor wants them safe. I'm sure he has the power to do it."

"That's not the point. They're not with me—us!"

"But they're going to be all right."

"Would you stop doing that."

"Doing what?"

"Changing the subject."

"I'm not."

"You are. I'm talking about why I want to get them back. You're telling me it's not a problem. Stop it!"

"It is a problem, but it's not the problem you think. We'll get them back. That's the problem. Worrying about it ..."

"Well, I am worried about it. They're little children, torn from their mother."

"And father."

"You ripped yourself away."

"Now who's changing the subject?"

"It's the same subject."

He threw his hands in the air. "What?"

"The subject is whether or not you care about them."

"I do care."

"Then why don't you act like it?"

"Releana, horrible things happen all the time. The twins are having a horrible thing happen to them. It happens. They'll go on. It's just part of life." I stared at him. "It's true. We all suffer. That's just part of what it means to be alive. It's to be expected. That's the point. That's *my* point. They're suffering. But what are we going to do? Keep them safe from all suffering. For what? So that they'll think the world is safe, when it's really not?" His voice began to strain, and his fists began to clench. "So they can think life is good and whole and that you can be happy when there's just so much, so much, so much . . . I mean, better they learn it from us than from the world later on. Better now, than later, because the world isn't this place you think it is, Releana. It'll cut you and scar you. And it hurts . . ."

"J'role . . .?"

"But it's all right. You see? Because the scars are who we are. The scars of life define us. Without the pain and the scars, we wouldn't know who we are."

"No . . ."

"That's the amazing thing. Life just hurts so much, but that's where we get our strength from. It's from the pain . . ."

"No . . ."

He stared off at the stars, his words tumbling out quickly, trying to convince himself of something. His eyes became wet and glistened, though he did not cry.

"They're all right, you see, not because everything is right. But because that's just part of what it is. Their being *alive*."

"J'role, please . . ."

"The Therans, you saw them. The beauty of their castles. Their physical beauty. Overgovernor Povelis, flawless to the point of being repulsive. That's wrong. That's their distortion. They try to build so much perfection into their lives that they become unnatural. And the charm you told me about—needing to keep Torran and Samael perfect. That's perverse. They should be scarred. We all should be scarred. That's natural. That's the way of it."

"J'role! Please! You're frightening me!"

He stopped, looked at me, confused. "You really don't know this?"

His eyes. I thought of Wia's comments about his eyes. There was something wrong about them. He seemed to be staring at me from a different place, a different world. As if he stood on a vantage point of another plane, large enough only for him, viewing the world in a way none of us could ever understand.

"J'role, you've never said—you've never said anything like this . . ."

"I thought you knew." He touched his fingertips to his chest.

I shook my head.

His head sank down, his shoulders folded forward. "I . . . I sometimes . . . I sometimes don't make sense to people." With that, he turned and walked away, his body a trophy of a broken spirit.

"J'role . . .," I said, but he kept walking. I did not pursue him. I had no idea what I might say.

Hours passed. The dark jungles below seemed even darker; dangerous pools full of ink waiting to be used to write a tale of mutilation, betrayal, and death.

I waited and waited for some impulse to inspire me to

rise and go back to the village. But it never came. Matters of the human heart seemed so hopeless. I remember thinking that night, "And if I rescue my boys, will they be dead from sword or disease in another year's time?" What was the point, I wondered, when nothing seemed to work out?

# 17

Life in the crystal raider village carried on, with all of us doing the usual tasks. There is no point in listing the details of the work—not that it was tedious, for in the midst of it I was fully engaged and somewhat happy. Work has always been a relief for me.

I will note only this then: that J'role performed his stories with the same intensity each night, but it was only during these performances, and when playing with children, that he seemed truly alive. At all other times he seemed drained of energy, as if a slow disease had begun to consume him.

At no time did he approach me. For my part, I remained silent as well. What were we to talk about? It seemed that the only matter left at hand was the dissolution of our marriage, and though my mind said to destroy my bond with him, another part of me refused. The same part of me that had kept me always waiting for him, I suppose.

Two weeks passed.

Some trolls had gone off on an expedition into the caves of Twilight Peaks and had returned with sacks full of crystals. I was dividing the stones by size and shape—a task the trolls thought I could handle well enough—when a cry came from one of the trolls posted on a cliff above the village. These lookouts served the primary purpose of keeping an eye out for neighboring crystal raiders who might attack the Stoneclaw village.

But in recent days hopes were running high that they would soon spot Vrograth and the fleet returning.

The trolls suddenly stopped work, whatever the task at hand, and stood about. They began speaking quickly in trollic, the noise passing throughout the village like birds flying in formation. Then an abrupt stillness as the trolls all looked west, their heavy hands held up to shield their eyes from the light of the setting sun. The amber light of early evening turned their still forms into stones carved into the shape of people.

I too stood still, staring in the same direction as the trolls. Within moments I saw a line drifting in the sky, though I quickly realized the shape of the line was a trick of my eye. In reality it was a series of dots floating near one another. I felt a presence beside me, and turned to see Krattack. I didn't know whether it was an illusion or really him, but I'd decided a few days earlier it didn't really matter.

"It didn't go well," he said. The wind picked up a few strands of his gray hair and moved them about from side to side over his barren scalp. He wore his ragged blue magician's robe covered with the pattern of jungle vines.

He sounded upset and this surprised me. Did he mean not enough ships were lost to fulfill his plans? Or did he feel loss for the lost ships? I looked back out across the sky and saw between five and ten ships. "I can't tell how many . . ."

"There are only nine ships. Six lost. I have no idea how many sailors and warriors."

"How many ships did you expect to be lost?"

"Six. It's still a sad day, whether I guessed correctly or not. The men and women who died have families here. There will be so much sadness." His voice trailed off. His wry distance from the unpleasant realities of political machinations seemed to have vanished, and he was in the middle of pain now.

As the ships sailed closer I could see he was right—

nine ships total. The trolls began craning their necks, looking for the rest of the fleet. A soft murmur began, and they turned to one another with questions; no answers could be found.

The ships sailed closer, and cries of excitement rose from the deep throats of the trolls as they recognized the flags or the patterns of the sails on some of the ships and realized that their fathers or mothers or sons or daughters or brothers or sisters had most likely survived, for their ships still sailed. Their muscles relaxed, and their stone-like vigil ended. But around these many other trolls remained still. Some simply lowered their heads, and I saw them moving their lips, most likely asking Garlen to give them comfort in this time of their despair. Others slipped to their knees, as if a presentiment they'd been holding for the last two weeks had finally been confirmed.

Those who found in themselves the ability to rejoice—or at least retain optimism—set about gathering herbs and ointments and other medications for wounds. Others began feeding fires and preparing stew and roasted goat for the returning warriors.

When the ships reached the mountain, they floated down gently upon the massive ledge that formed the heart of the village, one after another, lining up next to each other. Then screams filled the air—terror and remorse, wailing into the darkening sky—as the fears about death became reality. The sounds traveled up to the early evening stars; the pinpoints of light were cold and unresponsive. The trolls raised their arms upward, and beat their chests and cried and cried.

Happy trolls dragged loved ones off the drakkars. These trolls embraced each other fiercely, whirling around one another in a cluster if the family was large.

However, I noticed that it was only the adults who exchanged these outbursts of emotion and physical energy. The children held themselves in several lines formed fifty feet or so back from the area where the ships docked.

Their small, stocky bodies—small for a troll, some only five feet high—remained almost impassive, yet I saw them straining, wishing to be with the adults. On their faces smiles formed with hesitation, as if afraid that by revealing happiness they would be breaking the taboo that limited a crystal raider child's emotional expression (which, indeed, they would). Other faces were very still, and I saw chins trembling and eyes filling at the edge with tears.

None of the trolls gathered around the drakkars, neither adults nor older children, took notice of the youngsters. Even my companions from the Theran ship seemed far more caught up in the dramatic outpouring of despair and exuberance at the center of the village. And I was not much better, for though I noticed the children, I did not act.

J'role, however, was different.

Your father has always been different.

He stepped up behind a young girl, her body perfectly still, one hand covering her eyes so as not to reveal her pain. Her body was thick; she wore a red jerkin with bits of fur sewn in around the neck. I would not have thought much of it, but I knew that among the troll children, such an outfit was worthy of pride.

J'role touched her shoulders. As if he had cast a spell around her, her shoulders began to heave up and down, faster and faster, until she abruptly spun around and embraced his legs and hugged herself to him.

Then, more magic. Without looking at him directly, those children in pain began walking toward J'role and the girl. He knelt down and stretched his arms out wide, and the children gathered around him. J'role tried to embrace them all, a lightning rod for pain. Soon they clustered around each other, a mob of despair, their big bodies several layers thick, sobbing and shaking.

My throat tightened for it was such an unfortunate

sight, yet so beautiful. Horror and beauty balanced so perfectly in tableau.

These thoughts were interrupted, however, by the scream offered up by Vrograth to the clan—to Twilight Peaks, and to the stars.

"We will have our vengeance!" he cried. "The invaders will know our pain!"

# 18

Bonfires burned, massive and towering, shifting pillars of heat that turned and twisted, mimicking the frenetic bodies of the trolls as they danced around them. Five fires in all, built from large tree trunks gathered several hundred feet down the mountain and carried back up in the drakkars. The trunks, leaning against each other, shaped like large cones pointing to the sky, contained the bodies of those dead the crystal raiders had been able to bring back.

Vrograth's fleet had attacked the floating castle and its escort of two stone ships. He hadn't considered the discipline of the Theran soldiers. Hadn't considered the fire cannons that could rip apart a drakkar if they scored a solid hit. Hadn't considered the thick stone hulls that could smash into a drakkar even as the trolls tried to board the Theran ships.

The dead were many, and most of the corpses did not come back. The loss of the bodies was especially grievous to the trolls. Krattack explained that the crystal raider custom demanded that the dead be burned in the funeral pyres at their village. So many trolls lost in mid-air, their bodies left ruined and broken on the ground far below, was a tragedy.

So those corpses that were brought back were burned, fifteen in all, and the air ran thick with smoke and the stench of burning flesh. My eyes teared from the acrid and overwhelming smoke that swept out from the flames, even though I stood a good distance away from the ceremony, as did all of us who were not part of the clan.

The children were involved now, in their own, removed way, and formed a large ring around the fires and their parents. Their circle moved, all in one direction, and the children stomped their feet and raised their hands and cried out to the sky. The motion was rhythmic and controlled, but the cries formed an undulating, ghastly tone. I thought of the villages located far below, buried under the canopy of jungle leaves along the base of Twilight Peaks. Could they hear the strange wailing that flowed down the cliffs of the Stoneclaw village? Did they wonder what strange monster had arrived in our world, and were they now barring the doors of their huts, sending their children to bed with strained words of comfort? Or did they know of the trolls, and realize that such cries floating down through the night meant some of their number had died? But even if they knew this, would they know that the ceremony was for more than grief? Would they know that the Stoneclaws were whipping themselves into a frenzy for battle?

The children formed a sparse ring around the adults. The adults, hundreds of them, wore nothing but crystal armor. Those who did not own such armor wore nothing. It was, Krattack explained, a time of war, and for the crystal raiders, a time of war meant that nothing else mattered, not even clothes on your back.

Krattack was within the ring of the children, and he, with all the hundreds of adults, moved around the funeral pyres. They too stomped their feet and shook their hands and cried out in anguish at the sky. But on occasion, Krattack stopped and began a slow dance, with careful gestures and sudden, abrupt slices through the air with his arms. As he did this dance, those around him would notice him, and one by one, they would follow him. Only those in Krattack's immediate area could see what he was doing, and only those around him followed. So the mass of the village was wild and loud and screaming, and in a small pocket there was stillness, led by Krattack. Then the old troll, his naked flesh gray with age, but his muscles still thick and powerful, would suddenly shout up at the sky. Then his followers would do the same and all of them would once again be stomping and shouting.

The energy created by the trolls was palpable, and though I had never seen it before in a group, I knew what was happening. They were calling upon one of the Passions to infuse their souls with energy. Specifically Thystonius, the ideal of conflict. Krattack, I realized, was a questor of the Passion, something I would not have guessed.

We all call upon the Passions, in one way or another, throughout our lives. Sometimes purposefully, sometimes not. A man who lusts after a woman he sees in a market is full of the Passion of Astendar, whether he meant to call Astendar to him or not. Sometimes we do it on purpose. The same man who perfumes his body with the scent of flowers to draw a woman to him is purposefully calling upon Astendar, for he is focusing his body and his thoughts to being attractive.

And there are the questors, those who commit themselves to the ideals of one Passion. They live imbalanced lives, for they know conflict, or creativity, or greed, or domination too well, at the expense of the other passions that make up a whole person. But they are rewarded for this imbalance, for the Passions bless their devotees with powers—much like magical powers, but only for the purpose of bringing physical manifestation of their ideals to earth.

But never before had I seen a mass of people all working in concert for such a goal. All thoughts and efforts of physical exertion were turned to the matter of conflict. Soon the trolls began slamming into one another, sending each other reeling throughout the giant circle formed by the children. The cries grew louder, the thrashing more and more pronounced.

The frenetic dance thrilled me, called to me, though now, looking back, I do not know why. My small, human body could not have lasted long in the orgy of fury. Yet such was the intensity that I longed to be a part of it, as if I might be able to draw in the energy and sustain myself through the violence.

And so I passed through the circle formed by the children. I cannot tell you what actually caused the final decision. At the very least it was a chance for dramatic, physical action, and after weeks of waiting, I was ready to do something.

But this explanation sounds too rational, and I do not think my intellect was working as it usually does. The sounds and cries and random motion of the mob, combined with the finely crafted ritual dance of Krattack, took possession of a different part of my thoughts.

I maneuvered my way between two troll children as they danced. They seemed both awake and asleep. Entering the circle proved a jolt to my senses, and for just a moment the heat from the fires seemed ready to scorch my flesh from my bones. The circle of children had somehow trapped the heat and kept it from dissipating into the night air.

I became dizzy, for all points of reference vanished against the constant motion of the trolls, who rushed to and fro, stomping their feet and slamming into one another.

A warrior crashed into me. His breastplate of red crystal—now blood-black in the firelight of the pyres— cracked against my head and sent me to the ground. Dozens of massive troll feet rushed through my vision, and I rolled over onto my back. The pain in my head was sharp, as if a long edge of glass had been cut through my skull. My tongue, oddly, felt thick.

A hand grabbed me by the wrist, large and strong, and

dragged me up to my feet. Krattack stared at me. Suddenly I felt safer. Better. Several trolls stood clustered around us. J'role stood there as well, though I do not know how he got so deep into the circle without my being aware of it. I hadn't seen him for some time. His eyes were large black circles. I don't think he recognized me.

My own sensibilities were disintegrating. The fall had just fled my memory, and I once again eased into the delight of being in the dangerous mass of trolls. The intense heat of the circle seemed quite comfortable now, almost like a fever not accompanied by illness.

Krattack, J'role, and several other trolls were involved in the slow dance I had seen Krattack perform earlier. At that moment I knew two things. First, that if I did Krattack's dance, I would be enriched with the Passion of Thystonius. Second, I very much wanted that to happen. I did not know how I knew those things, but I longed to be stronger, to be able to throw myself into combat unscathed. Not for reasons of self-preservation, but because I simply wanted to push myself to limits of physical endurance I had never experienced before. All these desires rushed into my head. They were not my desires. Or rather, they were the desires of a part of me, the part of me that was Thystonius.

I glanced at J'role.

A thought . . .

Pain. I wanted to feel intense pain and survive. I wanted to walk away with the memory of agony burned into my thoughts. J'role had done this. I knew it suddenly. The secret from his past he had never shared. Agony.

He had once been mute. He walked into the ruins of Parlainth and came out again with his voice. He never told me what had happened in there.

Pain. Something dug deep into his emotional flesh, a silver hook, its tip cold and sharp. It had dug into his emotional flesh and ripped something out. The scars had toughened him.

Sometimes I hated him so much, but part of that was envy.

I danced.

I followed Krattack's lead, moving my right arm slowly, first before my face, and then behind my back. A simple movement. Yet in the strange surroundings of the dance I *felt* the muscles in a way I never had before. Krattack then raised one leg, like a bird about to take flight. The small group clustered around him did the same, as did I, and again my muscle—my bones—felt *clear* to me.

The screams continued around me. Grunts and groans and hasty motion and the red glare of the massive flames; the residue of burnt flesh swirling in the air, and I could taste it now, bitter on my tongue, and that taste of death inspired new sensations of life. My entire body shook, not as if from a fever, but as if the ground—the mountain— shook, and its earth-shaking vibrations traveled up my flesh, gripped my heart tight, and jostled it firmly, shaking out the useless and keeping only the core of life.

My sorrow for my sons, my self-pity, and everything in my heart that dragged me down each moment slipped away as my flesh and muscle and bone took flight. My heart, last of all, followed, and as I continued to imitate Krattack's motions I felt a new kind of exhilaration. It was not joy—which I knew well from moments of love, or the birth of my children, or the learning of my first spell—but the promise of victory.

I looked up.

Astounded.

At the center of the hurricane of troll flesh stood a giant human woman, sixty feet tall at least.

# 19

She wore a suit of silver armor so well polished that it reflected the scene around her with absolute clarity, though
the curves of the armor distorted the details. The flames
and frenetic trolls warped and wrapped around the metal.
Thus, it seemed ablaze with hot red light, and the bodies
of the trolls crawled around her, rushing up and down and
back and forth across the silver surface.

Her hair was long and black and coiled around her
neck, writhing, as if alive. Her face, strong but smiling,
white teeth gleaming, looked down at me. Her large eyes
were hazel, and reminded me of the mix of blue and
green one sometimes sees in the sky at a clear sunrise.

I almost turned to those around me, wondering if they
too could see the fantastic apparition standing in the
midst of the violent chaos, but did not, for fear that she
would vanish if I turned away. From the periphery of my
vision I saw no change in the wild motion around me,
making me suspect she was my vision alone.

On her hip was a sword—thirty feet long at least, its
pommel encrusted with rubies the size of babies. The
woman leaned down toward me, her outstretched hand
covered in a glove of silver links. As she bent toward me,
the reflection of firelight from the pyres slid down her
length. I could see clearly that her belly was a lovely, tremendous bulge.

She was pregnant, and the armor had been fitted to
give the child within her a place of safety.

I smiled at her in delight, and her smile widened. Her gloved hand came closer—its size making it seem as if it were rushing toward me at a terrible speed—but it did not crash into me. Not that I would have moved. The image mesmerized me, and I would not have moved even in exchange for the secrets of spells I only dreamed of possessing. Her fingers stopped, brushed against my cheek, and I felt the surge of a hundred monsters rush through me. I thought of the two of you, and instead of feeling concern for you, or rage at those who'd enslaved you, I felt at overwhelming desire to *hurt*. The desire was connected to the Therans, but the goal did not matter. Your freedom did not matter. What mattered was moving my muscles and bones, pushing them as far as they could go in conflict against others. The Therans were just an excuse. There could be others. There would be.

Pain would be my mark. The more pain I felt, the more I had succeeded. Not pain unto death, for that would mean defeat. But as much pain as I could withstand. I would burn myself as much as I could endure, and what could be more challenging than that? What could be more wonderful?

My perceptions of the universe melted, sight mixing with sound, touch with taste. The cries of the trolls around me became dark shadows floating with wild abandon to the rhythm of the stomping feet. I screamed with pleasure, though the noise that tore from my throat appeared before me as a scarlet wraith, winding around my body, lifting my arms and legs, turning me into a marionette of brutal pleasure.

Thoughts could no longer survive in my mind; my body had become too hot. Barely aware of what I was doing, I leaped into the air and slammed against a troll wearing armor of fur and sharp crystals. The stones raked into my flesh, and the pain was exquisite. What can I say? It seems insane, but there was something so wonderful about the pain. A reminder of being alive. An acceptance of being alive. A surrendering to being alive. For life is so full of pain and dependent upon our fallible flesh.

Trolls smashed into me, knocking us into each other, then to the ground. Their jagged crystal armor tore open my right arm and the blood flowed freely. The raw nerves tingled in the night air, as if silver needles danced feverishly along my flesh. With my left hand I brought my blood to my lips.

I reeled at the taste. So, so sweet. The droplets flowed across my tongue, alive, like insects crawling in my mouth.

I screamed and screamed and threw myself at the trolls, flayed my flesh for my efforts. Bled. Knew each part of me that could be hurt easily, and then found those more carefully protected.

At no time did I feel as if I would black out. Thystonius sustained me. My flesh began to heal even as I rushed for my next wound. It was that way for all of us. The blood flowed freely. We all knew pain. But none died, and the injuries were temporary. They were true wounds. They were wounds inspired by our Passion of conflict. They gave us a taste of battle, and we hungered for the real thing.

# 20

Vrograth threw his head back and laughed. He stood on a mound in the middle of the dance. "My warriors!" he screamed, his voice harsh and tired, but so full of life! The energy caught all of us full in the chest, lifting our Passions. I wasn't even one of his warriors, but at that moment I would have done anything he asked. "We will avenge. The Stone Sailor will suffer. We shall kill. Tonight we leave. Tonight we sail for their false mountain and destroy them!"

By "false mountain" I knew Vrograth meant Sky Point. At last! It was as Krattack had said. Finally I would go after my children. So deep was Vrograth's fury, the Therans would not stand a chance. I would fly with them. I knew it. There was no choice. I would accompany them, and they would let me kill the Therans. And if I died in the attempt, at least I would have lived.

But here Krattack surprised me once again. "Great Vrograth!" the inscrutable illusionist said, "How many more shall you lose to the might of the Therans?"

Missing the true question in his advisor's words, Vrograth shouted, "As many as it takes to destroy them!" A sound like a gale rushed up from our throats as we cheered the response.

"No, great Vrograth!" said Krattack, and his voice now floated in and out of the crowd. The effect was disturbing, and many of us began to calm down. "You will lose everyone. Days ago you engaged in direct conflict with the Therans. They killed a third of your numbers. If you do this again, you will lose another third. And then another third. And then another third. You will lose a third each time until only you and the clan's children are left!"

"Then I shall give the children swords, and they shall die as well!"

We all thought this was the most wonderful idea in the world, and cheered once more to show our appreciation.

Krattack spoke again, not one to be daunted by the words of others. "Great Vrograth! Your passion for war is a wonder, and your people do you proud. But you must focus the energies of war. As they are now, they will be wasted."

The pregnant giantess looked down at Krattack with suspicion, as if she might have to swat him out of the way to let the party began again.

"I want to KILL!" screamed Vrograth, and we repeated the words.

"But how do you want to kill them? Choose carefully. Patience might be your best path, mighty warrior!"

"Patience. Bah! Patience! What can patience do?"

Suddenly Krattack swept his arm toward me—really. His arm flew off his body and rushed toward me. Trolls jumped out of the way, clearing a path. The arm grabbed me by the shoulder and pushed me toward Vrograth. The one-armed Krattack said, "She can tell you what patience can do!"

Vrograth and the giantess both stared down at me. My body burned for pain and the release of rage, but I felt Krattack's hand against me, and this cooled my flesh and allowed thought to return.

At first I had no idea what the troll was talking about, then, with strange clarity, I understood, and knew my place in Krattack's plan. I decided to help the old troll, for it seemed that it would help me as well. "Great Vrograth," I began softly, overwhelmed and disoriented.

"Louder. Please," begged Krattack with a whisper in

my ear, though he stood dozens of feet away. "Presentation is everything."

"Great Vrograth!" I shouted. "Patience bested you several weeks ago when you and I confronted each other." Vrograth began to dismiss me with the wave of one of his massive hands. But I cried out, "You are mighty, Vrograth! I am small! But with patience I bested you. I waited, and when I struck, I struck for victory!"

Not knowing where these words came from, I thought Krattack was using his magic to influence me. But, remembering well the odd moment in the years afterward, I realized that we are often given the gift of words when we least expect it, when the words are truly worth speaking.

Whatever their inspiration, the words had a pronounced effect on the gathered mob. All began to settle, though still breathing heavily. Even the giantess seemed pleased, for she smiled at me.

"Listen to her," shouted Krattack, and his arm was back on his body. He walked with sturdy steps toward Vrograth as he went on. "This woman is not like us—she is not one of us. She does not depend on her bulk and massive strength. Yet she survives. Yet she wins. We are like her to the Therans. If we wish victory, we need to learn her wisdom."

Vrograth did not trust this bit of logic. "What can this little one teach me?" But around me I heard grunts of approval for Krattack's statement.

His reference to me as a "little one" pushed me into anger. I am short, even for a human, and I do not hide from the fact, but he used the term in such a dismissive way. Though reigned in, the Passion of Thystonius still flowed strongly in me. I charged up the mound, running low. Vrograth spread his arms, ready to catch me as I tried to knock him over.

But I did not intend to knock him over. At least not in the way he thought. For once in my life, I had no hesitation about how to use my spells effectively, and a plan quickly formed that melded my magic and muscle.

As I rushed up to him, I blew my breath on the ground and cast the ice breath spell. The sheath of ice formed behind me as I kept on running. Vrograth did not notice this, for he was intent on chasing me. When I reached him, I ducked in between his thick legs, still casting the spell. The icy surface spread out over the mound and under his feet. He gave a startled gasp as I kicked him in the rear, knocking him off balance. He slipped forward, teetering for a moment. Then his legs slipped out from under him and he slid down the mound, landing finally on his rump.

A great cheer went up from the trolls.

And another, when Vrograth struggled to get up and slipped on the ice once more. This time laughter accompanied the clapping.

I felt terribly happy, but of course my troubles were not yet over. Vrograth scrambled off the ice and stood up, furious. The Passion of Thystonius was still strong in him as well. He prepared to charge me. Reflexively I grabbed some dirt from an un-iced portion of the mound. If he came at me, I would send earth darts into his forehead.

But Krattack appeared between us—suddenly, with a silvery burst of light. "Great Vrograth! Certainly you can charge her and win. That is what the Therans will do to us. But we are her size, and we must find the clever ways to best them, as she has bested you. Will you learn from her?"

Vrograth stared at the illusion, ready, I was certain, to charge through it and rip me apart. But several other trolls came up behind their leader. They touched his arms. He shrugged them off. They whispered to him. He shook his head.

More and more approached him, until he was surrounded by his people, all of them speaking with great excitement. Countless voices tried to reason with him.

Finally he bellowed, "Enough!" and all the trolls quickly stepped back. He looked up at me and said, "Very well. Krattack say I listen to you. I listen. But I am chieftain. Do you understand?"

I nodded, realizing how easy it is for people to lead from vanity rather than respect for the people who follow them.

# 21

He spread his arms, as if with generosity, but on his face I saw nothing but spite. "What wisdom does the little human offer?"

"The first piece of wisdom is this: We have to attack them in small battles. Their fortress, Sky Point, is too well defended to attack directly. We must chip away at their fleet." The words came from my mouth, but I had never before spoken of matters strategic. It seemed only common sense—but Krattack seemed to think my common sense would carry the day. "Sky Point is where the true wealth is—the Theran magic, the Theran treasure of stone and metal. But that is the greatest prize. Second are the flying castles, which are filled with treasure as well. And last are their stone ships. These we must attack first, in isolation, for they are the weakest of the . . ."

"What challenge to attack the weakest?" demanded Vrograth.

"The challenge," shouted Krattack, who looked for a moment as if he might be about to pummel Vrograth with his old hands, "is in the long-term goal. In sustaining the patience. She speaks wisely. Hear her out."

"Patience is not way of crystal raiders!" Vrograth screamed, and suddenly, despite his size, I clearly imagined him as a little child, four or five years old, who had gotten his way for far too long. It seemed he might start stamping his feet at any moment. Some of the trolls around him nodded sagely, but others seemed uncertain.

Krattack said, "Often patience is not our way. But our world has changed. The Therans . . ."

"Therans, Therans, Therans. For months you speak about the Therans! When I was a boy I remember you speak about Therans! All your life you tell us Therans come. Now they here. Why things different? We attack. We kill. We raid."

"They are different because the Therans are here now. They live life differently than we do, and they wish to force that life upon us."

"We will kill them!"

"We *might* kill them," said Krattack, teeth clenched. "But we might not. The arrival of the Therans is the test of the people who live in this land—this land of Barsaive. The entire land will change because of their presence. Either they will rule us, or we will force them out—but all of us will be changed."

"What do you mean 'we'?" J'role asked, loudly, for he had been too long removed from the center of attention. "Do you mean the Stoneclaws? The trolls of Twilight Peaks? What 'we'?"

"It is of no consequence now," replied Krattack quickly, shooting J'role a scathing glare that said, "BE QUIET!"

Krattack obviously had his own reasons for holding certain portions of the discussion in reserve. The clan was set in its ways, and the old illusionist wanted to walk them through each new idea slowly. I realized now that Krattack had encouraged my battle of patience against Vrograth as a way to introduce the effectiveness of patience to clan. Each step had to be introduced carefully for fear that the trolls would balk at the entire concept.

To the group of trolls I said, "The second point of wisdom is this: match their strengths."

"We have enough strength," said Vrograth.

"Their ships are of stone, yours of wood. They will best you."

"We will not use stone for ships!" said Vrograth, and I knew immediately I had touched on a sensitive point.

"No," said Krattack, "we will not. We have not the knowledge nor the means of labor to produce such ships as effectively as the Therans."

"But there is the ship we arrived in," I declared.

"Precisely," said the old illusionist. "It can be repaired, perhaps, and . . ."

"We will not sail such a ship. The earth is not meant to fly!"

"Wiser words I have not heard," said Krattack carefully. "And no Stoneclaw need soil his hands with this endeavor. But there are those among us—Releana's people from the ship—who are under no such prohibition. They could refit the ship and join us in our efforts. They could crew the Theran vessel. And some trolls could sail the ship if they wished."

An excitement bubbled up through my chest. We *could* do that. Perhaps. I didn't know if we had the knowledge to repair the ship. But we might. We might get our own vessel. The ship would be an extraordinary help in searching for the two of you.

And more than that. There was an excitement in the thought of controlling the ship. I remembered my desire to hide aboard the drakkar several weeks earlier, and now it seemed that I might be able to sail without hiding. To have my own ship, sail where I wanted, and save my two boys. What more could I ask?

Vrograth thought the matter over. "How long repairs?"

Krattack turned to me. "How long for the repairs?"

I was an elementalist magician, so they thought I would know. But I had no experience working with airships. Fearful, however, that if I hesitated, Vrograth would revoke my opportunity to rebuild the ship, I said quickly, "Two weeks."

"Two!" Vrograth said scornfully. "We must go to war now."

"Patience," said Krattack.

"I hate this patience."

"Yes," said Krattack, "but you hate the Therans even more. Two weeks."

With a heavy, forlorn sigh, Vrograth nodded.

The giantess had vanished. But I had the feeling I would see her again.

# 22

Two weeks was not enough time to do the job properly, but it was all there was. We made do.

I studied the ship for a few days, and had one of the drakkar shipbuilders accompany me. He explained how the drakkars were build by first carving the wood and assembling the ship. Then elemental air was added, sewn into the wood by elementalists using obscure spells I knew nothing about. I said as much to the troll who accompanied me, and she looked surprised.

"Krattack said you were a fine shipbuilder. He's been saying it for weeks now." She was plump and placed her hands on her waist, like a mother trying to decipher the first lies of a child.

Krattack's words startled me, but I'd learned to react fast when confronted by the old illusionist's deceptions. "Yes, yes. But I mean ... I'm used to having a shipyard prepared to work on stone airships. The facilities here ... Your people know so much more about using crystal than I do. We'll need to use them to repair the ship ... That's what I meant."

She looked at me carefully, then turned back to the ship. "Yes," she said, running her thick fingers along one of the ship's fissures. "We can use the crystals to fill the cracks."

"Exactly," I said, though until that moment I did not know if such a thing was possible.

\* \* \*

We worked very hard. The trolls—those Krattack could persuade to help—cut crystals for us and gave me instructions about airship building. They knew how to build wooden airships, and how to manipulate crystals with magic, but they had never combined the two before. The thought of stone flying bothered them very much. My job was to listen to all the information they had about the two separate arts, and synthesize it to repair the ship.

With a great deal of care, J'role and the others of my band of former slaves fit the stones into the cracks, carefully setting them so they formed a smooth surface. There was no time to get the colors to match, so the ship soon had multicolored fissure lines running through it. As the cracks were filled, I cast the spell of elemental air binding over the stones.

I ought to have been more tense than I was when weaving the magic. Our lives would, after all, depend on successful repair of the ship. Besides, I was tapping the etheric plane, still without the protection of a magician's robe. It would take months and months to build a robe, not to mention magical supplies the clan did not have. I would have preferred to have taken a robe from one of the clan's magicians and re-attuned it to my aura. But none of the magicians, not even Krattack, would grant me this boon. That is how valuable the robes were only thirty years ago.

But I accepted the risks. There was little choice. And I had a great time. The challenge of the work was delicious. Magic, after all, is where my senses flow into the Universe, and there is no greater experience than this. (Carrying the two of you in my belly was equal to casting magic, however, for your senses flowed into me, making *me* the Universe. Not a sensation to be dismissed.)

J'role and I were so intimate that we could work effectively without having to speak to each other. I would simply look at some earth I needed for a spell, and J'role would scoop up a handful for me. He expected no thanks from me, and he received none. If he needed help holding crystals in place while brushing them with the special adhesive the trolls used for mounting their crystal work, then I would be there. We would stand with our hands nearly touching, our faces only inches apart, grim and focused on the work at hand. The other members of our group often laughed and joked with each other. Not us. We carried between us a focus that let us work at an incredible rate. Which is just as well, for we had little enough time as it was.

I remember distinctly the last day of work. My two weeks had passed, and I had to finish that day, for Vrograth wanted blood. J'role and the others had fitted the stone to the cracks, and all that remained was for me to weave the stone of the ship to the crystals, and then the elemental air into the ship.

Storm clouds and rain turned the day dour; the ship's hull gleamed with a layer of water. I wore a blanket over my head, which quickly soaked through. J'role was with me, silent as ever, holding my magical supplies in a box, covering the contents with his own body. The rest of our group had taken to living inside the ship, and they prepared the interior of the vessel, cleaning the blood stains from the walls and floor and stocking it with food the trolls had provided. Krattack had seen to it that some of the more daring trolls agreed to serve on our ship, for we needed help handling it. These trolls worked inside with the others. I was glad, for it would give our little crew, made up of twelve former slaves and ten trolls, a chance to get to know each other before battle. Every so often I could hear deep laughter coming from within the ship.

Melding the stone to the crystals was easy enough, for the two items were from a similar elemental source. I simply allowed my magical thoughts to enter the ethereal plane, and from there, to pass into the elemental plane of Earth.

To my astral sight, the thick gray stone of the ship appeared as rows of dots so tightly packed together I had to strain to see them. The Therans used heavy rock, denser than other rock I'd seen, and again I wondered at their ability to get the stone ships into the air. Luckily, most of the ship's magic had held through the crash, and I would not be required to repeat their process whole and from scratch.

The crystals were dots as well, but they formed fine lines and delicate patterns. The different colors of the crystals revealed themselves by the pattern of the angles, the way wood grain flows one way or another.

J'role seemed no more than a ghost standing beside me. I could see his aura, of course. I perceived what I had always perceived when I looked at him with astral sight. His body was in fine health. But his emotional state revealed itself as something like a child, and within the child was a flower—a tall sunflower—but blackened and dead from lack of water and sun. Or, at least that's how I thought of it. Magicians say that a person's aura presents a truth. It does, but one that comes in strange symbols that must be interpreted by the magician viewing the aura. People examining people is a very imprecise art, and magic only helps a bit.

I pressed my hands against the dense stone of the ship and could feel my astral fingers press into the material, like a hand working its way into thick mud. I would not be able to pass through the hull, of course. But my astral body could manipulate the material as if it were clay. Gently my fingers pushed the dense stone toward the beautiful lines of the crystals, and began mixing the two patterns. It would never be a perfect combination, of course, but I only needed the edges to fuse. Like a bricklayer applying mortar to stone to make a wall, I took the two stone elements of the hull and forged them into a whole. Unlike the bricklayer, however, I needed no mortar. The stones themselves would fuse under my magic.

Soon the edges bled together. I repeated the process

along all the cracks in the ship, and when I slipped out of astral space I was delighted by the effect on our mundane plane. The crystal had fused into the ship's gray stone, forming wondering veins of glistening color. Although very odd, it seemed perfectly natural. Which, of course, it was after I'd worked my magic.

"Done," I said.

J'role remained silent and I looked at him. He wore no shelter from the rain, and the water had drenched his hair and was streaming down his long face. He looked pathetic, and I could not help think that with his performer's sensibility he must know that quite well. "All I've wanted is to make you happy."

I started to leave. I'd had enough of the man. He could help me try to save the two of you or not, but I wasn't going to spend any more time trying to soothe his wounded sense of worth. He could get someone else to do that.

"Releana!"

I stopped. I felt tears in the corners of my eyes, and the rain that poured down around me only seemed to encourage a good cry. Why did it have to be like this? Why had I wasted so many years on him? Why couldn't I just find the means to throw him out of my life? What is it about people that keeps us together when all we want to do is be apart?

"Please. Don't turn your back on me. Please don't . . . I don't have anyone but you."

I kept my back to him. The rain was cold against my back, and I shivered under the red blanket I wore draped over my head. "You have your sons."

"I can't be a father." He said it simply, with surprise, as if he couldn't believe I hadn't realized this most obvious fact years ago.

Now I turned. "You are a father."

"I love *you*."

"I don't want your love if you can't love your sons.

J'role, what is wrong with you? Why are you like this? What is wrong with you?"

"I . . ." In one of those rare moments, he fumbled for words.

"This isn't normal, you know. Parents care for their children. That's what we do."

"I know."

"What is it?" I stepped closer to him. I so desperately wanted to understand. He was a good man, in his own way. He had so much love and caring in him. Compassion at least. "You can take care of the Stoneclaw children. Why not your own?"

He clutched his hands to his chest, and his chin wrinkled up and the rain on his face mixed with his tears. His face, always so expressive, now seemed the Universe was crying for his pain. "I'm afraid."

"Afraid of what?" I could taste it. Something was coming. He would tell me something now. A clue. Or the whole story. Something had happened to him. Before we met. Or maybe in Parlainth. When he got his voice . . .

*When he got his voice.*

"J'role," I said quickly, afraid he'd interrupt me, "you've kept something from me for years. And I'm your wife. And this thing . . . It's keeping you from being the father your boys need."

He nodded, his shoulders hunching over.

"When you regained your voice, you could finally speak, and you were free in a way you hadn't been before. But now you've got to use your voice. You've been practicing all these years. And now it's time to talk. Now it's time to say what's really important."

An incredible struggle took place inside his thoughts, and under his wet flesh his muscles tensed and loosened and clenched and strained, reflecting the turn and toss of his inner dialogue. His face became a living map of the battle. It was not like watching one person become thoughtful. In that moment J'role was dozens of people.

Each expression on his face turned his features—by some trick of emotional chicanery that only J'role understood—into someone completely different. I wondered several times if he might speak, but with the voice of someone else, depending on who his face revealed at the moment.

I wondered if there were many people in his head. I know I have two voices in my thoughts, the person I consider *me,* and another voice that sometimes encourages me, sometimes admonishes me. I wondered how many voices J'role listened to.

He stammered, finally. "I can't."

"Why?"

He looked straight into my eyes then, and I don't think I've ever seen an adult or child so frightened in my life. "It's too dreadful, Releana. Please. Don't ask me to talk about it."

The way he asked me this, there was no way I could insist.

"All right. All right. But I can't be your wife anymore, J'role. A husband can't . . . I don't have words anymore. You either understand or you don't."

He nodded to show me he understood. But he did not.

# 23

The rain continued into the next day, when we lifted off into the air in search of Theran ships to raid. The rain fell heavily, and though we traveled in airships, it was through a sea of water after all.

J'role, disturbingly, was in a wonderful mood. His attitude toward me had become something like a goofy friend of the family who had a crush on me. Or a recent acquaintance who had respect for me, but couldn't let on yet because we didn't know each other that well. He cavorted over the slippery stone deck to the amazement and delight of the rest of the crew as he entertained everyone.

Everyone but me.

Krattack was the last addition to the crew. "This ship is much safer," he said as he came aboard.

"I didn't realize you went on raiding parties."

"I don't. This is war."

"My search for my children is a war? A tiny fleet of ships against the Therans is a war?"

"You're thinking about it all wrong." Now, more than ever, Krattack looked like he might be a sage. A gray-gray sage, with deep lines cutting into his flesh, his huge mouth home to massive yellow teeth. "You're thinking of war as it is when it's underway. Or even more precisely, what it's thought of when it's recorded in the history books, when the perspective is closed and everyone can comfortably say, 'Well, this was a war.' And of course such an image doesn't match what is happening here today. It would be almost preposterous to think these events would lead to a war."

"But they will?"

"Oh, yes. Just remember, if we knew how things would turn out when we started them, there'd be no reason to bother with the beginning and the middle. We could just be happy ever after with the results. But the actions we begin invariably turn into something else."

"You seem rather certain."

"I am. But only because I'm certain I'll be surprised before it's all done."

I looked around for J'role, suddenly worried. He was nowhere to be seen. Everyone was working. Some of the crew kept an eye on the sail, keeping it tight to the wind. Some watched the compass and manned the wheel. And the rest were below, rowing. J'role was probably with them. Working.

Then I saw him, on the mast, hanging from the yard-arm. He'd hooked his ankles over the pole and was hanging upside down, out over the edge of the ship. He laughed and laughed and laughed.

# 24
___

Another letter from your father, another request to come see me. I haven't even had time to make up my mind about the first request.

But something extraordinary came with the letter. A long manuscript introduced by a dragon named Mountainshadow. Or so it claims. It might be some elaborate hoax on your father's part.

It purports to tell of J'role's past.

I have to decide if I want to know that past now.

The more I write of this story, the more I simply want to leave him completely behind. I have a few years left. Couldn't I spend them without J'role crawling around in my thoughts?

# PART THREE

# Scars and Blood

# 1

Though Krattack had made me the Prophet of Patience, impatience clawed at my flesh from the inside out. I wanted to fight the Therans; I wanted to rescue my children. All this time I wasn't even sure whether you two were still alive, but I forced the question from my mind. I knew if I thought that way I would lose all resolve. Or become a mindless fury driven by blood lust. I did not want that. Despite all my growing thirst for combat, I did not want to become a crystal raider.

We sailed for more than a week, spotting Theran ships and floating castles in the distance, but never finding a single ship that would serve our purposes. We also saw the drakkars of several other crystal raider clans flying the skies. There seemed to be an uneasy peace among the airborne trolls. As long as they could freely raid the lowlands, they stayed away from one another. But Krattack assured me that if a crystal raider clan found itself desperate for goods and treasures, they would not hesitate to raid another clan.

The rains came and went, though not with any of the ferocity that had forced us to land on Twilight Peaks two months earlier. Below, the jungles glistened sharp green. Buried beneath the leafy roof were dozens of villages and towns. I sometimes spotted farmlands exposed to the life-giving light of the sun. The world seemed calmer from the perspective of the ship. Everything in miniature. When I spotted people down below, they were so small I couldn't make out their faces, saw only little figures going about their business. Hidden from me was their pain and jealousy, their anger and their fears.

Being captain of the ship filled me with a sensation wholly unexpected. As I stood on the bow of the boat, watching the land beneath me roll by, watching the clouds around us, pink mountains drifting lazily, I felt a tremendous rush enter my spirit. It was like the sensation of a dream where one flies—except that it was real.

The unexpected part was that I suddenly found myself in a position of responsibility, and it wasn't bad at all. When I had imagined stowing away on one of the Stoneclaw drakkars a month earlier, part of the fantasy had been to be utterly free of responsibilities. To leave everyone behind and not *care* anymore. Yet here I was making decisions about the crew shifts for rowing, the distribution of food, doing the best I could to learn the rudimentary techniques of air sailing, and I didn't mind at all. It was fun, in fact. For with the responsibility came the sense that it was *mine*. I wasn't stuck in some horrible life, though I'd ended up as captain by a perverse twist of fate. Instead of seeing my quest for the two of you as some task forced on me by the Therans, I saw it as a choice I brought to myself. I saw my giving birth to you in the same way. And it was how I saw falling in love with J'role.

For so much of my life I'd viewed everyone who'd wanted something from me as people who charged into my life with demands they had no right to make. Now I saw myself as part of the process. I had given in to those requests, and was an accomplice, not a victim. It was my choice as to how to proceed. I could float through life one way or another. The winds would buffet me around, of course. And I might not reach my destination. But the course I strove for was mine to set.

I was searching for you not because you were helpless. Not because the Therans had stolen you. Not because

J'role hadn't been around to help protect you. Those were the circumstances. I was searching for the two of you because I chose to.

One morning, at dawn, Wia roused me from sleep. "We've spotted two Theran ships. No others about."

Pink light filled the cabin through the portholes, turning the walls the color of a dream. An excitement coursed through me; my breathing quickened. I remember now that I gave no thought to the possibility of death—either my own or that of members of my crew. It seemed as if nothing could be easier than attacking two Theran airships.

"Wake all hands," I said to Wia, and she left quickly. I slipped into my armor—furs provided by the trolls—and walked up to the deck. The sun had just crested the horizon behind us. Ahead of us and to the north floated mountain ranges of clouds illuminated fiery gold. It seemed as if one could really sail to them, land, and discover a new world of pure beauty.

Our ship cast a shadow forward through the mist of the high altitude, and like a dark beacon, it pointed toward the two Theran mining ships. The sunlight turned their hulls fiery gold.

There are moments in life where you are suddenly lifted out of the daily concerns, and you find yourself part of something larger—a thread in the fabric of the universe that connects you to something bigger than you could ever have imagined. In that moment I knew I was suddenly part of the history of my land. Krattack's war would take place, and I would be a part of it.

To either side of the *Stone Rainbow*—the name I'd given my ship, after the multicolored crystals that ran along the hull—floated the nine remaining Stoneclaw drakkars. All of our ships flew at different heights, and at least five hundred yards apart from each other.

The trolls usually communicated by shouting or, when too far apart for that, a simple series of signals sent with red cloth. From Vrograth's ship I could just make out blurs of red. This signal was read by a ship closer to Vrograth's, and they passed it on to another ship and so on until a troll on board my ship could read it clearly. Though the trolls had explained the codes, I had decided to always let a clan member read the signals for me, for fear of making a small error with horribly dire consequences.

As the troll stared off at the twisting flags, he translated. "We attack now." Then he squinted, as if he could not understand the flags, and said, "Now, now, now." Smiling at me he added, "Vrograth very hungry for blood."

I was, too; the desire for it rested on my tongue, and I welcomed it. My fights in previous years had all been with mindless monsters or the cruelly intelligent Horrors. Or with those who had threatened me first, to which I immediately responded with violence. Never before had I hunted out a battle in this way. My breathing quickened. I felt my flesh become warm against the cool, high air. I touched the dagger on my belt. A dagger I'd found on the corpse of a Theran sailor.

# 2

"Prepare for battle!" I shouted. The cry echoed throughout the ship as my crew passed it along.

From below the trolls at the oars began a rhythmic war chant. Their voices, deep and rumbling, traveled up through my bones, and I thought back to long ago when I was a little girl and my father used to sing me to sleep. Till today I'd thought it was the gentleness of his voice that had made me sleep so peacefully, but now I realized that what had comforted me was its *strength*.

The ships picked up pace, and the wind rushed faster over my skin. I called for J'role, and we headed for the fire cannon mounted on the ship's bow. The trolls were unfamiliar with the weapon, but J'role and I had been around fire cannons during our journeys on the t'skrang riverboats. Although we lacked training, we had seen them used, and had practiced firing our cannons while we patched up the *Stone Rainbow*.

At the base of the cannon rested a stack of golden orichalcum boxes containing elemental fire. J'role flipped open the back of the fire cannon as I lifted the lid of one of the boxes. Heat immediately rushed out, the fiery glare of the coal blinding me, even in the bright morning sky.

I closed my eyes and perceived the world not with my flesh, but with my astral senses. Before me glowed the elemental fire, taken at some time by Theran miners from a crack between our world and the elemental plane of fire. Seen in astral space, it burned white hot and shrieked off white sparks like shooting stars.

I scooped up the coal, using my knowledge of magic to buffer me from the heat, and placed it in the cannon's coal chamber. I then reached into the sack on my hip and removed some elemental air—also pilfered from the ship's storeroom—and twisted it into the shape of a fuse. This I carefully shoved down the small tube that led into the fire coal's chamber.

When I finished I pointed the cannon toward the closer of the two Theran ships. During our practice sessions back on Twilight Peaks, we had tried to hit the side of a mountain, just to see if we could get the cannon to fire properly. Now, looking down the length of the cannon, lining up a shot on a ship that appeared no bigger than a cart, I was overcome with despair. There was no way I would hit the ship. I did the best I could, however, and moved the cannon a bit to the left, and then a bit to the right.

"Hurry," J'role said. "If we wait any longer the trolls will block our shot."

I looked over the rail of the ship. He was right. The other ships were closing quickly on the Therans.

"I told them . . .," I began.

"No difference. We've got the shot now. Take it."

I looked down the cannon one more time, setting its tip on the Theran ship, then remembered just at the last moment to pull it up a bit. A t'skrang sailor had once explained to me that the further the target, the higher one had to aim above it. The fireball, like any object, would fall down as it flew forward.

"Now."

Although he could not see the fuse of elemental air, J'role placed the lit torch near the back of the cannon.

The flames from the torch rushed toward the fuse, like fire pulled up a chimney on a winter night. A strange sight, for in mid-air a tiny flame slowly snaked its way closer to the cannon. Finally the flame reached the tube leading down into the cannon.

A moment of silence. I steadied my shot.

Then a tremendous roar as the elemental air inside the small coal chamber burst into flame and made the elemental fire even hotter. The cannon roared as it spewed forth a fireball.

I stood, tense. The fireball spewed flames and sparks as it went. Within seconds it became a small dot. Fireball and sunlit ship melded into one, and then the fireball smashed into the ship's deck.

Cheers shot up from the trolls, and their voices carried through the air like distant echoes. "Let's get off another one before they get too close," I said.

"They're already . . .," J'role began.

"Too bad. Let's do it."

He didn't say another word, and we loaded, aimed, and fired again. Experienced sailors could have done the job faster, but we did well enough. This time the fireball smashed into the ship's castle. Again the fire washed over the ship, like a raindrop of blood. I saw shadows move quickly around on the deck, and then a sailor, his clothes on fire, fell off the ship and plummeted toward the ground. His arms and legs moved frantically, as if he hoped somehow to find purchase against his fall.

The sight stunned me. I understood clearly now how Vrograth had lost so many of his people and drakkars. In fact, I wondered that so many had returned safely. The sight might have made me turn from the thought of continuing the fight, but instead it made me cold inside. Another part of me took over—a part whose existence I was aware of but did not like—sealing my compassion away. I could do anything now, with no thought of the implications until it was all over.

The drakkars had all closed. A fireball shot forward from each of the Theran ships. One crashed into a drakkar, sending flames along the thin wooden hull. Some of the trolls jumped up and began beating down the flames with their cloaks. The other shot—from the ship I'd hit twice—went wide past Vrograth's vessel and plunged earthward.

Then Theran sailors, much more practiced at firing the cannons, got off two more shots almost instantly. Two balls of fire raced toward us. "Down!" I shouted. "Everybody down!" Then I dropped to the deck and rolled until I had tucked myself against the corner of the ship's bow.

Bright red light flashed overhead, then warmth bathed me. I shrieked in agony as fire licked its way up my legs. J'role was on me a moment later, smothering the fire that burned the furs I wore. He turned me wildly one way and then the other. The motion only made a dim impact upon my perception. Nearly all my attention went to my legs; the flames had burned off my flesh, and the stench of my own burns overwhelmed my sense of smell. The muscles, exposed now to the open, cool air, seemed horribly cold and hot all at once.

I felt a tearing at my throat before I realized I was uttering a long, endless scream. J'role shouted for Crothat, the questor of Garlen on board. He was a young troll, and still new to the ways of his dedication, but a novice healer was better than none at all.

But Crothat did not come. When I stopped screaming long enough to breathe, I heard several more cries of pain from the other side of the ship's castle.

"I'll go get Crothat," J'role said, and stood.

I grabbed his hand and held him back. I bit down on my lips as I tried to get the focus to speak coherently. "No. He's either in trouble . . . Dying . . . Or helping the dying . . ."

He began pulling away. "He'll help you first . . ."

My hand had tightened around his, like a baby gripping

its mother's hair. "Don't leave me. Please." Only as I said the words did I know how terror had dug itself deep, deep into me.

Already my flesh had gone numb—not just where the fire had struck me, but along my entire body. J'role still tried to pull away from me, and it seemed so absurd to me, because all I wanted him to do was stop moving away and to plant himself and look at me. To be with me. I felt myself slipping away from life, into the void of a world without flesh and color and love. I didn't want to die without someone noting my passing.

"Releana, I've got to get help." Now he looked at me, and spreading over his face was a terrible fear. "Don't die. Do you hear me? You cannot die!" If possible, fear claimed a stronger hold on him than on me.

I let his hand go. "Get help."

The *Stone Rainbow* continued to rush toward the Theran ships. I heard many shouts and cries of the trolls on other ships. The boardings were about to begin. The voices of Theran sailors floated into my ears as well, as they barked orders and began to prepare for close combat. I heard the blast of their fire cannons several more times, and fireballs crashed into our castle, cracking it and sending shards of thick stone scattering across the deck.

J'role returned with Crothat. Terrible burns ran down the right side of the young troll's face, down his neck, and onto his right shoulder. The flames had peeled back his gray-green flesh, revealing streaks of pink muscle charred black. The muscles had bubbles that sank slowly as he examined me. He looked terribly frightened, but determined.

"You need to help yourself," I began.

"Quiet, Captain," he said, his voice straining with a high pitch. "Please, let me just do something."

He placed his hands on my shoulders and I saw a shimmering in the air behind him.

More shouts. The firing of the cannons. Screams.

I felt myself in a nightmare, the kind where one is doomed to remain inactive while one's fate is determined by the chaotic actions of others.

And then three Theran sailors appeared overhead, magic carrying them across the gulf between ships. They tumbled through the air like acrobats, swords drawn. They plunged toward the deck, blue armor gleaming hot in the morning light.

Despite the fact that they had come to kill me, their appearance made me gasp with amazement. I remember thinking, How amazing and terrible are the ways of our people!

J'role and Crothat had their backs to the Therans, but saw my gasp of surprise. J'role started to turn just as the Therans landed.

## 3

J'role whirled around, unsheathing his sword as he moved, raising it high as two of the Theran sailors slashed down at his back with their blades. The three swords all clanged against one another. The blows of the Therans forced J'role down onto the deck.

Meanwhile, the third Theran sailor swung his sword at Crothat. The troll ducked, but not quickly enough, and the edge of the blade bit into the burn wounds along his right shoulder. The young troll howled in pain, but without pause he pushed himself up to his feet and stretched out one long arm at the Theran sailor. The Theran took a desperate swing at Crothat, but in his fear the blow cut wide. With shocking abruptness Crothat slammed his hand against the sailor's neck and sent the man reeling back into the rail of the ship, whereupon the Theran flipped over the edge. His scream faded quickly.

The sailor's companions took little notice of his fate, for J'role was on his feet again and the three had joined in intense battle. All three grunted as their swords clashed against one another. Crothat drew his crystal sword from his thick cloth belt. The blue stone caught the sun's light and, combined with my pain, blinded me for the moment.

When I could see again, a Theran lay dismembered on the deck, his blood a spray of droplets against the wall of the center castle. The other Theran turned and ran, with J'role chasing after him.

Crothat dropped to his knees beside me, wincing

against the pain in his shoulder. He moved me so my head rested in his lap and said, "Close your eyes and let Garlen come to you."

"You're hurt . . ."

"Please, human. You speak too much. Do it."

I closed my eyes. I heard him mumbling words in his troll tongue, and though the words retained their harsh consonants, his tone soothed me. Screams and shouts continued to fill the air, but I began to relax. The troll's big hands touched my arms, and a warmth spread through my flesh. Soon this warmth reached my burned legs, and even there a comfortable coolness took hold.

I sensed a bright light beyond my eyelids, and opened them.

The pregnant giantess with the silver armor had returned. In her silver armor was clearly reflected the morning sun and all the fighting on the ships around us. She was smaller now, no more than nine feet, and stood at my feet, looking down, stern-faced.

"I thought you were Thystonius," I said to her, for I knew Crothat was calling upon Garlen. My voice sounded thick and far away, and though I knew what was happening was real, I also knew it was taking place far, far from the *Stone Rainbow*.

"*That* windbag of random violence? Not likely." She sounded like a mother with too many demands on her time—not angry or dismissive, but to the point. "And I've never seen you before. I've sensed you, I've been there when you've been hurt before. But we've never met."

"But I saw . . ."

"You saw what you thought you should see. We're Passions. We don't look *like* anything. You've decided at this time in your life that the essences of conflict and care are similar. So we look similar. It's happened before." She leaned down, very serious now. "One of my questors here is trying to heal you."

"Yes."

"He doesn't do this lightly, you know. He is suffering himself. He could heal himself."

"Yes. I've told him . . ."

"But he wouldn't listen. He's young and somewhat stupid. Because he's wasting his time on someone who doesn't necessarily want to live."

My mouth opened in surprise, for I had no idea what she was talking about.

"Don't do that. I hate that. When a Passion speaks the truth, you'd think people would listen. Recognize it as a truth. I'm a life force that winds its way through *everybody*. That should carry some authority."

She paused. I had no idea what to say, so I remained silent.

"Well?"

"I don't . . ."

"Feel it inside of you, woman! I'm that part of you that wants to protect and take care of you and others."

"Yes, I know, but . . ."

"What kind of life are you living? What is this sex with blood? What is this pain for affection?"

I'd never, ever spoken of the matter with anybody. Never put it into words. Not even with J'role. Garlen coming out and naming those years of confused feelings about J'role's sexual desires—and my cooperation— threw me into complete confusion. This time, though, she waited. The screams had died away, though I could still see the reflections of the battle in her silver armor. If Crothat still held my head in his lap, I was no longer aware of it.

"I . . . It is something J'role started."

A part of me had hoped that by throwing the blame, Garlen would let the matter be. She waited for me to go on.

"I didn't like it at first. But in time . . . He seemed to like it so much."

"Wait, what was that part before about him liking it? 'But in time' what? In time *what*?"

"In time I liked it."

"Out of curiosity, out of my own desire to find out if you'll *ever* listen to me unless I put in one of these dramatic appearances, have you ever admitted this to yourself? Or has it always been a matter of J'role victimizing you, forcing you into something you don't want to do . . ."

"But I don't want to do it . . ."

"But you like it! You just said . . ."

"I like it while I'm doing it. But if I wasn't doing it, I wouldn't miss it."

She knelt down before me now, the pregnant belly close to my flesh, her large face only a foot from mine. I was a child against her. A child caught in a web of deceptions I'd created to justify why the sweet meats were missing; a deception I couldn't untangle to keep my story straight.

She said softly, "You can't even say the words, can you? You name-givers have this wonderful language given to you by the Universe, and you hop all around your mouths with 'it' and 'thing' and other imprecisions. Obscurity is your last refuge in the face of the Passions in your soul rising up to confront you." I stammered something inconsequential. She dismissed it. "What do you do to him? What is this 'it'?"

"I hurt him."

"Yes?"

"Bite. Cut him with fingernails. Draw blood." As I said the words, I felt my passions begin to rise.

"You taste it even now, don't you? You want to do it. Despite what you said."

"Yes."

"What do you want to do to him?"

"Hurt him."

"Yes?"

"Humiliate him."

"Yes?"

"I want him to know . . ."

"Yes?"

"What he does to me."

"He cuts you?"

"Yes."

"Yes," she echoed.

"He doesn't cut my flesh. He leaves me. He cuts *me*."

"Yes. What do you want to do?"

"Hurt him."

"That makes you feel better?"

"Yes."

"Yes?"

Tears began to well up at the corners of my eyes. "No. No, it doesn't make me feel better. It makes me even with him. We're just clawing at each other. Not better. Even. Even in our pain."

"Yes."

"Yes."

"What makes you feel better?"

"My boys."

"Yes."

"Myself, learning my magic."

"Yes."

"Helping the people in my village. Building Horvak's furnace. Figuring out how the Universe is made, using that knowledge. Helping people."

"Yes."

"Making."

"Yes."

"Protecting."

"Yes."

I reached out my hand to hers, touched it lightly. "I don't

know how to heal. I want to heal myself. Something's gone terribly wrong."

"Yes." She paused, looking at me kindly. A bit of sadness. "There's a choice coming. Be ready."

She vanished.

# 4

My flesh was whole once more, though the skin was pink where I'd been burned. I had only a moment to enjoy the lack of pain when Crothat threw me from his lap with a scream. A spray of blood rained down on me, and the troll dropped to the deck with a heavy thud, his large eyes open and lifeless.

Reflexes took over and I rolled across the deck and put my back up against the ship's rail. A quick glance at Crothat revealed two heavy crossbow bolts protruding from the back of his head.

I looked up and saw his killers. One of the Theran ships had risen slightly—just enough to get a clear shot over our rails. The ship had only just started its rise. I realized that my conversation with Garlen had taken little—if no—time at all from the battle around me.

I had little time for reflection. The two cross-bowman—a female elf and female dwarf—grinned at me as they cranked their weapons, readying them to slip in bolts and fire them at me. I thought for a moment about casting a spell, but decided against it. The encounter with Garlen had unnerved me, and the risk of calling a Horror into my head was too terrible to contemplate. I desired a new magician's robe so much! What good was magical knowledge if it only led to potential disaster?

I scrambled to my feet and rushed toward the stern of the ship, keeping the Stone Rainbow's central castle between me and the rising ship. The sound of clashing blades came from ahead, and I drew my dagger from its sheath.

As I turned the corner around the castle, I saw several badly charred trolls lying on the deck. Some dead. Some still dying. Others, trolls from my ship and elves and humans from the Theran vessel, lay bleeding. J'role and four trolls had positioned themselves at the ship's stern, keeping their backs to it. Seven Theran sailors, all armed with swords, had them pinned in place. The sun, level with the fleet battle now, cast the rising ship's shadow across the fury of swordplay.

I rushed forward, moving silently as J'role had taught me. "Screaming a war cry," he once said to me, "is for those big enough to frighten without needing to scream a war cry. People like you and me should get up there as quietly and efficiently as possible, and kill them before they even know it."

So I crept as quietly as I could. But quickly as well, for the Theran ship would soon pass the *Stone Rainbow*'s castle and spot me. J'role and the trolls from my crew saw me approach, but none revealed my presence by either word or facial expression.

I had just reached the backs of the Therans when the ship cleared the castle, and cries of alarm showered down from it. The Therans before me began to turn, but I plunged my dagger deep into the back of one of them, and he screamed out in agony and crumpled to the deck.

As he fell I tugged my blade out of his back. Strange, dizzying emotions overcame me. Memories of bloody sex with J'role flooded my thoughts. One a murder, the other an act of sexual arousal. How? What had I been doing?

# 5

What *had* I been doing? Passions! So many ideas and questions I've washed from my thinking ever since the end of the Theran War when your father and I parted.

The massive letter from the dragon sits on my table, still unread, not far from where my hand writes these words. It waits like a Horror, coiled and ready to spring. It's as if I'm standing once more on the edge of Twilight Peaks, staring out across the ink-black jungles at night, comfortable at the precipice, neither falling forward nor retreating in fear, but unable to move.

The dragon's letter threatens to knock me over the edge.

# 6

Crossbow bolts slammed into the stone deck, shattering and skittering on impact. One of the trolls jumped forward and took a bolt in the shoulder that would have split my skull. He groaned heavily, ripped the bolt out of his flesh, scooped me up in one arm, and rushed me to the doorway of the castle for shelter.

The remnants of the crew numbered five trolls, J'role, and myself. That wasn't counting those who remained below on the oars—a mix of trolls and my original group.

A few more crossbow bolts slammed into the stone surfaces around us. The Theran ship sailed on. Black smoke billowed through the air; many drakkars burned.

"We've got to end this," I said.

"Retreat?" several of the trolls asked in astonishment.

"No, no. Everything." I had no intention of retreating. And I realized I'd rather die trying to hurt the Therans than return alive having accomplished nothing. "We've got to bring the *Stone Rainbow* around and gain on the Theran ship. Can't let her escape."

I didn't even give the order to move, the trolls simply took it upon themselves to act *now*. Several ran to the sail lines, others to rudder. "Come," I said to J'role. "Let's get to the cannon. We're closer now." We ran to the bow. A fireball hissed by my face, missing me by only a few feet, warming my flesh.

The rowers had slowed the ship's pace as we'd floated toward the Theran ships, and now as I ran I screamed,

"Row! Row!" over and over again at the top of my lungs.
"We need speed NOW!"

From below the troll rowing chant began, and the ship
lurched forward, nearly toppling J'role and me backward
as we ran. They'd drawn on magic to increase their
speed, and it was working impressively. The sail swung
wildly to starboard, picking up a gust of wind, and we
rushed after the escaping Theran ship.

As our ship swung around, the other ships involved in
the battle came into clear view. To my surprise, only two
drakkars had actually caught fire. The crews of the ship
were working madly to put the fires out, and it seemed as
if they would succeed. Three undamaged drakkars hov-
ered around the other Theran vessel. Several dozen trolls
had boarded the vessel, and I could see that the fight was
winding down. Rich red blood streaked the ship's gray
stone. Bodies and portions of bodies lay scattered about.
Trolls with terrible gashes in their flesh leaned against the
rails, breathing in air quickly after their desperate fight.
The only Therans I saw were the dead and dying.

More trolls were jumping onto the ship, healthy and
ready to plunder. Of course, this meant fewer trolls who
could help us with the ship the *Stone Rainbow* now pur-
sued. I made a note to myself: if I survived I'd have a talk
with Vrograth about priorities. Looting *after* complete
and certain victory. Two of the drakkars did break away
from the potential plunder, however, and began to float
toward us to join the chase.

J'role and I loaded the cannon again, and as our ship's
bow turned to face the fleeing Theran ship, I took steady
aim. "Fire!" I said, and J'role touched the torch against
the fuse of elemental air. The cannon fired and the fireball appeared with a tremendous hiss. I had tried to hit
the ship's sail, thinking it the best target. Instead, in my
inexperience, I'd sent the fireball rushing toward the
ship's rudder. This proved to be a stroke of luck, for the
fireball slammed into the rudder, cracking a portion of it

off. The impact also turned the device sharply, sending the sailor at the wheel to the deck as it spun.

The effect of all this made the Theran ship suddenly begin listing to port. Its sailors rocked back and forth, and some of them lost their footing completely. The sudden turn brought the ship perpendicular to the *Stone Rainbow*'s path and allowed us to close tighter on the ship. I fumbled with the elemental fire coals, taking much longer to reload this time, for I was both excited and anxious.

J'role suddenly cried out and I turned to find him grabbing his chest. Glancing back to the Theran ship, I saw a magician in a black robe decorated with silver raindrops sitting on the ship's castle looking for another victim. He saw me, smiled, and immediately began the gestures of a spell. I grabbed the torch from where J'role had dropped it on the deck and waved it toward the fuse. Then I dropped the torch and grabbed the cannon, hoping to aim it before it fired.

I jerked the cannon and lined up the shot on the magician, then pulled it up slightly, trying to compensate properly for the arc of the fireball's flight. Just as I did that, I felt my body tense terribly, as if my bones had frozen inside my flesh. Then my arms began to move against my will. I knew immediately that the magician had cast bone dance on me.

But I tried to resist the spell and hold the cannon on my target. Sharp pain flowed through my limbs. Time stretched out, thoughts of blood and sliced flesh and passion and love twisting and warping in my head. If I could have surrendered to it, might I have enjoyed the control the magician exerted on me? That's what J'role did. Surrendered to me. To give one's self over to someone else meant no longer being responsible. There was an appeal in that.

Outside my thoughts, a mere moment passed. My hands, under the influence of the magician's spell, tried to twist the cannon back toward the ship; to fire it into my own crew.

Needles dug at me from the inside out as I resisted.

Seconds passed.

The cannon fired.

The magician scrambled up as the fireball rushed toward his ship. It would not have hit him in any case—my aim was not yet good enough. Instead it crashed into the mast, sending an elaborate network of fissures running up the stone pole. A splash of fire caught him on his robe and he dropped down to the ground and rolled on it to put it out.

# 7

"Faster!" I screamed. The strain of the cry tore at my throat.

"We'll ram them!" J'role shouted as the ship lurched forward once more. He was up on his feet again, the effects of the spell over.

"Exactly," I replied. Then I shouted back to the helmsman, "Bring us up!" Other crew members conveyed the orders until they reached him. The *Stone Rainbow* rose slightly. "That's it!" I shouted, hoping my inexperienced calculations would prove correct. "Prepare to board!"

The ship held its incline as we closed on the Theran vessel. We drew our weapons—I my dagger. I had only one goal: the magician. If the robe was not too badly damaged, I *might* be able to re-weave it to my own aura and finally be free to cast spells again.

Those trolls available for raiding gathered around J'role and me. We formed a total of seven. Luckily the Theran's crew had been sharply reduced by the efforts of the other drakkars. And one of the two drakkars that had followed us was making good time and would soon be with us.

But impractical or not, dangerous or not, I would leap over the side of the *Stone Rainbow* and attack. I felt the lust for conflict rising in me, and the sensation of the war dance filled my muscles. I looked forward, gasped. In the air, just beyond the Theran ship, floated the woman in silver armor, oversized and pregnant as always.

She smiled at me.

Thystonius? It seemed I should be able to distinguish the Passion of conflict from the Passion of healing, yet I kept imagining them as the same image. Were they the same? For me at least?

I had no idea.

Crossbow bolts sliced the air before us as the bow of the *Stone Rainbow* slammed into the Theran ship. The mast shattered against our momentum and crashed to the deck, crushing the corpses.

I turned to leap over the side of the ship, expecting the trolls to already be on their way. But they waited on my order. One of them gave me a toothy grin. "Captain?" he said.

I laughed. "Attack!" I screamed.

"ATTACK!" the trolls and J'role echoed, and we all launched ourselves into the air, suspended, it seemed, for a glorious moment as the sheer stupidity of what I'd done bubbled up in my soul and made me laugh again.

Then down to the deck of the Theran ship. I landed hard, surrounded by the gruff grunts of trolls doing the same. Their crystal armor and swords and maces glittered in the air around me. The shadow of the *Stone Rainbow* passed over us as the ship continued on, crewed only by the helmsman and rowers.

Therans rushed us, swords drawn, shouting oaths in a language I could not understand. Elves and humans and dwarfs stood against us. They were good, very good. But I tell you this: a crystal raider doing what he loves best— fighting for spoils—is a fire in a sea of oil.

We drove the Therans back, forcing them to the port rail. Soon more of their number came upon us, rushing us from behind. Little matter. The trolls cut them down quickly, and I became ill at the sight of one body after another cut to pieces by the troll's weapon skills. Then a drakkar came alongside us. More trolls boarded. I saw panic in the eyes of the Therans. Each one wanted so much to live, yet realized only now that he might not see the sun set.

With my companions seizing control of the ship, I decided to seek out the magician. I feared the ship might soon begin to sink, and wanted to get the robe before I had to abandon ship. As the magician had yet to show himself, I assumed he was wounded from the fireball, perhaps seeking shelter below deck.

I waited until I saw a clear path through the scrimmage. The path was not straight, but with harsh twists and turns, I managed to clear it without a single Theran striking me. When I reached the door to the castle, I found it unguarded, and took this as a good omen. Already my body prickled with excitement at the thought of gaining a new magician's robe.

Fortunately, I already knew well the layout of the ship, for it was of the same design as the *Stone Rainbow*. Because magicians are usually granted upper status in most societies, I decided he would probably have one of the better cabins off on the port side.

Here there is a moment I remember with shame.

As I ran through the narrow corridors, it occurred to me that the rowers on the ship would be slaves, just as I had been a slave. And each one would desire freedom as much as I had desired freedom from the yoke of the Therans. I knew—or part of me did—that I should first go down to free the slaves and then resume my personal quest.

But another part of me knew that if I did not get the robe now, it might be months before I could make another one, even if I finally got Vrograth's cooperation.

I knew many, many things, all of them justifications for my selfishness. This knowledge carried me past the stairs leading down to the slaves, and toward the area where I believed the magician waited.

I turned a corner. A Theran elf and I ran into each other, my face slamming into her chest. The dagger was in my hand, while she must reach for her sword, panic on her face. Too late. Even as she drew the sword, I drove my blade into her stomach, and twisted it as my father had taught me.

A long moan poured from the elf's mouth, and her long face turned suddenly lifeless. Blood from the wound flowed over my hand. Her corpse leaned into me. I lowered it gently to the floor. The fact of what I'd done was impossible to ignore; I was too close to the corpse. I did not know why we so often do horrible things to one another, but I'd learned that once done, I simply had to go on.

I thought that the elf might have been accompanying the magician to get him to his quarters, which meant he might be nearby. I began searching the cabins, one after another . . .

In the fifth room I found him.

# 8

He lay on the bed, his back to me, still wearing the robe. Black, with silver tears and shiny black eyes just barely visible. He moaned softly as I opened the door, turning as I entered.

He was a strong man with a handsome face. Mid-forties.

"Vestrial!" The magician called, and I thought I saw the shadow of something enter the cabin, the presence of Vestrial, Passion of manipulation and deceit.

Something seized my mind. A Horror, I thought at first. But the man said, "Carry me safely and alive to the ground under your own power."

As if I had suddenly awakened from a dream, a new truth confronted me. It seemed perfectly normal that I wanted to carry him to the ground. I had no idea how I might do it, but it was all very clear. A part of me struggled with the orders, knew that the desire to do the man's will was the dream. But the powers granted to the man by Vestrial won.

"I don't know how to do it," I said.

He had begun to sit up, wincing in pain from the burn wounds along his right arm, and stopped abruptly. Through gritted teeth he said, "Cast metal wings and we'll fly down."

"I don't know that spell."

He looked at me with astonishment. The shouts of the sailors drifted between us during the pause in our ex-

change. The clashing of swords and cries of battle came closer, and I imagined the Therans fighting a running retreat, taking shelter in the lower decks of the ship.

"You're an elementalist! I saw your aura! You must know metal wings. What would you be doing in an airship without metal wings?"

"I didn't mean to be here. It's kind of an accident." In the back of my thoughts I wanted to rush him and kill him. The sensations burned like dying coals in my muscles. But my desire to carry him to the ground took precedence over all other objectives. First I had to figure out how to do it, and then fulfill it.

"Over there," he said, nodding with his head to a stone cabinet set into the wall. He cradled his burned arm.

I walked over to the cabinet and found several leather bags and metal boxes—all in a variety of shapes and sizes.

"The silver box," he said, "I think. With the ruby on the top."

I picked up the box. It felt cold in my hand, but the metal was smooth and pleasing to touch.

"There's a bit of a grimoire in there. I think that's the one with metal wings. When you read it, you can cast it."

"I don't have a robe."

"No, you don't. That's your risk. And don't think I don't know why you came rushing in here looking for me. Now help me up. It sounds as if the ship will fall to the trolls soon."

Indeed it did. The fighting had died down, but I heard the cheers of trolls from the upper deck. I went over to magician, and supported him by slipping his arm over my shoulder. Then we walked out the door. Again, I wanted to shout and call for help, but I could take no action but those that would help me carry him to the ground.

We made our way down the corridor, and when we reached the cargo hold we entered it. He had me lead him to a large door, and said, "Here." I leaned him against the wall. Then he said, "Go bolt the door we just came through."

That had nothing to do with getting him to the ground, so I refused. I didn't want to prevent the crystal raiders from finding us.

"Do it or I'll kill you with a spell. It's a manner of death you've never even imagined, I promise. Everyone I've used it on has been quite surprised."

It wasn't his melodramatic threat that got me to do as he commanded. He was a nethermancer, and I knew they carry the vilest of the art's spells in their heads. But, if I died, I couldn't get him to the ground. I bolted the door and returned to him.

"Now, open this door." He took in ragged breaths, and his flesh went pale as he stood against the wall. If he died, I wondered, would I be forced to carry the corpse to the ground, or would I be freed of the power?

I pulled a bolt back on the broad door, and it fell forward, forming a loading ramp. But the ramp now opened out into thin air. Storm clouds gathered outside. Above I saw a drakkar floating alongside the Theran ship's upper deck.

"Open the box and learn the spell."

I opened the box and found three smooth, flat stones. Upon each was a spell, written in tiny, neat letters. Metal wings. Wall of fire. Whirlwind. I already had wall of fire, but not the other two.

"Hurry."

I hurried. I pulled out the stone with metal wings on it and placed the box on the floor. Then, after kneeling on the floor, I began studying the stone. The grimoire's owner had bound the magical writing to the rock and it took me a moment to see past the stone.

I heard the deep voices of trolls outside, and then their pounding on the door of the cargo hold.

"Hurry," he said again, his voice now no more than a whisper.

The words came clear to me with a minute or so of work. I would not "know" the spell, because I had not the time to transfer it to my own grimoire, but I could read it and cast it right then. I stood and cast the spell.

A strange weight began to build upon my back. It surprised me, even though I knew the effect of the spell. It grew heavier and heavier, until I could feel my bones changing shape and growing into something completely unfamiliar. My shoulder blades hunched together, and I had to lean forward to keep myself supported. Within moments I could turn my head to either side and see the gray-metal wings that grew from my back. The feathers looked carefully sculpted by the hands of a craftsman, each with small lines and ridges.

The magician smiled, then hobbled over behind me. He wrapped his arms under mine, and then clasped his hands behind my neck. It was uncomfortable, but not intolerable. "Now," he hissed. "Now!"

I hobbled forward so that we walked out along the loading plank. I heard shouts from above, and looked up to see several trolls noticing the magician and myself. They stared at us over the edge of their drakkar, and as I looked up into their faces I hesitated.

The magician pushed me forward, and the two of us fell over the edge of the plank and tumbled down through the air. The world spun wildly around me, a blur of jungle green and storm gray.

"Flap!" the magician screamed, his voice filled with fear. At the back of my neck his hands loosened for a moment, then clasped themselves back together. He groaned in agony—staying on my back under the pain of his burn wounds was not easy.

The command to bring him safely to the ground echoed in my ears, and my own desire to live influenced me as well, and I spread my wings. Though I'd never used the spell before, and had no experience flying this way, I found I could fly as well as I could walk. From our plummet, we suddenly swept up, like eagles out flying for joy.

"Down," hissed the magician.

Down we went. Whatever feeling had overwhelmed me while flying on board an airship could not compare with this sensation. I rested on *nothing*. The only detriment to feeling completely free of all responsibilities was the grumbling magician on my back. I longed to have no one needing me. To be free of gravity and everyone seemed a wonderful goal.

We raced to the ground, approaching in a wide spiral. I glanced up and saw the Theran ships and the drakkars. The battle seemed to have ended with the trolls victorious.

But where was I heading now?

# 9

We landed at the edge of a jungle.

Roughly.

The wings and the magic could only help me fly, so landing was the business of my legs and my own dexterity. I tried to hit the ground running, but I mistimed the approach and tripped. The magician and I sprawled across the ground, he with a loud cry.

I turned to face him, freed now from the command, ready to claw his flesh from his body with my nails. But he was already composed, and had begun forming a pattern in the air with his hands. I reached down to grab some dirt to cast earth darts.

Too late. His spell shimmered around his hands, and then an enormous pain filled my mind. I blacked out.

Rain dripped down on my face, and it took me a few moments to remember what had happened.

When I did, I scrambled up. The wings had vanished from my back, and I could move quite easily. All around me was deep jungle, dark and textured with endless grays.

I turned, looking for the magician. He stood there, resting against a tree, smiling. He had dragged me into the jungle, hiding me from those who might search for me.

I charged him.

He called upon Vestrial again.

This time it didn't work.

The smile sagged from his face. He held up his hands

to fend off my blows as I began to pummel his face. Fury so filled my senses that all I perceived was the pounding of my hands against his face, and the blur of the hands as they hammered him again and again. Then they were around his neck, choking him.

Just barely, under all this, I heard him speak to me. His voice was strained, for I did everything I could to crush his throat between my hands. But his tone remained calm and, most important, convincing.

"The last thing you want to do is hurt me," he said. "What you want to do is relax. You do not want to hurt me. Do you know what I can do for you? Think about that. What can I offer you?"

I did not think about it. I did everything in my power to put his words out of my mind, for I know that the questors of Vestrial are the most manipulative of people, that they could lie about the weather and most people would believe them.

Yet despite my attempts to block his words from my ears, they wormed into my thoughts. Soon my grip had loosened. Not enough to release him, but enough so he could relax a bit.

In that instant he called on Vestrial once more.

I heard him speak, and heard his voice in my head.

"Fly me alive and well to Vivane."

I did.

# 10

It took us several days of flying because I needed rest between flights. Periodically the magician and I would struggle as I tried to run away or kill him in between his use of Vestrial powers, but he invariably won. His force of will combined with Vestrial's aid and my exhaustion made him an invincible foe.

So I found myself enslaved again. First at the hands of the Therans, then trapped by the crystal raiders, and finally by a lone nethermancer. Add to the list the years enthralled by the madness J'role and I shared, and it seemed I had never lived a day of freedom in my life.

The magician's contempt for me grew and grew as we traveled on, until I became no more than a pack animal to him. And, obviously, a pack animal he had no intention of keeping healthy. By the time the blue spires of Vivane appeared on the horizon, his hands were digging deep into the back of my neck as he clung to me. He seemed to have forgotten that people are only meant to bend certain ways, and that by forcing my head forward he twisted me completely out of shape. My words of protest fell on deaf ears. "Just fly straight," he would say. "I'll tell you when to turn."

Thus, it was only by chance that I espied the city ahead of us at all. An upwind had caught my metal wings and lifted us straight up. Vertical for a moment, I saw the city. The red, evening sun caught the shiny blue towers and turned them a glittering black. From the air the sight was spectacular, and I gasped with pleasure. "Enough!" he said, and forced my head down again. "Just get me there!"

I flew on. I knew that to the south of the city stood Sky Point. Beyond that, across thick jungles, stood the village where I had lived with the two of you. I wondered once more where you were, and if I would ever see you again. It seemed certain that I would be executed once we arrived in Vivane. The task of finding the you two would fall to your father, and I did not think he was up to it. I feared for you both. I feared for your father, for his secret, buried in his soul like a thorn, kept him from finding the life I think he so desperately sought in his stories. And I feared for myself, for I knew that if I died, I would have failed you. An ugly epitaph.

As we got closer, I saw a flying castle docked at the tallest spire of the city—the Overgovernor's castle!

The spire was part of a huge palace, which I knew to be the home of Yorte Pa, the city's magistrate. It seemed that the Therans had taken over the palace and made it their own. Most likely they had taken over the entire city. If the castle was docked at the palace, the Overgovernor might have taken up residence there. If he had, you boys would be there as well.

I flapped my wings a few times, increasing speed as we reached the city walls. Guards on the walls, a mix of Theran and native forces, raised crossbows at us. But they spotted the magician, and the captain of the guard ordered their weapons lowered.

"There," the magician said. "On the castle wall."

But I had only to get him safely to the city. *I* would choose where we landed.

I turned and headed toward a wide balcony set into the palace. A large fountain stood in the center of it, and water poured down from the mouth of a dragon that coiled around a iron mountain.

"What are you doing!" he shouted.

I ignored him.

A set of glass doors led into the palace, and as I rushed toward them I could see myself fully in the reflection of the window. Small and round, with the long gray wings that grew out of my back. My focus shifted through the glass doors and I saw guards rushing toward us from within the palace.

I began to turn, thinking that I might be able to move fast enough to avoid the crossbow bolts of the guards. But this plan vanished from my thoughts immediately, for behind the guards on the other side of the glass doors I saw the two of you . . .

I could not see you clearly, but I recognized your fair hair, the shape of your faces. Dressed in short white tunics, you each held a silver tray.

I increased my speed.

"Stop!" the magician screamed. I felt a tug at my thoughts. I had to get him to the city safely.

I already had.

I smiled.

As I rushed toward the glass doors, momentum carrying me forward, I turned on my back and tucked myself into a ball. In his panic, the magician clung more tightly to me.

We smashed into the window, the man's back taking the brunt of the blow. He screamed in terror and agony. I rolled up quickly; blood poured from his back and he writhed on the floor. The guards pulled back in surprise, and the two of you turned toward the violent sounds, dropping your trays as you saw the silhouette of a winged monster rushing toward you.

I'd been living with the trolls for some time. Blood and dirt caked my face. Ferocity possessed my body. I think I gave a crystal raider battle scream, but I do not remember.

You both began to cry.

The Theran guards reclaimed their composure, raised their crossbows and fired. One missed me. The other caught me in the arm.

Hot pain bit through my flesh, but I continued.

The guards dropped their crossbows, and pulled out their swords.

I took to flight, rising just above where the blades cut through the air. Of course, even though the room was large, the ceiling was not high enough to make flight practical. I slammed my head and the wings into the ceiling, then tumbled back down to the floor.

But now at least I was near you. On my knees I scrambled for you, arms outstretched. I cried out your names. I wanted to fly away with you, and if not that, then simply embrace you one last time before the guards drove their swords into my back.

The two of you recoiled in terror.

"Samael. Torran," I whispered, holding my distance.

Your faces changed, softened. Torran, you stepped forward a bit, taking Samael's hand. Silver flakes still decorated your faces, forming intricate, identical patterns. "Momma?" you said, tilting your head to one side, your expression suddenly very adult, as if I were the child who had become lost.

The door to the room slammed open. I stood up, thinking more guards had arrived, but it was Overgovernor Povelis storming into the room. His perfect white skin seemed to writhe on his body as he approached. "What is going on?" Four guards came in behind him, all armed with swords. I feared that if I grabbed you two and tried to escape I might get you killed. I remained motionless, biding my time for the right moment to act. The tension of the moment combined with my exhaustion made me shake, as if with fever. You were right before me, but I could not hold you.

When the Overgovernor saw me, he stopped. "What is *this*?"

I do not know if you remember, Torran, but you stepped forward decisively and said, "My mother. And you leave her alone!"

"Ah, yes," said the Overgovernor, staring, recognizing me. "Come to rescue them?"

I did not speak.

"Actually," said the nethermancer, who had been helped up by the guards, "she brought me here. She was helping a group of troll raiders attack two mining ships. They were using one of our ships, Overgovernor. *The Pride*. The ship lost in a storm several months ago." The Overgovernor thought for a moment, then remembered. "The trolls used the lost ship to attack in conjunction with their usual long boats. She is more than a prisoner. Most like she is a slave from *The Pride,* and she has information about the organized attack made by the trolls."

The Overgovernor raised his hand. "I'm sorry. Perhaps I have misunderstood. Did these barbaric raiders *win*?"

"Yes. They targeted two mining ships and flew in quickly. This one fired *The Pride*'s fire cannon against us."

He stared at me as if I were a slug. "Who do you think you are?"

I swung around, striking him with one of my wings, and grabbed the two of you, one in each arm. He fell to the ground with a cry. The guards charged forward.

I raced for the window, and you both began to scream. But it all ended very quickly, for the guards set upon me, the edges of the their swords cutting my flesh. One cut across my side, very deep, just above my hip. An abrupt dizziness overtook me, and I lost consciousness.

# 11

They put me in a box with a small door in it, the only light coming through the cracks in the door frame. Each night a small slot opened and a bowl of mashed rice was placed inside.

Days passed, then weeks.

I only discovered this later. Time soon lost meaning within the confines of the box. After several days I would fall asleep, wake up, and have no idea whether I had been asleep for twenty minutes or eight hours. A panic settled over me, and I thought I had been forgotten—forgotten by all but the hands that passed me food through the slot each night. (Was it each night? Perhaps they varied the feeding times? I had no idea.) The box stood up straight, and was not wide enough for me to sit, so I would lean against the walls, legs bent, my body pressing down and the bones straining.

I took to screaming, striving to get some attention. After death, with time, we are all forgotten. But to be forgotten while we're alive is too terrible to contemplate. The darkness of the chamber closed around me, and often I could not be certain if my eyelids were open or not. I sometimes did not know if I was asleep or awake.

Soon I began to confuse where and when I was. One time in particular kept coming back to me. I thought I was back in Blood Wood, a prisoner with J'role in a deep pit. That was where we first met, J'role and I, as prisoners of the elf queen. Your father was mute at the time, and in his eyes was a terrible anger. But I also remember thinking I had never seen so much sadness in anyone's eyes. Yet there was something about him that promised he would never surrender. He might be knocked down, but he would always get up. It was that attracted me, intrigued me.

In my confusion I began speaking to him.

"Why do you keep leaving?" I asked him.

"I have to go."

"Why?"

"Don't make me answer that."

"Why?"

"You'll rip me open. You don't want to do that."

"Why?"

"What's inside. It's too much for you to bear."

I slammed the door again and again. I could not feel my fist any longer. My legs had long since gone numb. "How dare you . . . How dare you tell me what I can bear and what I can't. Don't you love me? Don't you care about us?"

He touched my hands, and I felt hundreds of needles press against my flesh. "I do. That's why I don't tell you. Don't you understand. If I tell you, you'll leave."

"J'role. If you *don't* tell me, *you* will leave; you always leave. If you tell me, I might stay."

"It's mine. It's all mine. Don't ask me to give it to you."

"It's ours. We're married. It's *ours*."

His hand pulled away from mine. He vanished.

My cries for help or attention were in vain. I remained trapped, alone with J'role, for a long time.

# 12

When the door opened, torchlight rushed into my eyes, peeling my sight back, blinding me.

"I told you," a woman said.

"I didn't disagree with you," said a man.

"You said it wasn't her."

"I said I didn't know."

"Well. Let's get her up."

I kept my eyes shut but could still see a hot red glare. Two pairs of hands grabbed me roughly by the wrists and dragged me out of the box.

"I knew the paper work around here was getting too thick," the woman said.

"Didn't say it wasn't."

"You said we hadn't lost her."

"We didn't. She was right here. The whole time."

"I'm free?" I asked, though it came out as a sort of whisper.

My captors laughed. "In a way," said the woman. "Free of the box, at least."

"Where are you taking . . . ? Where are my boys?"

"We're taking you to Overgovernor Povelis," the man said. "And I don't know where your boys are."

"He has them. He has my boys."

"Then you'll soon be reunited."

The sun beat down, hot and clawing at my exposed flesh. Around me the stench and constant thrum of the city crowd.

I could see now, just barely. From the platform in the city square I glimpsed the merchants and traders and shoppers and beggars of Vivane. A crowd had gathered around the platform, and many among them stopped to stare at me. Chains attached to scaffolding held my wrists high above my head. My clothes were rags, and I felt terribly vulnerable. The Overgovernor stood beside me. To his right were two guards. One held a whip. Many more guards, standing at attention, surrounded the platform.

And, of course, the two of you stood on the balcony where I had landed weeks earlier. You were down at the proceedings, crying and crying and crying.

"You understand I can kill you whenever I wish."

I nodded.

"We have not been able to find your troll companions. Where are they?"

"Why do you care?"

"They have become . . . a nuisance."

I looked up into his face, saw that he was trying to hide something between fear and annoyance. I realized that the raiders must be more than a mere nuisance. "I have nothing to say to you."

"Yes, yes, yes. But let's cut through the noble sentiments, shall we? I can kill you. Your children. I can torture you. Torture them. Which one, I wonder, is the magic to unlock your tongue? Tell me now, and we'll save ourselves a lot of time."

I looked into his eyes. His pale skin seemed loose on his face, and I thought he might be some kind of monster masquerading as a person. It all came too easily to him.

"You're not working very hard to gain my help."

"I'm not going to gain your help. I'm going to take it. Now, we know that the trolls are crystal raiders from the Twilight Peaks. But we don't know which clan. The expedition we sent to the mountains never returned, and we know that an attack might touch off resistance from all the raider clans—which is *not* something we want to do.

We only want *your* clan." He leaned down close to my ear so his breath was hot against my flesh. "Which clan? And where is it located?"

I found the energy for a terribly smug smile. "They are hurting you, aren't they?"

"Minor problems."

"But your people, they don't like minor problems, do they? I'll bet there's some official back in your homeland looking over reports you've written on this area's progress, wondering why you're having 'minor problems.' I'll bet he's wondering why you've allowed there to be minor problems, and if you're really the person to be handling these minor problems. And you're not going to last long if they continue. Isn't that so?"

He stepped back from me, the mask hiding all emotion suddenly dissolving, revealing fear and rage. "Take her away," he said to the guards. "Take her away and rip the flesh from her body."

# 13

One of the guards, a woman, turned me so my back faced the Overgovernor and the crowd. The chains that held my wrists coiled around one another as she turned me, and the shackles bit deep into my flesh. I heard the slither of the whip sliding over the floor as the other guard pulled it back, then the rush of the air as he snapped it back. I braced myself for the blow—tried to—but pain shocks the body and the heart even when we know it is coming.

I gritted my teeth, letting no more than a grunt escape my lips. You two began calling out for me . . .

There is no need to go on. You saw it all. The blood, my cries that I could hold back only so long. Again and again the whip snapped at my flesh and soon the pain overwhelmed me. When finally I began to beg for mercy, the Overgovernor ordered the whipping stopped. He approached and asked, "What is the name of the clan? Where are they located?"

In this lull I collected myself and found strength again, though the pain ate at my back like thousands of biting insects swarming over flesh. I simply hung limp, letting the chains hold me up.

"Again," the Overgovernor said.

The whip sang through the air as it snapped. Again and again and again.

"Get the children," the Overgovernor finally said to a few guards at the base of the platform. Then he ordered the other guards to turn me around.

They did. I found myself facing a fascinated crowd of onlookers. The pain of a few moments before was almost equalled by the shame of standing half-naked and helpless before strangers.

"Not the boys," I gasped out, barely able to concentrate enough to make words.

"Yes, the boys," the Overgovernor said in a dismissive manner. "I made it clear what would happen . . ."

"Not the boys."

He lurched toward me. "Then tell me."

"Not the boys."

"Again," he said.

I think the Overgovernor mistook my refusal for the physical strength to actually endure the torture. In reality I was probably very near death. The whip blows now tore at the front of my body, across my face and neck and breasts. It was much like drowning. The tip of the whip rushing toward me like water, and I turned my face away to avoid it.

I looked up to see you on the balcony, but guards had already led you away. I thought I would never see you again.

Then, a sight caught my attention. Black dots from the east rushing closer to the walls of the city. I thought at first it was a vision, for the blood in my eyes and the agony of my flesh had totally blurred my sight. But as I stared, the dots grew in focus and became ships.

Drakkars.

And a stone Theran ship with a rainbow of fissures lining the hull.

Cries came from the city's walls. The crowd turned from me toward the approaching ships with gasps and shouts of astonishment. The Overgovernor stepped toward the edge of the platform, as if those extra few feet would let him analyze the situation more clearly.

"Get a magician," he said to the guards. "Send word to Sky Point. We need the ships here immediately."

The two guards hesitated. The man finally said, "Overgovernor, the ships aren't at Sky Point. They're not available."

Between gritted teeth, the Overgovernor demanded, "Where are they?"

"They're out . . .," the woman guard told him. "They're out looking for the troll raiders."

# 14

I was forgotten.

Above me, sailors boarded two Theran airships moored to the city's high spires. Captains shouted instructions to their crew. Sailors threw lines off the edge of the ship. Before me the crowd shook off its surprise and took on the mantle of panic. Merchants began sealing up their shops. Wealthy shoppers and slaves and artisans began to run from the bazaar.

But not everyone was panicked. Even in my pained condition I noticed some among the swirling crowd looking to each other with smiles. Hands touch the pommels of swords. A few men and women gathered and whispered among themselves like conspirators, then took off in different directions.

"Kill her," the Overgovernor said. "Quickly." With these last words he stepped down from the platform. The way his hands flexed suggested distaste, as if the whole situation had been disgusting enough before, but unbearable now. He seemed to want to wash his hands of it all.

Thinking of him as I record this moment, I wonder at how confused his Passions seemed. He always seemed on the verge of something else. There is no doubt in my mind that in his desperate attempt to please his superiors and his bureaucracy he must have betrayed himself at nearly every turn, so that by the time he reached success, he was no longer truly alive.

A group of guards quickly surrounded him and led him

off to the palace. They moved warily, keeping a sharp eye out on the crowd, and I realized that though the Therans controlled Vivane, they certainly did not feel safe in it.

The male guard pulled a knife from his belt and stepped toward me. The blade caught the bright sunlight, and in the light I saw my life, a brief shimmer of gold that would vanish with the thrust of the blade. Then whoops and hollers filled my ears and the guards turned. A half-dozen men and women bearing swords surrounded us. Before the guards could react, the rebels cut them down, their blood sinking into the platform's dry wood.

A woman cut a large ring from the female guard's belt and starting trying keys to free my wrists. Meanwhile, she quickly told me her name.

"Releana," I mumbled in return.

She finally undid the locks. "Well, any enemy of the Overgovernor is a . . ." She stepped back and looked at me, a smile growing on her face. "Did you say Releana?"

I nodded and carefully lowered my arms. I wanted to rub my wrists, but my muscles were too weak.

"J'role told us to look for you."

"J'role?"

"J'role."

The shots of fire cannons rang through the air. I looked up and saw that the Stoneclaw clan had arrived, catching the two Theran ships just off the towers where they had been docked. Already the trolls had boarded the Theran airships, swarming over the vessels and slaying the crew.

But the true test would be how the trolls stood up against the floating castle that remained docked at the palace. I saw dozens of guards on the castle walls preparing the fire cannons.

"My children. My boys."

"Twins, yes?" asked a man.

I nodded. "The Overgovernor is keeping them. His own slaves."

"We'd better hurry then. He might try to leave in the *Preserver*."

I looked at him quizzically.

"The *Preserver*. The castle. They name them like ships."

"Yes. Hurry," I said stumbling forward.

"We'll get then," the woman who had freed me said. "You, take her to Quarto's basement . . ."

I mustered whatever strength I had left and stood myself straight up, stretching my muscles painfully to do so. "No, I'm fine. I'm going. They're my *children*." My voice was deep and pained, and the others stepped back and looked at me carefully.

"All right," the woman said. It was clear she didn't want to waste time arguing. "Let's go."

As we made our way through the streets of the city, I took a count of the raiding drakkars and realized they numbered close to twenty ships. Either the trolls had stolen ships from another clan, or they'd forged an alliance of some kind. I remembered the Overgovernor saying an expedition had been sent to Twilight Peaks. Perhaps they'd presumed too much when dealing with a crystal raider clan, and had sparked enmity with them. Certainly Krattack, if anyone, could exploit such a situation, drawing the clan into an alliance with the Stoneclaws against the Therans.

Some of the drakkars attacked the two Theran airships, some deposited trolls onto the city's walls, and the rest of the drakkars, along with the *Stone Rainbow*, approached the *Preserver*.

This last group rushed the *Preserver* from a high angle. The castle was still docked at the palace, high enough to be seen from anywhere in the city, and still had no maneuverability. The *Stone Rainbow* led the attack, using its stone hull to shield the wooden drakkars as best it could from the fire cannons.

The sailors manning the castle's fire cannons turned

their weapons up, but in the moment it took them to do it the troll ships had gotten much closer. The crystal raiders nearly dropped out of the sky onto the castle. The air filled with fireballs, but only a few struck the troll ships, and even fewer did serious damage.

Just when it seemed the ships would crash into the castle, they began to pull up again, leaving behind a trail of trolls jumping from the ships down onto the castle walls.

Meanwhile, my group raced through the streets. Clashes had erupted all over the city. Theran guards and city guards battled citizens in leather armor and armed with old swords. A full uprising was underway.

We reached the palace. The castle floated overhead, casting its huge shadow over us. The trolls had pulled their drakkars a safe distance from the castle. I searched the sky for the *Stone Rainbow,* but could not find it.

"Come on," one of the rebels said. "We've got to find the Overgovernor now!"

We rushed inside . . .

Or rather, the others did. My weeks spent in the "box," as well as the torture I had just suffered, made it impossible for me to keep up with them, and they forgot about me in the tumult of the moment. Still, I hobbled along, leaning on walls as I went. I felt a wet stickiness under my hand and realized that the blood from my wounds had run down my arms and now trailed along the walls.

Around me echoed the sounds of combat—clashing swords, screams of agony, shouts for help. Down one hall I saw cooks fighting guards with long kitchen knives; down another I saw slaves overwhelming guards with their sheer numbers and beating Therans to death. I moved on, not drawing much attention from either faction. The seriously wounded were not the main concern of anyone present.

I reached the base of a massive stairway. The Overgovernor's voice drifted down from the balcony above me. "I don't care how! Just clear a path! Get me to the *Pre-*

*server!*" I stumbled across to the other side of the broad
stairs and saw him standing with several guards—a few
trolls and an elf. Drops of blood covered their red armor
and their faces. All had nicks and scars over their flesh.
The Overgovernor shouted to guards on the other side of
the balcony, separated from him by the stairs.

"Yes, Overgovernor," the guards across the stairs from
him called. "We'll gather some more troops." They ran
off.

"I can't wait for them," the Overgovernor said to the
four guards around him. "We've got to get to the castle
now. She might have to leave without us. Come on. If we
get to the other tower, we can signal them to pick us up.
The rest of the guards will create a diversion."

He turned to move, and I saw that two of the guards
each held a child—the two of you. Torran, you fought
with all your might against the grip of the troll. Samael,
you let yourself be held, but kept your gaze moving, always looking for a means of escape. Then you saw me.
You almost cried out, but I raised my finger to my lips.

As the Overgovernor's group walked on I climbed the
stairs as quickly as I could. My legs felt as if they had not
moved for eternities, as if I'd been recently raised from
the dead and had not yet acclimated myself to life.

By the time I reached the top of the stairs, you and the
Therans were out of sight. However, I saw the glitter of
silver on the floor. I remembered the silver flakes on your
faces. Moving down the corridor, I found a few more
flakes.

Following the silver trail, I walked on.

# 15

The fighting had become sparser, the sounds of combat coming from only a few areas. I passed through the corridors unhindered, sometimes going down the wrong corridor, but always, eventually, finding the telltale sign of silver glitter—sometimes just a few flakes that caught the red torchlight—on the floor.

Eventually I reached the base of a stairway that spiraled up into a tower. Though I saw some silver sparkle resting on the second step, I no longer needed the trail. You both were crying, and your shrieks rushed down the stairway to my ears. I could have cried myself in frustration. You sounded so, so far away and I had no idea if I'd be able to catch up to you in my weakened state. To have traveled so far to reach you, and then fail only because I no longer had the strength to move seemed too cruel.

I felt someone behind me.

She was back. No longer a giantess, but still pregnant, and still wearing her silver armor. Her black hair trailed down around her neck. Her curved, armored body reflected me, so that I appeared not only ruined, but monstrous.

"Who are you now?" I croaked. I feared her, for I was sure she would expect too much of me, or accuse me of failing.

She smiled. "I am Thystonius. Who else would I be?"

"Garlen came to me, and she looked exactly as you do now."

Her eyes twinkled. "You must be a very confused young woman."

I felt anything but young, and said so.

"Thirty," she replied. "You are but a child. The Passions are still alive in you . . ."

"My children?" I said, interrupting her. I began walking up the stairs, clutching the railing, dragging myself up.

"Wait." She touched my face, and in that touch all the weariness in my body melted away. More than that, I longed for more weariness; I hungered for the exhaustion that I had just endured. I wanted to compete with the Overgovernor and his guards and exhaust myself in the process. I looked down at the scars and cuts and blood on my body. All remained. This was the Passion of conflict, not healing or comfort.

"Thank you."

"What will you do when you get them?"

"Go home. Raise them," I said in a harsh whisper as I began racing up the stairs.

As I turned the spiral she stood waiting for me.

"And the Therans?"

"What of them?" Just then I heard you two shouting for me to come and I ran faster, the thrill of the potential fight growing stronger and stronger in me.

I turned another spiral, and she stood there again. "Don't you need to protect your children from them?"

"Others will do that. I just need to raise them."

I turned the spiral again. "Oh, really," she said, and vanished.

All my pain returned. I staggered a few steps forward, collapsing to my knees. I saw that the top of the tower stood only a short way up the spiral staircase. Sunlight painted itself on the wall above me. Your cries came loud, and I heard the gruff voices of the trolls calling, "Here! Here!"

"Thystonius," I mouthed.

Nothing.

I whispered her name, allowing just enough air to escape my mouth for sound.

Still nothing.

"Please."

I realized I was whining. Passions do not respond to pleas. There was nothing to do but go it alone.

I stood and with one heavy step after another, walked up to the top of the tower. I heard many voices—the sound of battle. I moved more quickly. "Hurry!" the Overgovernor shouted.

With the last few steps I came into the center of a large, round room surrounded by windows. Large glass doors opened to the west onto a curved balcony. At the balcony floated the castle, its drawbridge extended, offering access to the Therans and you.

You were all walking across the drawbridge. Beyond the gate of the castle I saw many corpses lying about the courtyard—Therans and crystal raiders. But the crystal raider attack had been routed. Trolls were abandoning the castle, leaping off the walls into drakkars that risked cannon fire to pick up their comrades.

But the battle was not yet done. Just as you all walked onto the drawbridge, the *Stone Rainbow* sailed down. J'role and a half dozen trolls dropped onto the drawbridge, blocking the path of the Overgovernor and his guards.

"You," J'role said, pointing at the white-skinned man, "have something of mine that I want back."

The Overgovernor looked J'role over for a moment as everyone drew their weapons and hefted them. "You're the father?"

"That surprises you?"

"I would have expected someone a bit sturdier. You don't do justice to your wife."

I moved toward the balcony. I had traveled only half way across the room when more guards ran from the courtyard of the castle. I expected a blood bath; all the weapons, combined with the crystal raider's indifference to children, could result in your deaths from a few sword strokes.

Putting the last of my energy into getting to the drawbridge as quickly as possible, I arrived just as the fight began. None of the Therans noticed me, for their backs were turned to me. The trolls who'd been carrying you suddenly dropped you, and the Overgovernor grabbed your hands and held on tight. The thought of that pale, soft flesh touching my children so repulsed me that I charged into him from the back, knocking him to the ground.

The drawbridge shook. The *Preserver* was leaving.

I grabbed each of you by the hands and looked around for the *Stone Rainbow*. It floated several hundred yards off from the castle in an attempt to avoid cannon fire. But it sailed closer now, coming to pick us up from the drawbridge. The problem was that the Overgovernor and his troll guards cut us off from your father and the crystal raiders.

The Overgovernor stood, pulling a silver dagger from up his sleeve. "I ordered you killed," he said with distaste. He stepped toward us. Your small hands clung desperately to mine. "Momma! Momma! Let's go, let's go, please, let's go!"

The *Stone Rainbow* was not yet near enough. I turned around. We were only a few yards from the tower. If only I been able to copy the metal wings spell into my grimoire so I could cast it at will . . .

My legs buckled as the Overgovernor slammed into me, driving his dagger into my right thigh. I rolled over, slamming my fist into his face, sending red blood streaking over his white flesh. You two helped by jumping on him. I screamed for you to look out for the blade, but Torran, you who had been working so diligently to remove it from the Overgovernor's hand, almost took a cut across your right arm.

The Overgovernor cried out, for he had almost blemished one of his prize slaves. During his moment of anguish I kicked him in the face and sent him reeling back to the edge of the drawbridge. He nearly fell off, and the two of you rushed over to knock him off. Your small bodies had adopted the warrior's tough stance—fists clenched, faces with solid grimaces. It might have been comical had I not been so terrified for your safety.

Both the Overgovernor and I cried out—he called for his guards, I calling to the two of you. One of his trolls turned around, the guard's sword smeared with blood, saw what was happening and rushed toward me. Seeing this massive, battle-lusting warrior rushing toward us, you two immediately retreated to my side. I scrambled up. To the right, the *Stone Rainbow* approached. We would be dead before it arrived. Behind us—

"MOMMA!" It was you crying out, Torran. "We gotta *jump!*" You tugged on my arm, pulling me toward the edge of the drawbridge that faced the tower. Seeing no other choice I scooped you both up, which made my shoulders almost seem to pop out of their sockets. I nearly lost my balance. But I didn't, and made a swift run for the tower. We were about ten feet from the balcony now, and moving further away with each step. No matter that I thought we didn't stand a chance—I had to try. I had to keep the two of you safe. You had your small arms wrapped around me, and Samael, I remember you kissed me on the neck.

I reached the edge of the drawbridge and jumped off.

That was when I saw her—I do not know which it was—Thystonius or Garlen—just for a moment, floating in the air, her massive hands under my feet, supporting me as I jumped the distance to the balcony.

We tumbled to the floor. I looked back and saw the troll who'd been pursuing us stop at the edge of the drawbridge. His momentum carried him forward as he tried to stop. He waved his arms for a moment, flapping like a bird, then fell, plunging to his death.

J'role craned his neck, trying to see through the swordplay if we were all right. I waved to him. He smiled. The *Stone Rainbow* sailed under the drawbridge, and he and crystal raiders jumped down onto the quickly moving ship.

The Therans rushed into the castle, dropped the portcullis, and sealed the drawbridge. As they sailed away, I dragged myself into the tower, seeking shelter in case the Overgovernor decided to fire the cannons at me out of spite. We made out way into the tower, and I collapsed on the landing at the top of the spiral stairs.

You asked me if I was all right. I told you the truth. The two of you knelt down on either side of me, touching my forehead gently, as I had done so many times when one of you had a fever.

# 16

The looting began immediately.

I found out later that over the previous three months—the time I had spent in the "box"—J'role had set up the crystal raider attack with the rebel groups of Vivane. He had actually been in the city during my imprisonment, but had no idea I was so close. Krattack had arranged for the Bloodrock crystal raiders to join in the attack.

Now there were dozens of trolls in a city they considered conquered. According to custom, they set about taking whatever they wanted. They gave considerable attention to the palace, whose halls contained all manner of splendid baubles, some brought in before the invasion of the Therans, some after.

The citizens of Vivane, however, considered themselves freed, not conquered, and the actions of the trolls caught them completely by surprise. Soon both sides were fighting over treasures each considered theirs.

As this new conflict raged, I led you two through the streets, looking for the gate of the city. I had fill enough of trolls and raiders and Therans and simply wanted to go home. Numerous fires lit the darkening city, and I heard the screams of Theran soldiers and those who'd betrayed their city to the invaders. The streets were oddly empty, for most of the inhabitants of the city were hiding behind the safety of their locked doors.

The one thing I did not want was a confrontation with your father. I was too weak to put up with his words and his logic and his exhausting pleas for affection. Somehow my mind had twisted events so that everything that had happened in the last few months was his fault. You might remember how tired I was.

A swath of deep violet covered the sky; the stars began to sparkle.

Suddenly, there was your father standing before us, framed by a huge bonfire. Smoke coiled upward, twisting and turning, then vanishing into the night. First he looked at me, smiling, so happy I was all right. Then he noticed you, and his face softened so much I thought he might cry.

"Where did you go, Releana? I've been looking all over for you."

"Let's not talk now. I want to get them home."

"We can fly there." He laughed derisively. "What were you going to do? Walk back?"

In fact, I *had* planned to walk back. But flying certainly seemed like a better idea. Easier. Weariness soaked into my flesh the moment I weakened to the thought of flying. Yes, flying would be better.

I realized that both of you had become tense. You did not recognize this man, and you wanted to protect me.

"Shhh, shhh," I said, trying to soothe you. "This is . . ." I faltered, uncertain how to go on.

J'role stepped forward, the fire behind him casting a red aura around his body. His arms outstretched, he said, "I'm your father."

You both froze, then looked at me for confirmation or denial of this startling announcement. I don't know what possessed J'role to suddenly confront you with this fact. Perhaps he was just so happy you were still alive. Perhaps it was the fact that he'd finally been given the chance to save your lives—or at least play a part in saving you. It has long been my suspicion that your father, and all men, believed love had to be earned with spilled blood and a deliverance from mortal injury. Maybe now he thought he could claim your affections.

Whatever the reason, he said it. You both gripped my hands tighter, though whether from excitement or fear I couldn't tell. Torran said, "Momma?" and Samael asked, "Daddy?" and in that moment, hearing those two words spoken together by our children for the first time, I became as confused as the two of you.

J'role knelt down in front of us. He did not touch either of you, but held his arms out wide, poised for a hug.

"Why are you doing this?" I whispered, too tired to raise my voice.

He looked at you two boys, a smile on his face. I wish I could say it was a smile of joy. A pleasant smile. But he might just as easily have been looking at prizes. Trophies of an accomplishment from his lost youth. His smile, like so much about him, was not for you, but about himself reflected in you.

Yes, you were there, and so there is no need to tell you what you already know. But perhaps as children you were unable to grasp all the subtleties. I also know that you have forgotten much of the events I describe.

And I do it to turn you against him.

"I've been gone from them long enough, Releana." Your father looked from one of you to the other, back and forth. I saw him wanting to say your names, but hesitating again and again. Then I realized he could not tell you apart. He did not know which of you was Samael, and which Torran.

"Are you really our daddy?" Torran asked, lowering his voice, trying to sound as cagey and strong as an adult.

With no more than a croak, J'role answered, "I am."

"You're the clown who comes to our village," said Samael, suddenly laughing. "How can you be our daddy?"

"I . . ."

"Clowns can be daddies," countered Torran.

"Not this clown."

"Why not?"

"He's never said he was our daddy *before*."

"That doesn't mean he wasn't."

"Momma, why would a clown not say he was our daddy if he was?"

The question daunted my imagination—one usually well-versed in impromptu answers to the Very Large Questions children ask adults all the time. More than that, I saw no reason to try to answer. J'role had started it with his pronouncement. I decided to let him try playing parent for a while. "Ask the clown," I told you.

You hesitated for a moment, then Torran asked, "If you're Daddy, why didn't you tell us?"

"Well ..."

J'role looked to me for support. A deep, buried part of me wanted to come to his aid. I ignored it.

"Well, I am your father. I am your daddy. I've been ... You know how you get busy with something?"

You stared at him, uncertain.

"Releana!" a voice called. I turned and saw Wia running up. She came straight over to me and saw my wounds. "Oh, Passions. Oh, Releana. I'm so sorry. Are you all right?"

I nodded.

Then she saw J'role staring at her. She sensed immediately that she must have interrupted something. "What should we do?" she asked me.

"Let's go home," I said.

"All right."

With Wia at my side, I walked the two of you forward and past J'role.

"Is that Daddy, Mommy?" asked Torran, and Samael asked, "What about Daddy?"

As I continued to move on, I said, "Daddy and I have had problems."

"You mean you don't love each other," said Torran,

never one to mince words when he had a clue as to what was happening.

J'role, standing where we had left him, shouted, "We still love each other!" He looked down at the ground, his fists clenched. He didn't follow us.

"I really don't know," I said softly.

"But he's Daddy," said Samael.

"Daddy and I have a great many things to work out."

"But . . ." and with that, you, Samael, began to cry.

"Quiet," Torran said harshly.

"It's all right," I said, and tried to kneel down beside you. Instead, I collapsed and ended up sitting on the ground. I scooped you both up in my arms and hugged you tight. But I felt your attention being sent past me, to the man at my back.

Samael said softly, "I want my daddy."

I tell you, I was furious. That a man who had not been in your life at all should command so much attention. I wanted to lift you both up and shake you violently until I was the one who had the power of life and death over you. Not this imposter parent who had arrived on a whim and could not even explain his absence.

I reined it all in, however. "I want Daddy, too," I said, though I do not think I meant it. Maybe I did. I wish now I knew. "But not now. Maybe someday."

"Soon?"

"Someday."

Wia helped me up. We walked on. J'role did not come after us or speak another word. And neither did either of you for a long, long time.

## 17

We traveled on foot, and then by the good graces of a caravan driver, by cart. I became very ill. A questor of Garlen tended my wounds and my illness. The Passion did not manifest herself to me during this time, and I thought I had seen the last of her.

Finally we reached our village. We found, of course, burnt and ruined buildings. Weeds and vines grew up and down posts and stone walls that had been the village tavern, a barn, a home. Unburied skeletons, their flesh picked off months earlier by scavengers, lay half-buried in dirt churned up by rain storms in the intervening months. Weeds and wildflowers wormed their way over our fields. Nothing else remained.

"Where is everybody?" one of you asked.

Gone, of course. Enslaved, or escaped. It had never occurred to me that our home would simply not be there.

"I'm so sorry," I said out loud.

Torran said, "It's all right, Momma. You couldn't a' stopped it."

"She's just sad, Torran," Wia said. "She's full of sorrow. That's what she means."

We moved on, and eventually found residence in a village far to the west, near Death's Sea. I became the village magician, the previous magician having disappeared while looking for elemental fire along Death's Sea.

I took comfort in only one thing. J'role had no idea where we were.

We became members of the community, and the two of you made new friends. So did I, including an ever stronger friendship with Wia.

Compared to the roughness of the troll clan and their life, the gentler, talkative village we called home seemed a blessing. The focus was no longer on punching and boasting and raiding, but making sure we all got along well enough to protect each other against threats from the outside world.

Your nightmares came, and I comforted you as best I could. Until now I had always believed children were particularly resilient to the horrors of life. I thought that because their personalities were not yet fully formed, the simple comfort of a home could cure all painful experiences. But such was not the case. How many times would I rush into your room and find you both weeping uncontrollably in your sleep.

The horrors of childhood help *shape* a personality. They become part of who the person is. It isn't something that can be shucked off, because there isn't anything solid enough there yet to do the shucking.

So I held the two of you in my arms, trying my best to give you enough love to balance the terrors of being torn away from your home, captured and enslaved by strangers, witnessing horrible deaths, and viewing the scattered bones of the people who had once been our neighbors. I really don't know if my hugs and talks helped, but it was all I could do.

Months passed.

# 18

After the attack on Vivane, the Therans retreated to Sky Point. Their ground forces had been scattered between Vivane and Sky Point; the fleet had been divided up and weakened by Stoneclaw attacks. All in all, they were much weaker. The slave trade dwindled, and many people expected the Therans to soon leave the area.

That was not to happen. Not at all.

One day, on your eighth birthday, the Therans returned.

The village children had gathered for your party in the tavern courtyard. You two boys, along with the other young children of the village, ran about wildly, playing games involving a great deal of screaming. The rest of the girls watched your violent antics or else gathered in small groups and discussed which of you was nicer.

Then the cries of surprise and fingers pointed toward the air. Not one but *three* air castles flew toward us, escorted by a dozen smaller airships. I had just estimated their location as over the village of Branthan when the castles began pouring down a storm of fireballs. Just dropping them down onto the village.

Huge pillars of smoke immediately began to rise. I couldn't guess why such a small village would be the target of a major assault, but then I saw that the ships were still moving—moving toward us. The attack on Branthan was merely a passing thought.

"Let's get to shelter!" I shouted. Few of the other villagers had ever had actual encounters with the Therans, and so did not understand what the presence of the airships and their fire cannons meant. They didn't move in response to my warning, but instead looked from me to the flying castles and stone vessels.

I jumped up onto a barrel and turned to face them. "Listen to me. They've come back. The Therans. They've brought back more ships. This might be only a small part of the fleet! There might be more ships all over the land. But the key is that these ships are coming to hurt us!"

One woman said, "But we haven't . . ."

"It doesn't matter. They're out to ruin us. They're probably looking to revenge the attack on Vivane. They need to weaken us, destroy—"

"But what . . ."

"NOT NOW!" I felt embarrassed by my outburst and my position at center stage. The stares of the gathered villagers bored into me, increasing my discomfort. Each one seemed to silently ask, Who is this woman? Who is she to be so loud and order us around, when she only arrived in our community but a few months ago? Who does she think she is?

But my time spent among the trolls had given me training in such matters. I might lose face in the long run, with the community, with my standing as being nice, but there were times to give up nice, and I'd learned how to do it on Twilight Peaks. With all eyes still on me, I said, "Let's retreat into the jungle. If they don't try to hurt us, fine. But we can't count on that."

Some of the others nodded, and began gathering up their children. The village elder sent some of the village's fast runners off to the farms with the warning. The rest of us did what we could. We carried the sick and elderly. While the ships got closer and closer, I had to drag some people screaming from their fields, for they could not appreciate the threat that was upon us.

Finally, safe within the darkness of the jungle, we saw the Therans' terrible justice. Fireballs rained down from the sky, crashing into homes and barns and the village tavern. The balls crashed through the roofs of the buildings, then we saw the glare of hot red explosions through the windows. They dropped the fireballs into our rice paddies, ruining the crops and sending huge clouds of steam rising into the air. Among our fruit trees, the flames leaped from branch to branch, as if the flames grew on them naturally. As if we subsisted on fire and violence.

Around me people began to weep. Some tried to rush forward to protect their homes, but others held them back, tackling them and pinning them to the jungle floor.

I noticed that the fireballs were coming closer and closer. Soon they were smashing into the jungle canopy hundreds of yards ahead of us. "MOVE!" I screamed. "MOVE BACK!"

The terror of the moment gripped everyone, and with hearts beating incredibly fast and breaths of air sucked down our throats with tiny squeaks of fear, we fanned out. The crackle of the jungle flames rushed up behind us. The heat, trapped under the jungle canopy, rushed through the jungle and pressed against my back. I ran with the two of you, clutching your small hands, but you fell down repeatedly. "Please," I begged, as if that could move your small legs any faster. But protecting you was all I could think about. I had to move on. On. On.

Soon we became separated from the others. I could no longer hear their cries of panic as anything more than faint echoes through the dark jungle. Our loud, clumsy rout through the forest had frightened the jungle animals away, and we collapsed to the ground, exhausted. I wept and I could not stop myself. Samael, you curled up in my lap, and joined my crying. Torran, you stood in front of me, four feet tall, hands on your hips, ready to defend me from any danger that might present itself.

Ahead I saw the fire's glow, though it did not seem to be getting closer. We waited for a long time, then finally made our way back. Darkness had fallen. The bones of our homes, charred wood, glinted silver and black in the moonlight. The cries of people I could not see drifted on the warm wind.

You both remained silent, holding my hands, as I turned around and around and around, looking blindly at the ruined village. "What could possess people to do such things?" was all I could think again and again, for truly the attack against a peaceful village so confounded my mind I could not comprehend it. It seemed as if the Horrors had returned from their strange plane of torture and pain. But the Therans were not Horrors, supernatural monsters. They were people of my own world.

# 19

When your father found us three weeks later I thought that somehow the Universe had decided to wind in upon itself, with me as its center, squeezing me from my past. I wanted not freedom from all responsibility, as I had thought while with the trolls. I simply wanted freedom from those things that weighed on me in an evil way. J'role, the Therans, even Krattack, involved me in plots and plans that seemed contrary to my nature. It was not that I could not do them; they just seemed *alien*.

I had always viewed the world as a place where one sought bonds based on trust and intimacy. Where the goal of life is not conquest, but safety. Although I had adventured for some years before settling down to raise you two, those adventures, to my mind, had been about bringing greater order to the world. With fewer monsters running about, people would be helped. And I had wanted to help. I'd also wanted to keep up with J'role. I believed that if he wanted to adventure and throw himself into one mortal danger after another, then I should do it, too, if only to make our marriage stronger. Over the last several months I'd come to suspect that my desires for adventuring were different than J'role's, though I wasn't exactly sure what made me think this was so. But confirmation came with his arrival in our village. The smile he wore told me everything.

The *Stone Rainbow* landed in the village square, garnering such attention that your father stood on the bow much longer than he probably meant to, looking much like a statue, hands on hips.

The crew consisted of trolls and several other former slaves. They had long ago lost their original homes, and the ship had become their safe haven in a harsh world. I saw them moving about on the ship—striking the sail, cleaning the fire cannon—and had to smile. It was obvious that in just a few brief months they'd all become accomplished sailors. They were a solid crew now, and I was proud for them.

When J'role had enough of his preening, he jumped down from the bow onto the ground, landing with a roll and coming up with arms spread wide. The maneuver elicited applause, and he bowed.

I stood at a distance, glad you boys had gone off to work in the fields of one of our friends. While J'role was basking in the adulation of the crowd, I formulated my defenses. Just because he'd found me again did not mean I had to let him back into my life. Enough was enough.

When he'd finished shaking hands, he walked directly toward me. I hadn't even realized he'd spotted me at the edge of the square. But then, he had an uncanny sense for knowing my whereabouts.

He smiled—oh, how he smiled. There was nothing disturbing in it, exactly, and when he said, "I'm so glad to see you," I could almost believe his smile was one of happiness to see me.

But that it was not. The true joy was behind his eyes, buried deep in some part of him. I hesitate to name it, for it seems presumptuous of me. But it seemed to be the *man* part of him. There are the elements that bind us all together as name-givers, and then there are the elements that separate us. Sex is one of those.

He smiled and said, "War is raging across Barsaive. You're in great danger. They're looking for you. You and the boys."

*And I can help you.*

It was in his eyes, burning into my flesh as harshly as his smile. *And I can help you.*

I realized something, and the realization made me dizzy. I actually took a step back. It seemed suddenly to me that men *liked* wars. But not because of the usual theories often bandied about concerning their lust for war— that it lets them test their courage, or that it is an insanity that seizes them and they have to work it out of their blood through violence.

It seemed suddenly clear to me that men loved war because it made the world dangerous, and thus gave them a role as protector. In general they are bigger and stronger than women, certainly stronger than children. When the world is dangerous, they have a place. A place that makes them very important J'role smiled because I would need him now.

I said, "They've been dropping fireballs. Just dropping them."

"That's only a small part of it. All the while we were with the Stoneclaw clan the Therans were trying to negotiate with the Kingdom of Throal for a trade treaty. Just like the one they had before the Scourge. King Varulus said he wouldn't even sit down at the table until the Therans stopped the practice of slavery."

"That didn't sit well with them," I said as if in a trance, the obligatory tale of war's foreplay slipping from my lips.

"Not at all. They kept up the negotiations for weeks, then finally began attacking dwarven caravans and the farmlands around Throal."

"The dwarfs retaliated."

"Yes," J'role said excitedly, and he carried on from there, his tale full of mind-numbing details and facts about the nature of politics and war, all of it overstuffed with generalized theories about how Politics work, how War works, how People work. But rarely did any individual show up in his calculations, except as the representative of a force of history—A Soldier, A Politician, A Tyrant.

As he rambled on, I wondered if any of these people were parents. Did they have parents they cared about? Hated? Did they fight for someone they loved? What did they do with their time when they weren't plotting the ruin of all the rest of us who didn't care about their bloody ambitions?

"This isn't how you talk when you tell your stories."

He stumbled. "What?"

"Your stories. Especially the stories you told on Twilight Peaks. People acted from passions in your stories. They acted from love. All the actions sparked from personal matters."

"I'm . . . I'm not talking about stories . . . These are real . . ."

"Real? J'role, what is so real? Your speaking theories about how the world works? Your turning name-givers—name-givers!—into mechanical objects devoid of hearts, or ties to their home, their neighbors?"

A few villagers stopped to watch, quickly perceiving an argument was taking place; the men gathered around tightly, most of the women formed a looser, second ring.

J'role stared at me, suddenly taken aback. "What are you talking about? The citizens of Throal are tied to their kingdom."

"No they're not. They're tied to their homes. Their children."

"They fight for the ideals of the government."

"Only so they can live in peace with those they love. Few people fight for the love of an abstract, and it will only be those who have no one to love."

"That's not *true* . . ."

"So you say. You've said a lot, J'role. I've always assumed it was true. Now I know it's true in your own way."

Everyone realized now that the fight was a personal

matter, or at least that I was trying to drag it that way. The men looked down at the ground, into the air, anywhere but at what was in front of them, and then broke off as if they hadn't been interested in the first place. The woman left as well, but with a much slower pace.

"My way."

"What you consider love. What you consider violence."

"Violence?"

"What do you want? Why have you come here?"

He looked up, his brown eyes glinting with the sun's trapped light just for a moment. He remembered. "The Overgovernor. He wants you. He wants the boys. His soldiers are scouring the land looking for you."

"Thank you for the warning."

"Releana . . . You need help . . ."

"J'role, I don't want you dominating me anymore."

He pulled back, touched his fingertips to his chest. "I don't want to dominate you. I want to protect you."

I stared at him, giving him a moment to put it together himself. He said nothing. I shook my head, shrugged, turned, walked away.

"Releana!"

He ran up to me.

"What are you doing? They will find you."

"I'm sure they will. They're planning to dominate all of Barsaive. I'm sure they'll have no trouble finding me."

"You can't wait here. What happens when they do? Who will take care of you?"

I slapped him. No—I punched him. I meant to slap him, thought I would slap him, but my hand balled up. It slammed into his mouth and split his lip. A small trickle of blood ran down his chin. He touched it, his eyes opening wide at the sight of it, as if surprised to see he was mortal after all.

"Has it ever occurred to you I could take care of myself?"

"But you ... DAMN! Everyone needs help! I'm not being unreasonable. We all need help!"

"I have Wia. I have the village. We all help each other."

His voice became quite deep. "They won't help against the Therans."

I wanted to disagree with him, but I could not. It occurred to me that I might be putting the entire village in danger if I remained.

"Do you know what's happening out there?" he asked. He swept his arm northward, taking in the whole of the land. "The Therans have besieged the Throal Mountains. Nothing can get in or out. They're *starving* the kingdom."

My jaw tightened. I hadn't known that. It was too far away for anyone in my small village to know about that.

"This isn't some game I'm talking about. Throal is the one place that can stand up to the Therans, but the Therans caught Varulus off guard. He wasn't able to forge the alliances he needed to fend them off. But if Throal is destroyed now, it all ends. The Therans will face only small, factional resistance."

"I didn't know."

"No. You didn't." He folded his arms over his chest, hurt. Making sure I knew he was hurt. "I didn't come here just to protect you—though I do want to keep you safe—I also came to ask you to help. We need you. We need everyone."

"What are you going to do?"

"Break the siege. We have no choice."

# 20

The crew of the *Stone Rainbow* had begun helping to de-
bark slaves rescued from a Theran ship. Some of them
could barely move their limbs. Some had scars along their
backs layered over older scars, so their flesh seemed
nothing more than one massive scab. The Therans had
mutilated some—blinded them, cut out tongues. The pun-
ishments had become even harsher than since my time as
a Theran slave.

I really had no choice.

"I'll need to get some things together," I told J'role.

"And the boys."

I closed my eyes. How could I bring you two into this?
Then I said, "And the boys."

When I got to our home, I told Wia about what was
happening.

"You can't take them," she told me. We sat at the table,
facing each other, knees almost touching. Sunlight, warm
and gentle, lit her face and hair with a glow.

"Yes. I know what you mean. But it's the only way.
Povelis is looking for them. They're his prize."

"Is isn't easy making choices like this . . ."

"I can't leave them behind, Wia. I've got to protect
them."

"It's hard . . ."

"Yes, deciding *how* to keep them alive is as difficult as
actually doing it."

"Let's keep in mind . . . war. I mean soon we'll be at war."

"We? What . . . I didn't . . ."

A pause, neither of us knowing which one should speak next.

Wia said, "I'm going too. I'm not staying here."

"Of course. You want to go—just like me. But . . . I thought you meant you'd look after Samael and Torran. I didn't realize you'd go."

"No. I have to go. What they did to my family . . ."

"I know."

"I know why you want to go. You have to stop them. You want to protect your family. But I have no family to protect. I just have . . . I just want to hurt them. You know? We're the same, but different, because you want to hold on to something. To build it. I just want to tear down."

I touched her hand. "That's not true. You have us."

"Yes." She smiled. I felt graced by that smile. "We have each other. But . . ."

". . . Yes. It's different . . ."

"Yes. Different."

Another silence. I thought for a moment of Wia going to war, all the pain in her driving her into a battle from which she might never return, fighting until nothing remained of her. Nothing that would be considered alive. Finally I said, "I don't want to go without you."

She laughed, and I joined her. "No," she said. "No. And I wouldn't want to go without you. You know, it wasn't the fighting that was too much for me. It was how everyone else *saw* it. I can kill. I can do what needs to be done. But with the trolls, it was almost as if I were alone in the fight, because I didn't see it the same way everyone else did. You know . . ."

". . . Yes . . ."

"There's a way the trolls fought, even the women . . . That's why I want you there. Someone who will see it the same way I do. It's not the doing that bothers me. It's feeling like you're wrong because you don't react the same way everyone else does. The Passion of Thystonius. Just competition. Always that *competition*. What is that? I want to fight to get something done, to help somebody. Not to prove I'm a better fighter than the person next to me."

While Wia spoke, I remembered seeing my Thystonius during the troll war celebration. I hadn't mentioned it to Wia, or to anybody. It had been too strange. And private. But I wanted Wia to know what she meant to me. I told her about the vision, and also the visions of Garlen.

She listened intently as I related everything. When I'd finished, she said, "That's so strange." I looked at her and began to laugh. She joined in.

"It is," I said. Then, "I don't think the Passion of Thystonius is alien to us. But we all perceive the Passions as they make sense to us. I needed that Passion of supernatural competition to save Samael and Torran. But for me, at least, she came as a woman with children to protect."

"Yes. Thystonius didn't come alone. I've heard about people seeing Garlen as a pregnant woman, of course. But Thystonius . . . For you she wasn't *alone*. See? She had someone with her. The child in her belly. I'll bet the trolls never see the Passion of conflict manifest itself as anything but a stack of muscles." We laughed again. "The Passion is all about them, just them. Alone."

"I think you're right."

The door opened. You two came in. Torran, you said, "Momma, the clown is here. He wants to see you."

We all went, of course. After talking with Wia I realized I could not, did not, know how to separate my Passions to be a mother and my need to be a warrior, so I packed both and set out on the *Stone Rainbow*.

Despite all my fears, I let you peek up over the rail and stare out over the green landscape of Barsaive. The sun glittered its light over the jungles below, while storm clouds turned the sky gray to the north and west.

Samael said, "Momma, we're as big as everything! We can see everything!"

J'role came up to us, and stared off the bow. "Releana," he said softly. "I want . . ."

"Yes."

"Don't interrupt me."

"I wasn't interrupting, I was saying yes."

He shook his head. "I want to . . ."

He paused, stuck.

"Samael. Torran," I said, "This is your father."

You turned and looked up at the stranger. He no longer dressed as a clown. He wore black armor now, shiny and well polished, pirated from a Theran soldier. A long silver sword hung at his side. Both of you eyed it covetously. I became nervous.

J'role smiled, seeing your interest. "You want to learn how to use this?"

You both nodded enthusiastically, then quickly looked up at me to see what I thought of your response.

"J'role, I want them to study elemental magic."

"They should know how to use a sword, no matter what they study."

I swallowed. I didn't want to quarrel. Not in front of the children. "Come here," I said and led him to the other side of the deck. "What you pick up shapes what else you pick up," I told him. "If they learn how to fight with a sword, they'll start thinking as fighters."

"You don't want them to learn how to defend themselves?"

"I don't want them seeking out problems to defend themselves against."

He nodded at this. "All right. I understand. But if they want to learn . . ."

"We're parents. We can say no."

"But should we? We're going to war, Releana. The Therans. They should know."

Now I paused. "Yes. Yes, yes, yes." I looked back at the two of you. Your bodies, muscles, already getting so big. "There's really not much choice, is there?"

"Ships ahead!" called the lookout.

Off the bow, still floating like small dots, flew dozens of ships. "What are they?"

"Drakkars," J'role said with a smile. "Krattack has gathered a good dozen crystal raider clans in the effort to break the siege."

"Will that be enough?"

"No. But we've got several t'skrang crews along the Serpent running supplies for us. They've also lent us money to hire scorcher cavalry mercenaries . . ."

"Scorcher mercenaries?"

"Yes," he said with a laugh. "New development from the scorchers. They figured out it would be easier, and usually more lucrative, to get paid to fight rather than wandering around to raid. Some of the tribes at least."

"Looks like you've got it all set."

"No."

"No?"

"No. We have to win."

# 21

We sailed for many days, traveling north to the Throal Mountains. Scouting reports suggested that most of the Theran forces had gathered around Throal, though some air and ground forces continued the random attacks on the people of Barsaive. Apparently they meant to weaken the spirit of our people so that we would do anything to stop the slaughter. I'm sure that it did affect some people that way. But during those days I traveled with people who refused to surrender. The attacks only strengthened our resolve to drive the Therans out of our land.

I watched as J'role taught the two of you how to fight with swords. You practiced with short swords with blunted edges, but this did not assuage my fears. I wasn't so much afraid of you hurting yourselves now, but of what would grow inside you.

On the foredeck J'role rested on his knees, working with you, one after another. He taught you the basic sword cuts and parries, and you repeated them again and again. At first you were both so wild with the swords that I thought J'role would become frustrated and give up. You did not seem to want to learn how to sword fight as much as pretend to be amazing swordsmen.

But J'role knew how to handle this problem. Or rather, he seemed to expect it. His natural affinity for children extended to teaching, and when either of you got out of line, he simply gave you a long look, the expression in his eyes a mixture of harshness and disappointment.

AND IT WORKED! Time and time again you would settle down, glancing down at the ground and then back up at your father, awaiting his next instruction. I couldn't believe it, and I was deeply jealous. It seemed horribly unfair that this man who had been such a small part of your life should exert this much influence over you.

Here came this *stranger* and you gave him a growing and earnest respect. He told you to do something, and you obeyed not because you feared his anger or that he would take his love away, but because you wanted to please him. I felt a strange sensation in my belly, as if the connection that had tied us since your conception was now unraveling.

Of course, as the days passed, each of you did displease him on occasion. I remember the time you were practicing cuts and parries on the day before we were to meet the scorcher cavalry mercenaries. I had given up watching, for there was no place for me in the activity. But on this occasion I came out to see how you three were doing.

The rest of the crew was busy at work on the rest of the ship. I stood by the castle, leaning against the wall, the high air cool against my face. A heavy mist surrounded us, and droplets of water formed on my skin and cloak. Neither you nor your father had noticed me, and I suppose you thought yourselves completely alone.

Samael, you missed a parry, and J'role's sword touched your shoulder. He did not hurt you with the blade, for he used careful practice strokes. But a true fury blossomed on his face. I had never seen anything like it from him before, and I drew in a sharp breath.

He raised his hand then, slapping you so hard that you fell down to the stone deck. "What do you want to do?" he shouted. "Do you want to die? Can't you understand any of this?"

Too stunned to speak, I began closing the distance between us. Before I could get there, your father had grabbed you by the shoulders, Samael, dragged you up, and then put the blade of his sword against your neck. "Is this what you want to happen? Everyone is out to get you? Do you understand? You can't let your guard down for a moment!"

"J'ROLE!"

He turned, stunned to see me next to him. His face paled, and his eyes lifted skyward as if he had just entered a trance. He stood quickly. "Sorry." He said to me.

"What are you apologizing to me for?" I spoke sharply, and my body did not shake. But inside I felt the fabric of all my sense of reality slipping away too quickly for me to comprehend. Inside my flesh I felt my body begin to disintegrate, and a clear scream struggled to crack through my throat and rip out of my mouth. All of this I fought down, because I knew if I let it out I would lose control of *everything*. I had no idea what I might do next.

I'd thought I knew your father, the good and the bad. I thought I could handle each part of him; that's why I had struggled to work with him for so long. But suddenly a new part of him had just revealed itself—putting a sword to a child's throat!—his own son! If he was capable of this, what else was he capable of? Memories of his requests for bites that drew blood came back to me, and in combination with this incident, I realized I never wanted to leave him alone with the two of you ever again. I thought I had some special power to draw his pain, to soak it up and keep it focused safely on me—that is, keeping his fury away from the rest of the world.

Why had I assumed all of this? I do not know. I thought I had a power over him, to heal him. I do not know. I just don't know. Oh, if only I had known so many years earlier. If only I could have foreseen what would happen . . .

The two of you were in tears. You had dropped your swords and were beside yourselves. J'role knelt down before you. The panic grew stronger in me, and I thought I might just strangle your father on the spot. I knew the powers of his perverse charm, and his ability to apologize for *anything*. I didn't want him to begin weaving his habit around the two of you.

"Boys!" I said sharply, all my panic and energy rushing out in that one syllable.

Without hesitation the two of you fell in at my side and we walked quickly away, returning to our cabin. J'role remained on the deck, kneeling, drenched in the heavy mist.

# 22

Two days later the Theran War exploded and for three days it continued until its finish.

You were not only present, but you've heard the details hundreds of times, so I will not repeat them. And to tell you the truth, the details of the war do not interest me. Yes, a great deal of cleverness was involved, as well as deeds of bravery and strength. The crux of the strategy—getting t'skrang riverboats up the Coil River and directly into the mountain kingdom of Throal was brilliant. Not only did the success of that operation replenish the kingdom's supplies, but it gave them war materials they needed to successfully wage the battle against the Therans on two fronts—from within the kingdom and from without.

We might well have lost, and it's lucky we did not. But the stratagems and objective theorizing about the conflict are not what interest me.

I saw too many people die useless, senseless deaths. Airships shattered by the fire of Theran fire cannons. T'skrang riverboats sunk as they raced up the Coil. Ground forces smashing against each other like waves of water on rocks, shattering their bones and lives in repeated contests of endurance.

Others have spent years going over and over the matter. For me, it was simply something to be done with, so I could get back to the business of *living*.

So I will recount but two matters of importance, one from pride and one to do with your father. The first took place before the fighting began, the second at the close of the war.

# 23

The day before the final battle began, we held a war council on the *Stone Rainbow*. The ship had acquired an extraordinary reputation during the last few months, and as both a captured Theran vessel and a safe and strong ship, its choice as the meeting place of the various factions was both symbolic and practical.

J'role had arranged the tables of the mess hall into a large U shape, so that everyone could see one another during the meeting. There were ork cavalry mercenaries, their bulky bodies covered with chain armor decorated with feathers and paint. Crystal raiders, their massive troll bodies fidgety at the stateliness of the meeting. Quick-witted t'skrang, smiling pleasantly with sharp teeth as their reptilian bodies rested comfortably in the chairs. Dwarfs with battle-scarred faces who had just recently gotten past Theran guards to give us a report on Throal's defenses. Windlings, who preferred to perch themselves on the edges of the table. Elves and others, all committed to breaking the Therans stranglehold and driving their armada out of Barsaive.

The level of cooperation astounded me, for never had I heard of so many different factions working together for a common goal. They had been drawn from all over the province, and worked not for their own gain, but a shared goal.

A tense atmosphere hung over the meeting as an elven warrior from Throal, General Oshia, gave out the details of the upcoming combat. There were disagreements about some matters, but no one underestimated the danger. Those involved simply wanted to make sure they weren't throwing the lives of their followers away.

During a break I ran into Krattack out on the deck, though more likely than not Krattack had sought me out. I did not mind. I remembered him fondly since I'd last seen him. Of the people I'd met since the Theran castle flew over my home months earlier, he had been the most honest and the most interesting. He seemed terribly old now. The gray-green flesh now sagged along his large muscles. His eyes, once piercing, now seemed unfocused and carried a white shadow within them. His gentle smile—with a touch of his humor—still remained.

"You're very tired, aren't you?" I said to him.

"Somewhat. I just don't make a show of hiding it anymore."

"Retiring soon?"

"Dead soon," he said. Then, when I reacted with surprise: "Not anything strange about that. I am old. I travel with warriors. It's going to happen."

"You don't know . . ."

"I wanted to tell you that none of this would have been possible without you. Or, rather, I would have arranged it somehow, but you were the one."

"None of what?"

"This meeting. This cooperation."

"I'm not sure . . ."

"Of course you're not. You haven't been around, and to you cooperation seems perfectly natural. But trust me, this gathering of warriors was no easy task. Vrograth had his work cut out for him."

"Vrograth? I thought you were the magic behind this, old man."

"No. No." He twirled his fingers in the air. "I can work manipulations from a distance, but no one would take an old troll seriously. Warriors don't understand or trust talk of cooperation unless they hear it from someone who is as fierce and independent as they are. That's the only way they can really come to accept that cooperation may be the only viable option. Vrograth was the person to send to the front."

"I wouldn't think he could gather people into an alliance."

"Which is where you came in. You made quite an impression on him, you know. You bested him three times. First with your peculiar contest of patience— wonderful, by the way. I would never have thought of that. Second, during the war dance. And third, when we defeated those two Theran ships. The day you were captured you proved that your way of thinking worked well. In his own clumsy way he's tried to emulate you."

"Really?"

Krattack laughed. "No one would ever confuse the two of you, but he's done passing well at it. Anyway, thank you so much for not running off that night."

"You would have stopped me in any case."

He touched his bulky fingers to my right shoulder. "That, my dear is where you're wrong. If my words could not persuade you, you were free to go on as you wished. What would have been the point of holding you against your will? I needed someone who could speak to Vrograth from her heart."

"But I wanted to go after my children."

"Dying wouldn't have helped them. You knew that. Anyway, thank you."

"It's seems like you're the one who should be thanked."

"Both of us. But neither of us will be. The histories are written by men who think the killing and body totals are the most valuable part of a solution's conflict. The peacemakers are seen as extraneous elements, usually dangerous."

I smiled at his humility. "I doubt that, Krattack. *If* we win, your work will long be remembered."

"You're wrong, dear Releana. But I appreciate your kind words."

Krattack was right, of course. He died the next day, and no one speaks of him.

# 24

The raids on the Theran ships did not prepare me for the Battle of Throal. The number of people involved overwhelmed my sensibilities. The number of deaths I witnessed from moment to moment stretched the bounds of my sanity.

Airships flew like swarms of black birds around each other. Fireballs raced between the ships, brilliant red arcs of death seeking out their victims. Flames blossomed on drakkars and castles and stone airships. Men and women plunged to their deaths, some twisting and turning in pain as ragged flames ate their flesh and trails of smoke uncoiled behind them. The ships raced toward one other, the stone ships trying to ram the wooden drakkars. The troll raiders attempted to swing in close to the Theran vessels to board the stone ships without being struck. Sword fights erupted on castle walls. Riggings of ships became delicate stages for sword fights.

On the ground, hundreds of troops swelled up against each other in terrible, raging confrontations. Magic and arrows and swords stole the lives of hundreds.

The t'skrang riverboats made it up the Coil, navigating the turbulent and rocky water, delivering supplies to the kingdom. Later that afternoon the horde of Throalic warriors swept out from the kingdom, overwhelming the Theran troops stationed at the gates of the kingdom. Theran airships descended to support their soldiers, and with their attention split, the battle came our way.

I myself crewed the *Stone Rainbow*'s fire cannon, along with Wia. First I became numb, and then euphoric. The entire battle, which raged three days, turned me into something I no longer wish to remember. I felt Thystonius nearby—along with everyone present, Theran and crystal raider alike—though I did not see her. She loved the battle. She craved only that there be excuses enough for conflict and that people act on them. She infused us all with her Passion so we might fight harder and longer.

On the third day it seemed that we had won. The Theran fleet had been cracked in half. With their valuable armada weakened, I thought our victory was certain. Then I saw a castle rushing towards us—the largest of those the Therans had in the air. I did not recognize it at first, but knew it when it began firing on us.

The *Preserver*.

## 25

"J'role," I shouted, "Get us about. The Overgovernor's coming!"

Even as I screamed the words, I felt the ship lurching to starboard. We had little choice but to retreat, for we had become separated from the rest of our fleet while pursuing a Theran airship. The winds picked up around us, and large drops of rain began stinging against my skin.

"Drop the sails," Wia commanded, and we quickly climbed up to get the sails down. As we worked, I glanced over my shoulder and saw the *Preserver* getting closer and closer.

"Why did they stop firing?" Wia asked.

I looked back. It was true. My mind drew a blank in its attempt to answer her question. And then it came to me. "He knows we're on the ship . . ."

"He?"

"Overgovernor Povelis. He wants us. He wants the boys."

I left the others working on the sails and ran to J'role. "It's Povelis. He's coming for the boys."

He kept his eyes focused forward, trying to keep the *Stone Rainbow* on a course toward the rest of our ships. "The boys," he said softly. "Releana, this custom of the Therans, with the twins. Do you think it's true? I mean, can we stop him, no matter what we do?"

"I don't know. I don't." I remembered the fight on the

drawbridge in Vivane. I told J'role about it and said, "When the Overgovernor almost cut Torran, that's when I punched him. He nearly went over the edge. He would have died. But he didn't. The boys were still fine. So maybe."

"Or, they were almost cut. Just a little. Maybe the magic almost killed him to keep him in line. To remind him how important they are."

Behind me came a red glare. I turned to see two fireballs rushing toward us. Grabbing J'role, I slammed us both into the ground. The ship rocked wildly and flames rushed up over the stern.

J'role jumped up, grabbing the wheel. He tried to steer back toward the drakkars, but the wheel turned loosely in his hands. I looked out over the stern and saw that the fireballs had ruined the rudder. The castle loomed over us now, its massive, dark stone walls filling all the space behind us.

"I've got to get the children off the ship," I said.

Distantly, as if to himself, J'role said, "Yes."

Upon committing to fight in the war, I had found a copy of the metal wings spell and inscribed it into my grimoire. It was my plan to take the two of you in my arms and fly off with you. I rushed toward the stairs to the lower decks. Glancing off to my left as I reached the doorway, I saw that a dozen drakkars had broken off from the fleet and were rushing to meet up with us. There was no guarantee they would reach us in time.

# 26

I'd had to leave you boys in my cabin when the fighting began. As I rushed down the corridor to reach you, I was halfway there when the *Stone Rainbow* slammed suddenly to port. The sound of stone grinding against stone raked through my ears. The castle had rammed us. I fell into the wall of the corridor, catching myself just as the castle rammed us again. The sound of stone cracking open grew louder, and I heard the two of you screaming.

With the ship listing back and forth, I ran until I reached the cabin. When I pushed the door open, a gust of wind rushed past me. A long fissure seven inches across cut along the floor and up the wall. One of my crystal seals had split. The two of you were on the other side of the fissure, clinging to each other. The *Preserver* struck us again; the fissure widened.

I was completely unnerved. It was one thing to look over the edge of a ship and see the ground far below. It was another to see the ground far below from the room where one slept.

I heard shouts from above, and knew the crew of the *Preserver* had begun boarding us. If we were going to get away, it would have to be now. I jumped over the fissure, scooped you both up in my arms and then jumped back. Struggling with your weight, I ran out into the corridor, toward the lower deck's cargo door. All I had to do was open it, cast the spell, and fly away, as the magician had forced me to do months earlier.

We reached the door. I pulled the latch . . .

It did not open.

I tried again, and again, but I could not force it. Damage to the ship had sealed it tight. "Come on." Holding your hands, I led you forward to the stairs leading to the upper decks. J'role and Wia and two trolls met us from the direction we were heading.

"They're on board," said Wia. "We're dead. At least that's how it looks to me. The rest of the crew's given up the ghost on the upper deck."

"Hide," I said and the two of you turned and ran off.

"Overgovernor Povelis," a Theran shouted from somewhere up the stairway, "We have to leave NOW! The raiders will be here any minute."

"Not without the children!"

"But . . ."

"NOT WITHOUT THOSE BOYS!"

Footsteps clattered down the stairs. J'role, Wia, the trolls, and I drew ourselves up for the fight. Five Theran soldiers, their silver and scarlet armor dented and bloodstained, appeared in the doorway at the foot of the stairs. Behind them came the Overgovernor.

"Wait," he said to his men when he saw us. "Wait." To us he said, "I have little time here. If you give me the two boys, I'll leave you all alive. I'll just leave. I don't have time to fight with you."

His face betrayed such fear as I have never seen anyone reveal. It was as if he would die if he could not get the boys. And in his mind, that was the truth. Or perhaps it really was true. The ways of Theran magic are mysterious and unknown to me.

I felt a bizarre pity for him, but said, "Get off my ship now." Wind from cracks throughout the hull rushed down the corridors. I almost laughed, for it seemed ridiculous to use my crumbling ship as sacred ground.

"They're just your children. They are my *life*." His

white face contorted into deep anger, and he shouted at his men to attack us.

"J'role, what is it?"

"They can't be his life. That's wrong. Wrong. People can't . . ."

He felt silent. The Therans charged. I cast a fireball, and it caught the first two full in the chest. They fell back as the trolls by my side rushed up and engaged the others. I thought the fight would be ours, but then more Theran soldiers arrived. "Get them! Kill them! Find the boys. We will not leave the ship until we have them!" The soldiers seemed about to argue, then pulled the words deep into themselves and charged us. A magician was in the group, and he cast a spell to overheat our weapons. I cast a spell to manacle the Therans.

Swords and spells clashed until the trolls were dead, only a few Therans had fallen, and Wia and I lay bleeding on the floor. The Overgovernor walked up to us. "You see? The boys and I are bonded. I am safe." To his remaining soldiers he said, "Kill these two, and find the boys."

The *Stone Rainbow* groaned heavily once more, this time not from collision, but from the damage already taken. Thick cracks ran through the ceiling, and bits of stone rained down upon us. In the floor between the Therans and us a huge fissure opened—five feet wide— and the two sides of the corridor tilted down toward the opening. The corpses on the floor slid down through the blood and dropped out through the hole. The rest of us scrambled to keep our footing, and Wia and I worked desperately to pull ourselves further up the corridor.

The Overgovernor did the same until one of the trolls from our crew, now dead, began to roll down toward the hole. The body struck the Overgovernor in the back of the legs, and the two of them, their limbs tangled, tumbled out through the hole. The Overgovernor's fingers clutched at the edge of the hole for just an instant, then vanished from sight. All that was left was the Overgovernor's scream, and then we could hear it no more.

The soldiers on the other side of the crack took the opportunity to retreat, racing back up the stairs and back onto the *Preserver*. The castle sailed off and still threatens Barsaive today.

Wia and I took the time to breathe a sigh of relief, then stood up carefully, gripping door jambs to make sure we didn't slip and meet the Overgovernor's fate.

"How long do you think the ship will last?" she asked me.

"I have no idea." I called out for the two of you, but received no answer.

"It looks like the Overgovernor's luck wasn't tied to the boys after all."

"Yes," I said numbly as we continued climbing up the corridor, then suddenly fear came at me with icy claws. "Where's J'role?"

Wia looked around. "He didn't . . .," she began, with a glance toward the hole in the corridor's floor.

"No. He's been gone . . ."

I moved faster now, every part of my body and mind screaming to me that something was terribly wrong.

# 27

I tell you this now because you asked me about your father. Neither of you has memories of what happened, too horrible were they for any child to bear. I have never brought them back to your attention, for there never seemed any need. Now your father wants to see you again.

Now there is need.

I pushed one door after another open until I found the room where the two of you were hiding.

Blood was everywhere. J'role whirled around, streaks of blood across his face, a blood-stained knife in his hand. The two of you lay on the bed, bunched up against the wall because of the tilt of the ship. The bed's blankets were soaked with blood.

"What . . .?" I asked, just a gasp, unable to get out another word.

"They're safe now," your father said, almost like a boy looking for approval. "See?" He grabbed you, Samael, and turned me so I could see you.

Your once beautiful face ran with ragged, bloody cuts. Across your cheeks, down your neck, and into your shoulder. No magic could possibly heal all the damage done. Your eyes were closed, and your breathing shallow.

Very softly, I said, "You're insane."

He looked down at the ground, then at the ceiling, and then finally said, "Yes, I think so." I thought he might cry then, but instead he gestured to your bodies and said,

"He's scarred now, you see? He's got his scars now. Our scars make us who we are. The Overgovernor won't want them anymore, and they've got their scars."

I screamed. I continued to scream as I knocked your father to the ground and rushed to the two of you. You might die without help from Garlen *now.* I didn't know for sure. But both your faces ... So much blood.

I whirled on your father, dagger drawn. I wanted to kill him. The passion for violence rose up in me. Seeing it, he became filled with anger. "Don't you know what I've done?" he spat. He whirled, grabbed his sword from the floor, and placed its tip against my chest. I might be able to kill him, but it would be difficult. We faced each other, frozen.

Garlen and Thystonius appeared.

Mirror images of each other, eight feet tall, in silver armor. I could only tell them apart by a slight difference in expression. Garlen, her eyebrows creased in concern, Thystonius, her eyes gleaming with a hunger for energy.

"Save the children," said Garlen.

"Conflict is all you have left," said Thystonius.

I wanted both, but the Passions did not leave me that option. Both pulled me so strongly. But I thought this: What would I want to be able to do tomorrow?

I turned toward Garlen and lowered my head. "Please. I will follow your ideals until I am done with my life."

She touched my head and I felt her powers rush through me.

The *Stone Rainbow,* which had been in a slow descent from the moment the huge crack appeared, slammed into the ground, sending us flying around the room. More chunks of stone, large this time, fell to the floor. Huge fissures raced up the wall. Light spilled in. I scrambled up, fearing what J'role might do.

But he was already gone, vanished through the hole in

the wall. I could only see thick, dim jungle and gray mist outside.

You boys lay bleeding. Kneeling beside you, I wielded the healing powers Garlen bestowed upon me.

# 28

The Therans retreated to a small portion of southeastern Barsaive, their presence but a shadow of its former power. Both of you lived, but would always carry the scars of your father's action. Some of the alliances formed during the Theran War have held, and the might of Throal is growing. Vrograth's son, Kerththale, is the chief supporter of King Varulus among the crystal raiders.

You asked me to tell you about your father, and I have done so. After healing you, I discovered that you had no memory of what had happened with your father in the cabin, and I decided it was best that way. And later I learned that you had only dim memories of your encounters with him in the previous months.

He never came to see us again, nor have I heard from him since. Until these recent letters.

I have been true to Garlen these many years, but the one healing I have never attempted is that of healing your father. I think if I tried, he would destroy me.

Even now fire consumes the letter from Mountainshadow. I do not want to read it; I do not want to be drawn near J'role. I become weak when I am near him, my sensibilities confused.

I tell you this: I do not think either of you should go to see him, if that is what he has asked of you. I am afraid because he has renewed his interest in me. I am afraid for he has renewed his interest in you. And I am afraid for him, because there are things inside him, horrible things, that I do not believe he can defeat.

I wish so much I could be there for him. But there are some things we cannot do.

Even for people we love.

May the Passions remain true within you no matter what choice you make.

Love,
Mother

ROC                                    (0451)

# DARING ADVENTURES

☐ **SHADOWRUN #9: SHADOWPLAY by Nigel Fandley.** Sly is a veteran who has run more shadows than she cares to remember. Falcon is a kid who thinks he hears the call of magic and the voice of the Great Spirits. Together, they must face deadly confrontation between the world's most powerful corporations—one that could turn to all-out warfare, spilling out of the shadows and onto the streets themselves.                                              (452283—$4.99)

☐ **SHADOWRUN #10: NIGHT'S PAWN by Tom Dowd.** Although Jason Chase was once able to shadowrun with the best, time has dulled his cybernetic edge. Now his past has come back to haunt him—to protect a young girl from the terrorists who want her dead, Chase must rely on his experience and whatever his body has left to give. And he needs everything he's got, as he comes face to face with an old enemy left for dead.                                           (452380—$4.99)

☐ **SHADOWRUN #11: STRIPER ASSASSIN by Nyx Smith.** Death reigns under the full moon on the streets of Philadelphia when the deadly Asian assassin and kick-artist known as Striper descends on the City of Brotherly Love.  (452542—$4.99)

Prices slightly higher in Canada.

---